Northern Lights Writers Present

ROMANCE and MYSTERY

Under the Northern Lights

Featuring

Edna Curry	Denise Devine
Lori Ness	LuAnn Nies
Shirley Olson	Diane Pearson
Nancy Pirri	

Mystery and Romance Under the Northern Lights

by

The Northern Lights Writers of Minnesota

Lori Ness
Denise Devine
LuAnn Nies
Diane Pearson
Edna Curry
Shirley Olson
Nancy Pirri

Published by Melange Books, LLC

White Bear Lake, Minnesota 55110
www.melange-books.com

In For A Penny by Lori Ness, Copyright© 2011
Hotshot by Denise Devine, Copyright© 2011
Shadow Trail by LuAnn Nies, Copyright© 2011
Counting the Days by Diane Pearson, Copyright© 2011
Love, Fish and Fangs by Edna Curry, Copyright© 2011
Heal My Heart by Shirley Olson, Copyright© 2011
Candlelight and Silverware by Edna Curry, Copyright© 2011
Night Magic by Nancy Pirri, Copyright© 2011
Breath of God by Lori Ness, Copyright© 2011

ISBN: 978-1-61235-209-1

Credits

Editors: Lori Ness, LuAnn Nies, Nancy Schumacher, Denise Devine
Cover Artist: Becca Barnes

Mystery and Romance
Under the Northern Lights

present threat of wild animals, Riley and Helen don't give in, but discover true love beneath the northern lights.

Breath of God – Lori Ness   Page 166

In the early 1900's, Minnesota farm girl is forced by her mother's death to come to terms with the plans they'd made together and the expected role of a young woman. Betsy draws on the memory of her parents' love for each other to gain courage to face her future.

In For A Penny
by
Lori Ness

When he first mentioned the weekend visit, Rob talked of going alone. Slipping into his role of a surgeon preparing a patient for the upcoming ordeal, his words flowed. Like a distracted patient, however, Dorothy's hearing turned selective with only fragmented phrases washing over her: "Back before you know it"..."Only gone two days"..."We'll both feel better when it's over..."

"I'm going with you, Rob." Her firm tone silenced his unspoken protest. After a moment of staring, eyes narrowed, he scowled, turned, and stalked out of the condo. Biting her lip, Dorothy accepted this retreat, although she still struggled every moment with the knowledge that he'd walked out on her emotionally months ago.

So she'd laid down an ultimatum and now they were trapped together in the car, with unspoken awkwardness separating them from their destination.

As the sun glinted without mercy off the windshields of oncoming cars, stabbing through the protection of her sunglasses, Dorothy wondered whether, when Rob said, "we'll both feel better when it's over," he'd been referring to this weekend, their marriage or the birth of the new life stirring within her.

"Tell me about your grandfather," she said, the words spilling out and sending ripples to disturb the silence.

Rob hesitated. With her intimate knowledge of his thought processes, Dorothy could almost see him marshalling his words into orderly statements as though setting a row of delicate stitches. She waited with outward patience, the sharp edges of her fingernails gouging the palms of her hands.

As her husband swung the wheel in a turn, Dorothy's gaze snagged on his left wrist. Tanned, softly curling golden hairs, strong, but marred by the clinical precision of his TAG Heuer wristwatch. Her nails dug deeper—she'd been hoping he would leave it behind. The ever present symbol that time served as the master of their relationship stirred a faint nausea within her. She'd asked, no, begged, Rob to leave it behind on this trip.

"My grandfather isn't a guy you can peg into a hole. He's not someone comfortable in society and he's never had much money." The sting of the unspoken "unlike your family" echoed in Dorothy's head.

Another pause as Rob kept his gaze locked on the traffic ahead. "Ham's over eighty now and a widower."

The marriage counselor's admonition, "Pretend you're on a first date this weekend," jabbed at Dorothy. But communication between them had become a nightmarish blind date of walking on eggshells, fumbling for words and tense silences. She shared the blame equally but didn't know how to break the cycle.

Again, the sunlight highlighted her husband's capable hands as he maneuvered the Mercedes through heavy traffic spewing out of the city and heading north. The weekly exodus to wide-open spaces, one they'd never made. She continued to stare at Rob's hands. The hands of a healer, yet he refused to mend their marriage.

Dorothy yanked her thoughts off that gloomy track and launched another conversational probe. "What did Ham do for a living?" She winced. Her laugh sounded like a titter in her too critical ears. "I assume he's retired."

"Ham'll never retire, not completely." Rob snorted as a reluctant grin teased his lips. The car accelerated to move around a slower vehicle. Another moment, then Rob blurted, "He was a cowboy."

Dorothy hated the paper-thin defensiveness that coated his words, the subtle accusation of snobbishness. Then the import crashed in on her. "A cowboy?!!"

Her husband's studied attention to his driving left no room for her to maneuver. She blanked out her thoughts, determined not to let him win by getting angry and lashing back.

With one hand, she caressed her midriff. Such turmoil had to be bad for the baby. A baby scheduled to be born into a home so blessed with the material and yet so poor in the emotional. Would this tiny life be raised in a two-parent home?

As the miles murmured beneath the tires, cushioned in luxury, Dorothy pondered the mysteries of a failing marriage. When had the first unhealed wound appeared? Rob's schedule as a top-level trauma surgeon kept them physically apart much of the time, while his exhaustion and nervous tension from bearing life and death responsibilities nearly every day isolated them emotionally.

Dorothy knew she'd helped to create this division between them, that he viewed her requests for a reduced schedule as criticism or her frustration, when rare evenings together were interrupted with intrusive pages, as selfishness. Counseling had enabled her to see his side of the story but since Rob had neither the time, nor the inclination to attend counseling, she stood alone in her self-knowledge. Nothing she'd tried recently seemed to bring them closer together.

Until this moment, she hadn't realized how much she'd staked on this trip as a salvage mission. Rob might be able to avoid her emotionally but this weekend they were stuck together physically, without the beep of the ever present pager to allow him to escape, for at least 48 hours.

Dorothy blinked and raised her head. She massaged her stiff neck and stifled a groan. Somehow, she'd dozed off and missed a view of some of the lakes and rivers that Minnesota bragged about on license plates and official websites. She'd also wasted precious hours of potential bonding. Her mouth felt dry and a faint headache tingled behind her eyes.

She looked around. Wherever they were at, the road had been damaged by yet another severe winter, and not even the Mercedes' suspension system could level out all the bumps. Luxury defeated by an overwhelming force. Just like their marriage.

Dorothy had grown up in what Rob had jokingly referred to during their courtship as "the lap of luxury." Family holiday travel in Minnesota had been to glitzy resorts set on sparkling lakes where every need had been met with a smile. Places with spectacular views, everywhere you looked a vista of beauty.

Her parents had never vacationed in places like this backwater, she reflected, peering through the passenger window. When Rob told her where Ham lived, she'd imagined thick woods smelling of pine needles and "nature", not scrubby pines alternating with birches and tangled ditches that bloomed with orange, purple and yellow wildflowers. Or weeds, depending upon your viewpoint, Dorothy reflected.

After perhaps fifty or sixty miles, they passed through only the third town since Dorothy opened her eyes. More small lakes, more ditches, more wildflowers. She found herself wondering whether the names of those plants could possibly be as a colorful as they were themselves, trying to imagine where the people who lived in the small houses set well back from the road could possibly work. No big box stores or fast food restaurants in this "neck of the woods", as Rob used to say.

Used to. She yanked her thoughts back to the countryside. A bird flew alongside the car and then veered off, vanished. What did birds do after they raised a family? Fly south, find a new mate? No, Rob had once talked about ducks and geese that mated for life. This curiosity directed at something other than herself and Rob felt strange, yet welcoming.

"That's so strange."

Rob jerked his head around to stare and Dorothy realized, too late, that she'd said the word out loud. "I meant strange that there's so little traffic on the road."

"I told you before that this isn't a vacation paradise. No one in the Twin Cities has ever heard of—"

"Sibley's Corners!" Dorothy interrupted him, pointing to a faded sign that announced their destination. "We're here!"

"Don't sound so excited." Rob gave her a wary glance. "I don't know what you're expecting, but..." His voice trailed away.

Dingy houses huddled closer and closer together as though wary of open spaces as the Mercedes rolled through the town. For the first time, Dorothy realized that it must have been a dry season up north. Lawns looked patchy and brown, drowsing under the relentless afternoon sun. A too-thin woman in shorts and faded tee shirt watered a circle of petunias, the life giving liquid trickling from a hose that sagged in empathy with her shoulders. She watched the expensive car glide past, her face expressionless.

Two blocks past the woman, Rob swung the wheel and then slowed as he pulled into a narrow graveled drive. Switching off the engine, he dropped his hands into his lap. To Dorothy's surprise, she heard him draw a sharp breath.

Was he afraid? Her brilliant, driven husband, who'd put himself through medical school and faced down her family to get her to marry him, looked *nervous*. He wet his lips, reached for his travel mug for another drink, his stare fixed on the small, shabby house.

Dorothy turned from Rob to also study it. Peeling layers of various shades of paint gave it the look of a bag lady caught on the nightly news, an elderly woman bundled in layers to ward off the chill of a Minneapolis winter.

So cramped looking! The passenger door clicked open, breaking her concentration, and she struggled out, with Rob's hand to assist her, just an impassive, courteous attendant. The muscles of her back ached with tension and her temples throbbed.

With a flip-flop of nerves, Dorothy realized she shouldn't have come. If Rob was trapped this weekend, so was she. No hotels in Sibley Corners, Rob had informed her, his lips white and head held high. "So much the better," she'd retorted. Yes, so much the better. . .

The sun beat down on her uncovered head; a wave of dizziness washed over her and she grabbed at the sleek, hot side of the car. Rob had vanished.

As her head cleared, however, Dorothy saw her husband a few feet away, slouched in the shade cast by a spindly pine tree, his hands in his pockets and his poker stiff spine relaxed. Bewildered by this sudden shift in Rob's body language, she started towards him, her expensive shoes crunching on dried out needles. No grass underfoot, just sandy soil, burnt by the acid from the needles.

"Ham, this is my wife, Dorothy. Dorothy, meet my grandfather, Hamilton Forest."

Forcing a smile to her lips, she slipped off her sunglasses and extended a hand in greeting. As her eyes adjusted, her mental sketch of an ex-cowboy as lanky and laconic crumbled into dust and fell among the needles. Her husband's grandfather appeared to be an elf named "Forest"—or was he a gnome? The top of Ham's head only came up to Dorothy's chin, while bowed legs encased in ancient blue jeans and gnarled hands remained as the only outward signs of his former occupation.

Ham gave his grandson an enthusiastic hug before turning his attention to Dorothy. A startlingly deep voice boomed from his tiny frame, "Pleased to meet ya! You've lassoed a good man in my Robbie."

For a moment, she forgot her queasiness as she returned her host's smile. "Yes, he's quite a catch!"

Rob's swift glance and wary expression betrayed his doubts regarding her sincerity but his grandfather threw his arms around Dorothy and gave her a whole-hearted squeeze. Tears stung her eyes. Loving human contact after months of isolation. Her lower lip quivered and she bit down hard to maintain her composure.

Ham peered up at her. "I can tell she's a winner, grandson. As pretty as dogwood blossoms in the spring! We'll get along just fine."

Although Rob stood beside her, Dorothy sensed his subtle withdrawal, the shifting of his stance so their shoulders no longer touched. But Ham continued to beam as he regarded his visitors.

"What on earth are you working on?" Rob moved to bend over a saddle draped across a narrow board, a slim forefinger poking at the supporting legs. "What's this contraption called, Ham?"

"That's a sawhorse, Mr. Fancy Town Fella." Ham picked up what looked like a can of shoe polish and a ragged piece of cloth from the seat of a lawn chair. "I'm doing my daily polishing." He stroked the saddle's dark, moist looking leather. "Takes a heap of elbow grease to keep leather soft as butter. You gotta keep at it each day or it dries out, could crack."

A saddle, a symbol for a marriage? Dorothy rubbed at the tension banding her forehead. Too simplistic. *Stop grasping at quick solutions, real life isn't black and white*, she told herself.

"Still known as Handy Ham?" Rob punched his grandfather's shoulder with a playful light touch. "I'll bet you keep busy."

"Do most of my work for free now, Robbie. Someone's gotta keep the widder women in fuses and mowed grass."

A swarm of gnats suddenly appeared beside Dorothy, tracing invisible, cosmic patterns in the air, trapped in an endless cycle of futility. She choked back a laugh; on this trip she was seeing literary symbolism everywhere.

Ham noticed her grimace and jerked his head toward the house. "Come inside, children. It's hotter than a branding blaze out here!"

Fanning herself with one hand, Dorothy followed Rob. Her vision of staggering into a guest room and collapsing onto a cool white bedspread while lacy curtains fluttered in the breeze faded at first glance.

An open door to the right revealed a miniscule bathroom. Turning, she glimpsed a galley style kitchen through a doorway. The presence of a lumpy couch and a card table indicated that the room in which they stood served Ham as both living and dining space. The air smelled of dust and heat. Tears gritted like sand underneath her eyelids. No room here for three adults to spend the night—it barely looked big enough for one.

Rob had been right, she wasn't welcome. Sibley Corners lacked a hotel or even a motel, he'd warned her, adding that Ham didn't have space available for guests. But she'd been so desperate, grasping at this last chance to catch and focus Rob's attention. . .

"Thanks for putting us up, Ham." Dorothy could tell by Rob's sidelong glances that the room was even smaller than he remembered it. "Are you sure we won't crowd you? Is there a motel within a few miles? We could call for a reservation, take you out to supper—"

"Nonsense! I'm pleasured, Robbie. Don't get much company. All the local widder women bring over casseroles and hand knitted scarves at the drop of a snow flake. Those gals don't count as company, act more like a pack of wolves circling a downed calf." He arched bushy white eyebrows and smirked. "But I'm still able to dodge and jump—so far I've managed to keep a ring out of my nose!"

Rob grinned and Ham flapped his hand. "Now, boy, set a spell and tell me all about yerself." He turned to Dorothy and waved at the couch. "And you, Missie, just set and rest your feet. You must be plumb tuckered after travelin' from the Cities."

Rob and his grandfather seated themselves at the card table, leaving Dorothy marooned near the front door. She hesitated before crossing the dingy carpet to the couch where she was immediately sucked down into the quicksand of the stuffing. Her husband was already deep in detailing his daily routine to Ham, whose wizened brown face creased in a proud grin.

To disguise her intense interest in Rob's revelations of his days, Dorothy selected a magazine from the battered coffee table. Stockbreeder's Journal! Faded black and white photographs of bulls interested her much less than the torrent of conversation spilling from her normally taciturn husband.

"So you call yerself a trauma surgeon, Robbie. What's that when it's to home?"

Rob gave a husky chuckle. "It's a fancy name for a doctor that puts people back together after they get hurt in accidents. Hey, my patient last

Monday would have made you laugh, Grandpop. A big, burly guy, he told me before the surgery that he drives a diesel rig so he's never home."

Dorothy stiffened. The parallel seemed obvious to her—was Rob sending her a message with his choice of anecdote?

"—so this guy's in the habit of climbing on the roof to get out of range of her constant 'bellyaching' about him being gone. So I asked him as he lay there in bed, his leg in traction, 'What happened this time that was different? Did you fall off? And he said, 'Not until she beaned me with our son's baseball. Got something for a headache, doc?'"

Ham wheezed, his gusts of laughter threatening the stability of the card table that he pounded with a gnarled fist. "Bet you got a million stories to share with your wife each week, right, Dorothy? Must be tough on you with your guy gone so much."

Ambushed. She forced a smile to her lips. Rob never shared, but why should he when she had expressed so much resentment about his profession? She felt again the ache of having lost someone precious, the sting of throwing away something that could never be retrieved.

But Ham continued to beam at her. "But I suppose that's the life you two have chosen for yourselves. I can tell Dorothy's the strong, supportive type that she needs to be and, Robbie, you was a born doctor—'member your first patient?"

Guffawing, his grandfather hopped his chair around to include Dorothy in the conversation. "When Robbie waren't more than knee high to a grasshopper, he found this little bunny with a broken leg. T'was then he found his calling. He splinted the break and right away Mr. Rabbit's sufferings were eased."

Dorothy felt her jaw sag, picturing Rob in his surgical scrubs, a frown of concentration on his handsome face, bending over a ball of fluff. "A rabbit?"

To her surprise, Rob's eyes sparkled as he met hers, before switching his grin to Ham. "Better tell her the rest."

"Oh, yeah, see Robbie had to use his brain box, didn't exactly have a medical kit, so he splinted that poor leg with stalks of rhubarb from his grandma's garden. The patient ate the instruments of mercy, so to speak, and hopped off. Never underestimate the curative powers of rhubarb." Ham bobbed his head, still chuckling to himself.

Dorothy yearned to keep the banter going, basking in the light in

Rob's eyes when he'd looked at her. "Did he pay you in carrots?"

Her stomach roiled when Rob flicked an irritated glance in her direction, as if she'd intruded, thrusting in where she wasn't wanted. Somehow, in the past several months he'd managed to barricade himself behind invisible walls, leaving her standing outside, her fists bruised from pounding to be let in.

A sharp knock that brought Ham to his feet, the old man moving with the rolling gait of a sailor just off the ship.

After greeting the teenager clad in a faded red tee-shirt proclaiming "Mr. Quick's Pizza", Ham unfolded a bill from a roll tugged from his hip pocket and handed it over with an expansive grin. "Keep the change, Nicky!"

"Thanks, Ham." Nicky turned to include the visitors in the conversation. "My car knows the route here so well that my turn signal flips on all by itself."

"Quit yer kidding, sonny, and scoot, my company's chomping at the bit for a mouthful of supper."

Rob waited until the visitor had gone before asking, "Is pizza your meal every evening?"

He couldn't mask his concern and Ham's voice turned defensive. "I got this for a treat for you big city folks, Nicky's mom makes the best 'pie' in Minnesota. Hey, Nicky's just a kidder."

Greasy pizza and a can of generic orange pop served on a rickety card table didn't agree with pregnancy. Dorothy poked at the congealing slice on her plate while Rob and Ham caught up on family news. Ham kept trying to bring her into the conversation but for all the attention Rob paid her, she might as well have stayed at home.

She knew Rob felt guilty that he hadn't visited his grandfather since their marriage but did he have to take it out on her? Dorothy found herself frowning again and glanced up. Despite their proximity, her husband's gaze travelled through her as though her chair was empty.

With painful clarity, the finale from their last fight played on the mental screen inside her head. "You don't love me anymore—did you ever love me?"She'd spit those hurtful words at him, struggling to accept that he'd chosen an unending line of faceless patients over his wife.

Shivering, the memory faded to a dull throb at her temples. Glancing up, Dorothy saw Ham's deep-set eyes fixed on her untouched slice of pizza.

"You ain't et enough to keep a newborn calf steady on four hooves," he commented, forehead wrinkling into canyons. "How's Robbie gonna hug and chalk you at this rate?

"Hug and what?" Rob gave his grandfather a puzzled grin.

"If yer wife's healthy and plump, sometimes there's a little too much to get yer arms around in one go. So ya hug a little, mark your place with chalk, and keep hugging till you're done."

Rob pointed a long, capable finger at the remaining pizza. "Eat up, Dorothy. I'll never get that pleasure if you persist in starving yourself."

A fly buzzed at the window. "As if you wanted to!" The words burst out of a deep well of pain inside Dorothy. Naked longing mixed with hostility quivered in the echo of her words against the bare walls.

Facing her husband across the cluttered surface of the card table, she read the truth in his refusal to meet her imploring gaze. He mocked her because of his conviction that her love had died, his belief unshakeable while he remained secure behind the barricade of indifference.

Flicking a stubby finger at a milk bottle standing sentinel on the sideboard, Ham barked, "That tone of voice'll cost you a penny, Robbie!"

To Dorothy's bewilderment, her husband rose like a scolded child and fumbled in his pockets before displaying empty palms.

With a sigh, his grandfather reached into his back pocket and pulled out a shabby leather coin purse. Selecting a coin with shaking fingers, he handed it to Rob who strode over and dropped the penny into the milk bottle, a hollow clang against the glass.

Ham shook his head with a dissatisfied frown. "Now, now. You left out the most important part, Robbie."

After a brief hesitation, her husband bent to brush Dorothy's cheek with his lips, a cool, passionless kiss that burned and stung like a slap.

Maintaining a grip on her composure, she kept her gaze focused on the bottle, willing herself not to cry. The glass had a milky tint, as though through the years it had absorbed some of the liquid it was created to hold.

Ham bounced up and proceeded to clear the table by sweeping paper plates and napkins into a plastic grocery sack. When he'd finished, he dusted his hands together and beamed at his guests. "Who wants the first bath? Dorothy?"

Still struggling with her emotions, she attempted to hide her surprise. "Not yet, Ham. It's only six o'clock."

The sun seams shaped Ham's face into a walnut shell. It seemed apparent that the meal's tension hadn't escaped his notice; he clearly felt under pressure to provide some form of entertainment. "Ain't much to do after supper. We could listen to the ball game on the radio...get an ice cream...play poker?"

"I vote for ice cream." Rob already stood near the screen door, looking outside as if longing to escape.

"How about you, darlin'?" Ham turned to her, his smile anxious.

"Ready for ice cream!" Dorothy infused enthusiasm into her voice but she didn't want to go anywhere. She wanted to remain in close proximity with Rob, hoping to push him into betraying the anger underlying his polite smiles, opening doors for her, passing a slice of pizza. But she couldn't put Ham in the middle. Her mission this weekend seemed doomed to failure.

Hooper's Ice Cream Emporium featured high stools lined up before an old fashioned soda fountain that would probably cost a fortune to recreate for a movie set. Dorothy studied the chalkboard tacked up behind the fountain. A weekend special named "The Northern Lights" featured scoops of orange and green sherbet.

Ham introduced them to the other customers with pride as "my grandson, the doc, and his better half, Dorothy."

Dorothy's tummy had settled down but her back continued to ache. Since they were up north, she ordered the weekend special. Perched on a stool, she massaged sore muscles while studying the bay window fronting on Main Street. Spinning back to the counter, she touched the napkin dispenser, marring its shiny silver surface with a print of her index finger.

Their desserts arrived in moments and she closed her eyes as a spoonful of the blessed coolness melted on her tongue. Ham, who'd chosen a chocolate strawberry cone, was too busy licking for conversation. Rob had turned on his stool to chat with an elderly couple at a nearby table, bending to scratch their equally ancient cocker spaniel behind the ears as the dog lapped with concentration at a dish of vanilla ice cream.

The enormous wooden blades of an overhead fan provided a background hum as they sliced through the hot evening air. She felt as if she'd stepped into a colorized movie classic, where the tinkle of the bell over the door might signal the arrival of a young Mickey Rooney dropping by for a malted milk.

Dorothy became acutely aware of the cracked leather of the stool as it chafed the backs of her legs, the sherbet melting into a muddle in the bottom of her cup and Rob's studied avoidance. He seemed comfortable here, as he'd never been in her world. She realized with a twinge of nausea that she'd never tried to live in his.

In contrast to her growing misery, her husband grew boisterous, harpooning Ham by blowing the paper wrapper off his straw and contributing an entry to the tall tale contest in session at the counter.

The winner of the contest, an unshaven man in overalls, was awarded a free refill of his milkshake. He repeated the story for the benefit of each newcomer. "This heat is wicked. Last night, Elsie had a craving for a snack. I went out to the popcorn patch, peeled back a couple husks, and filled a bowl with already popped kernels."

Ham punctuated the latest burst of laughter by sliding off his stool. "Got to get these young folks ta home. Need their rest, being tuckered out from that fast city livin'."

On the stroll back to the house, Ham offered Dorothy his bed. A vision of the army cot she'd glimpsed earlier in the bedroom lent conviction to her refusal, which he accepted with ill-concealed relief.

"But you're my guests." His smile wavered. "I'm an old fool, never thought about where you'd lay your heads—"

"I'll handle the sleeping arrangements," Rob said, his voice firm. "Don't worry, Ham, we'll be fine."

Overhead, stars winked in the evening sky while the sounds of their footsteps punctuated desultory conversation until they arrived back at Ham's house.

Dorothy took up her host's earlier offer and soaked as much of her weary body as was possible in the tiny bathtub, tracing the hard water lines on its porcelain sides with her fingertip. Closing her eyes, she visualized the snatched, sweet moments when they'd made love while Rob was on the medical school treadmill, interludes that had dwindled into rare physical intimacy. By her continued insistence that she be placed first, she'd only pushed him further and further away.

Her parents' wealth and social status must have birthed fears in Rob that he wasn't good enough, but she didn't realize the truth until her careless words uttered in frustration and loneliness had torn their marriage apart.

Plucking at the chain, Dorothy lifted the plug. Water swirled and gurgled into a cyclone shape above the open drain, a grim parallel to a marriage's destruction. She'd never realized it before but such images were everywhere. Dorothy sighed, realizing with a shiver that a degree in literature hadn't equipped her for anything but seeing literary references in everyday life.

Hoping Ham had already gone to bed, Dorothy slipped on one of Rob's tee-shirts instead of the negligee she'd planned to wear. Although Ham had bragged about "birthing more hosses, calves and puppies than there's tumbleweeds on the prairie," she didn't want the poor guy scandalized by the sight of his granddaughter-in-law's bare legs.

When she emerged, she saw Rob kneeling near the couch. "Ham didn't have any extra blankets so I went next door and borrowed a couple of sleeping bags."

He'd zipped the two together and arranged them on the floor. Turning out the overhead light, he joined Dorothy on the makeshift mattress. With an apology in his voice, he said, "Ham was so excited to know we were coming that he didn't stop to think about where we'd sleep. If Rose were alive, our every need would have been anticipated."

She heard a yearning in his voice and whispered, "Rose?" This was the first spontaneous remark he'd made in weeks, a light gleaming through a chink in the fortress walls.

Rob hooked his wrist behind his head. "My grandmother. A gal from a Boston family of bluebloods who somehow ended up on a ranch with Ham. But she was practical and according to Ham, she learned fast. Sounds like she handled all the details while Ham did the dreaming. But they were so close, so in love. I remember thinking as a little kid that my house would be like theirs."

His voice roughened and he hurried on. "They lived in a cottage on the other side of this town. After her death, Ham sold everything and bought this shack. He said it all reminded him of Rose."

Just like everything in their house reminded her of Rob, plagued her with bittersweet memories. The sachet of dried rose petals that she'd brought on this trip was the remainder of the two dozen roses, their stems bound in a silver ribbon, delivered the morning after she'd accepted Rob's proposal. It wasn't until months later she'd learned that her starving medical school student fiancé had pawned his winter coat to afford the roses.

Roses. Rose. Rob's grandmother had given up her life for her husband. What had Dorothy ever given up?

"It's your fault," she muttered to herself.

But Rob heard and misunderstood. "You mean, the baby?" He snorted. "Be spontaneous in your sex life, that's what you told me that marriage counselor said. Look where that got us!"

A child needs a loving, stable home, not the raveled strands that bound her to Rob. His indifference to the news of her pregnancy had shaken her belief that the dying embers could be fanned into flame. The only thing he'd done on this trip regarding her pregnancy had been a couple of curt reminders to drink the bottled water he'd brought, to remain hydrated.

Insects buzzed outside; she longed for a breeze to stir the curtain at the window. Marriage counseling had come too late, she realized with the heaviness of sorrow. Rob felt bound to her by the new life and not by love.

Although she could feel the heat radiating from Rob's body, the distance between them seemed so great he might as well be sleeping in Minneapolis. The last year of stifled and pent-up communication separated them. The air remained breathless; a faint whiff of mosquito repellant rose from the material beneath her cheek.

Rob grunted, gave a soft snort before beginning to snore. Had other women lain beside him and watched him sleep, stroked back the rebellious lock of hair which fell across his left eye after making love?

Dorothy longed to believe that infidelity was responsible for his remote gaze—she could fight back against another person. But she knew in her heart that Rob remained physically faithful to his marriage vows. The love and cherish part had been ripped from the service, however…

Unable to bear the proximity to her lost dreams, Dorothy got up with careful movements to avoid waking Rob and wandered to the front door, which Ham had left ajar after locking the screen door. Gazing out at the darkness, Dorothy tried to empty her thoughts and relax.

"What's wrong?"

At the sound of Rob's voice in her ear, Dorothy shied like a startled horse and his warm hands closed on her bare arms, steadying her.

"Everything okay?" he asked.

She knew he referred to the baby and wished for one moment that he cared about her. "Just needed to change position—"

Breaking off, she stared at the colors that spattered the night sky, dissolving and reappearing. "So beautiful," she murmured. "Achingly, gorgeously beautiful. . ."

"Why do you think they have a special called 'The Northern Lights' at the cafe?" His breath, ice cream sweet, stirred her hair. "Rose and Ham enjoyed living here. Ham said they used to walk after dusk and dance along with the Northern Lights."

"How romantic," Dorothy whispered, her heart aching. She no longer wanted to force a confrontation but just wanted to turn and find that his arms were waiting for her.

For a moment, his hand cupped the nape of her neck and then it slipped away. "We'd better get back to bed. Such as it is." He said under his breath, "I never should have agreed to let you come."

"So I wouldn't see your grandfather? Or tempt you to love me again?" But the words remained unspoken, a leaden weight in her heart. She stood until the lights vanished, wiping the tears away with the sleeve of Rob's shirt, before going back to join him on the sleeping bags.

This was the first time she'd ever touched one of these things. Rob used to enjoying camping out, loved the Boundary Waters, according to Ham's conversation this evening. But had she ever asked what he preferred for vacation instead of insisting they go skiing at a Vail resort? Couldn't she have offered to do those things with him?

Combined with her demands that he choose her over his passion for his work, she didn't need a therapist to tell her what went wrong. Unfortunately, none of the professionals seemed to have an answer on how to repair her marriage. Wishing she could travel back in time and take her newfound wisdom with her, Dorothy fell asleep.

Crackling static awakened her from a dream of dancing ice cream cones. A sheet covered her bare limbs. Tasting fuzziness inside her mouth, she realized the sounds came from the old Philco radio on the sideboard. Dorothy yanked the sheet up to her shoulders and, rolling over, she squinted through a curtain of hair at their host.

Ham sat at the card table, with his back to her and his attitude of intense concentration. When Dorothy cleared her throat, he spun around, cheeks burning, averting his eyes from her sheet-wrapped form.

"Up already?" Shoulders hunched, he addressed the couch.

Rob groaned, stood, and twisted. Stretching, he rubbed the tortured muscles of his lower back. "Lying on your floor felt worse than bending over an operating table for ten hours, Ham. And where's that garbled static coming from?" He clapped his hands over his ears.

"Hog and cattle reports. I allus listen first thing. 'Bout time you was stirring. Let you sleep this long cause I knowed you was both beat like a dusty rug in the spring."

Draping the sheet toga fashion around her body, Dorothy bent to lift a change of clothes from her overnight bag, Her lips curved in a smile when a shrill whistle came from a bird outside the window and Ham hollered, "Don't mind him, he ain't whistling at your legs. He always does that tweetin' to make sure I don't lazy the morning away in bed."

Dorothy slipped into the bathroom to change. Dressed in shorts and a stylish maternity top, she emerged in time to see Ham place two glasses of water on the card table next to bowls of cereal. Rob, shirtless, stood by the lumpy couch. Her husband's body was anything but lumpy! She swallowed at the sight of his lean, yet muscular abdomen. Delectable as a piece of gourmet chocolate—she wanted to touch him, stroke his supple skin and press kisses against the strong line of his jaw.

How could he not want her as well? She closed her eyes against the overwhelming ache of rejection.

Biting her lip, she watched Ham survey the table with the care of a hostess checking on the place cards. "I'll get your water in a minute, Robbie," he promised.

Rob pulled a tee-shirt over his head, the bristles on his jaw scraping against the cotton fabric. "Since we're having cereal, Dorothy and I don't need water."

"Suit yerself. This stuff's powerful dry without it."

"We prefer milk." Rob took the few steps into the kitchen area and returned with a carton. Opening the top, he tipped it. Something resembling a lump of cottage cheese slid out and plopped in the middle of Dorothy's bran flakes, sending them flying like dried leaves in a gust of wind. Dorothy recoiled, gagging, from the sour smell arising from the bowl.

"Ham, this milk has turned!" Rob exploded, squinting at the freshness expiration date. "This expired over two months ago."

"Them little numbers don't mean much," Ham said with his voice defensive. Then he brightened. "Wait, we had that big storm last month, lots of thunder and flash. Lightning must have clabbered the milk."

It wasn't lightning that clabbered Dorothy's appetite. Choking and gagging, she made a dash for the bathroom.

After recovering, she and a subdued Ham sat on the couch while Rob cleared out the refrigerator, expressing scientific amazement over the variety of bacteria growing on the discarded items. Then he left for the nearest grocery store to stock up on food supplies and baking soda.

Dorothy's nausea had subsided, but Rob insisted she remain behind near the bathroom. His threats to hire someone to drive Ham to the store once a week, "if you can't make arrangements on your own" had sobered his ebullient grandparent considerably.

They moved outside after Rob left and made themselves comfortable in the shade, Ham seated himself in front of the sawhorse, his worn rag tracing aimless circles on the aged darkened saddle leather, while Dorothy settled herself on the grass. The ground felt softer than last night's bed on the floor but not by much.

"Rob's just worried about you not getting the proper nourishment or coming down with food poisoning," Dorothy offered. "He's afraid that you're not taking proper care of yourself."

"I know." He sighed. "Guess it's easier to order pizza than to fix my own chow."

A car rumbled by, then a peaceful silence fell. Dorothy felt her body begin to relax.

Ham sighed again, dabbed his rag into the can of polish and shook his head. "Truth is, Dot, it's plum hard to walk into a kitchen, any kitchen. Reminds me of Rosie."

"What specifically reminds you of Rosie, Ham?"

A reminiscent smile crossed his face and he said, "A sink, 'cause I can still see her washing up dishes. Oh, the pots and pans. She was allus rattlin' pots and pans. Sometimes I dream that we're in our old kitchen again, with her flipping batter cakes for Sunday breakfast, wearing her favorite apron with the tulips..."

Dorothy noticed the trembling of his gnarled hands and looked away, respecting his privacy. Plucking a blade of grass from the sparse lawn, she watched a ladybug stroll down the green gangplank until it descended to the ground with the dignity of a matron stepping off a bus.

"Why did you give up being a cow puncher, Ham? Cows started hitting back?"

His wheezing chuckles brought an echoing smile to Dorothy's face, but her thoughts were still centered on Rob. Why was she obsessed with breaking through her husband's protective reserve, attempting to force an admission that he wanted to end their marriage? Just flogging a dead horse, as her host would say.

A bee zoomed past Dorothy's knee, trailing a buzz like a mini sonic boom, pausing to fuss around the purple cup of a wild violet.

"'Twas hard to give up ranchin'," Ham said at last. "Riding fences, sitting up all night with a foal that's poorly, driving cattle to market…" A playful wink. "Hard to give up all that fun. But when Rose started increasing with our first, Robbie's Uncle Peter, Doc Baker, took me aside and said it would be a rough birthin'. No hospital within a hundred miles of our ranch. So I sold out for little more than buzzard bait."

Dorothy rubbed her knee, still stiff from a night on the wooden floor. Rob wouldn't sell his beloved ranch for her. He'd buy her a ticket and put her on the first train going back East. . . "How did you make a living?"

"Didn't have much schooling, but ranching had taught me how to shingle a roof and fix a water pump. Lots of folks too busy making money to potter around the house, so I set up shop and put my kids through college doing a little of this and a lot o' that."

His eyes crinkled as a soft smile curled his mouth. Dorothy guessed he was traveling back through time to a home populated with children, pets, and his beloved Rose.

"You know, I'll betcha we filled that bottle with pennies more times than a steer has burrs in its tail."

She blinked. "Are you talking about the milk bottle? Why did Rob have to put in a penny yesterday?"

"Family tradition, Dot. My wife and I started over, dirt poor, in a new town. Most days Rosie and I didn't have two cents to rub together. But the rule was no complainin' over rain squalls—we had to save our breath fer the gully washers!"

Dorothy coughed. "Gully washers?"

"Downpours that wash away the landscape and overwhelm a soul."

She felt her lips tremble and Ham reached out to squeeze her hand. After a moment, his age roughened voice continued. "As a reminder we was hitched for life, whenever Rose crabbed about toting water from the well or I turned up my nose at beans and cornbread three days running, we had to put a penny in the bottle and do somethin' nice for the other. In for a penny, in for a pound. The young'uns learned right quick that scratching at each other would short them a penny and they'd earn the privilege of making all the beds for a week. "

"What happened when the bottle filled up?"

His head nodded with the rhythm of old age. "Treat money. The kids allus voted to buy double-scoop chocolate strawberry cones." Turning back to his saddle buffing, he ventured, "Havin' trouble with my stiff necked grandson? Fergive an old man's killed-a-cat curiosity, but I noticed a mite of tension between the pair of you, on the order of two mount'in lions eyeing each other over a plump goat."

Her fingers trailed over the age-softened leather. "Ham, how do you let go of someone who's already let go of you?"

"Death's the only final lettin' go I ever heard tell of." He rubbed with vigor, head bobbing with each swipe of his arm. "Love ain't a rope you kin just drop and walk away from. Strong winds make a house on the prairie look dingy. "

He paused to rub his forehead. "Look, sweet pea, Robbie's a proud man. If he don't see a fresh coat of paint on the house, he thinks it's all weathered away. You've gotta chip through the grime—show him that underneath the paint's still fresh and new."

Love likened to a coat of paint? Had she stood in awe of a fortress's strength when all that stood between them was a few layers of dirt?

After Rob's return from the grocery store, they packed a lunch and went for a drive to a nearby lake. Rob rented a small motorboat and went fishing with Ham while Dorothy remained in the shade and did some serious thinking. Not the yearning and regrets type of thinking but about what it took for Ham and Rose to keep their partnership strong.

The rest of the day and throughout the evening, Dorothy kept quiet, encouraging the flow of memories between Rob and his grandfather. They went out for ice cream again after supper and this time Dorothy stepped out of herself and talked to Ham's friends and neighbors. This time she tried the chocolate-strawberry cone. Ham winked at her.

She kept looking up to meet Rob's puzzled gaze. Each time, she offered a tranquil smile, and, instead of regrets, the lightness of hope bubbled inside Dorothy. No more hand wringing and sighing, she told herself. You're a woman of action from now on. He's got to see it to believe it.

25

Cuddling next to Rob that night, she felt at peace as she traced the lines in the upturned palm of his right hand which instinctively closed around hers. He sighed in his sleep and she leaned in close, pressing a kiss on the corner of his mouth. He snorted, then smiled. She sighed but this was a sigh of contentment.

After a breakfast of bacon, eggs and milk that wasn't 'clabbered', they had a checker tournament that lasted until lunchtime. Dorothy spent the last half hour of their visit with Ham under the pine tree, rubbing the saddle with polish under his watchful eye.

"I'm sending you a cell phone, Ham, so I can talk to you while you're out here polishing," Dorothy said.

Rob nodded, his baffled gaze locked on his wife. "That's a great idea. We'll keep in touch at least once a week. And we'll be back. Soon."

"Make it before the snow flies, Robbie. I'll be knee deep in widder women, crocheted mittens and casseroles come winter."

After stowing the overnight cases in the trunk, Rob enfolded his diminutive grandfather in a gentle hug. "Goodbye, Ham. Expect us within the next month."

"We'd love it if you could come back with us for a visit sometime soon, perhaps stay for a week or as long as you'd like," Dorothy added.

Ham beamed. "Thanks for the invite, Dot. I just might take you up on it. Long as you got room for my saddle and my sawhorse."

He bustled into the house before returning to present Dorothy with an object wrapped in a brown bag left over from yesterday's shopping trip. She felt the smoothness of glass through the paper and the rasp of a leathery palm. "Don't forget the lovin' that goes with the givin' and may the rains wash the dust from yer home," he whispered, winked and gave her a smacking kiss on the cheek.

As a child, Dorothy remembered accepting a "blind man's dare", walking across unfamiliar territory with eyes closed, hands clenched behind her back. The memory of that excitement, coupled with the fear that at any moment she could trip and skin a knee or bump into an obstacle with the dare ending in disaster, rose up in her. The stakes were much higher now, the prize more precious than the cheers of her playmates.

On the trip home, she tried to relax as she watched the scenery glide past the windows, planning for the future, their future. Rob kept sneaking sidelong glances at her and she realized that she was no longer the desperate pursuer, but a mystery, and her relationship with Ham was something her husband could not get his head around.

She cradled her gift on her lap until they reached the outskirts of the city and moved into heavier traffic. With Rob distracted, she unwrapped the bottle and said a quick prayer.

As the car idled at a red light, Dorothy turned Rob's face toward her, smiled at his startled expression, and kissed him hard on the mouth.

He sat motionless. Then he drew a deep breath and tugged a penny from the pocket of his shorts. Leaning forward, he dropped it into the bottle, the metal of the coin ringing against the milky glass. "Ham gave me that coin when we were out on the water. He also informed me that a wife wasn't a seed you could just drop on the ground, walk away from and then expect a bumper crop."

Dorothy gave a nervous giggle and rubbed her stomach. "I'm growing."

He placed his hand on her "baby bump" and then bent to kiss her. She met him with equal passion and they clung to each other until impatient horns startled them apart.

As the car glided into motion once more, Rob chuckled. "That coin was the continuation of a wonderful family tradition, Dorothy. My way of saying that I'm definitely in for a penny."

"And I'm in for a pound, at least eight pounds of baby." She felt her lips stretch into one of the biggest smiles of her life. "I hope all our kids like chocolate strawberry cones—it's a family tradition."

The End

About the Author

Lori Ness wrote her first novel when she ran out of books that she liked to read. *Rosemary for Rembrance*, published by Harper Paperbacks under the name Christine Arness, was nominated for a Romantic Times Award for Best Contemporary Romantic Novel. Also under the name of Christine Arness, *Wedding Chimes, Assorted Crimes* was a hardcover published by Five Star.

Website: http://www.christinearness.com

Hotshot
by
Denise Devine

Cyndi Lauper screeched 'Oh-oh, girls just wanna have fu-hunnn....' on the radio as Meg Bristol sat in her Ford Fiesta on the I-35W entrance ramp, sandwiched between two eighteen wheelers. She took one look at the Friday morning rat race heading toward Minneapolis and shook her head. "Some days my life really sucks."

"I'm sorry about Tom Duffey," Nan O'Brien said as she curled up in the passenger seat. She reached over and turned down the radio, reducing Cyndi's voice to a high-pitched whine. "I never thought he could be such a jerk."

"That makes two of us." Meg cut a glance at her best friend. "I'm so mad I can't stop thinking about what a fool I've been, believing his lies." Her fists gripped the steering wheel. "Boy, I'd love to get my hands on him and show him a thing or two. By the time I got through with that lowlife," she pointed to the rig in front of her as it rolled onto the freeway, "he'd look like that Mack truck ran over his head!" She released an angry sniffle. "That would make interesting wedding pictures for his lucky bride, whoever she is."

"You're letting him off easy." Nan sucked down the last of her breakfast of Diet Coke. "If a guy dumped me like that, I'd aim lower than his face." She pursed her lips. "When did you find out?"

"I got the news this morning." Meg inched her car forward, wishing she could skip work. Given the circumstances, she didn't have the best attitude for dealing with people today, or her mid-year performance review, scheduled for 10 AM. "The coward emailed my Blackberry."

"You're kidding...." Nan blinked in astonishment as she slowly turned her head. "What did he say?"

The meter turned green. Meg sped her Ford down the ramp, searching for an open spot in the flow. A collage of cars, vans and trucks cruised bumper to bumper at seventy plus miles per hour. She signaled and merged into the stampede.

"Can't see you any more...getting married. Sorry." She swallowed hard, determined not to shed even one tear over the likes of him.

"That's so cold and cruel!" Nan reached down and dug a small cosmetic bag out of her purse. "I'll bet his fiancée doesn't have a clue that the jerk's been seeing both of you at the same time."

Meg rolled her eyes. "Well, I sure didn't and I dated him for six months. I wish someone would have warned me—" Her jaw slowly dropped as what she'd just said sunk in. "Hey, I think someone should warn her!"

"With 'someone' being you? Well, she has the right to know." Nan now held a small mirror in one hand and a brow pencil in the other. "He cheated on both of you." She stared into the mirror, studying her brow. "How are you going to find her? Any idea of who she is?"

"No, but I know Tom. He can't resist the urge to show off his latest trophy. He'll hit all of his favorite hangouts." Meg stared at the road ahead, formulating a plan. "I'll find them, and when I do, I'm going to let her know what a colossal fraud she's planning to marry."

At the Forest Bend over-pass, a massive Dodge pickup roared by and cut in front of her. The shiny blue four-by-four looked mean enough to gobble her pint-sized Ford for breakfast. Traffic suddenly stopped. Meg hit the brakes, her hands clenching the steering wheel as the pickup in front of her fishtailed to a screeching halt. In the next lane, brake lights decorated the freeway like Christmas in July.

Nan lurched against her seatbelt, her coppery curls dancing around her face. The cosmetic bag flew off her lap and hurled against the dash, scattering its contents on the floor. She glared at the back window of the Dodge and shook her head. "Where do pickup owners learn to drive anyway? In a demolition derby?"

"Maybe the right to invent your own rules comes with title to the vehicle." Meg tapped her fingers on the steering wheel. "This guy seems to think he owns the road."

Nan scooped up her makeup, dumping it in her lap. "Are you kidding? He knows he owns the road. This car is a mouse compared to his macho machine."

Traffic commenced at a snail's pace. Nan held up her mirror again and dabbed taupe shadow across her brow bone with her middle finger.

The car hit a pothole and her hand shot into the air--the lone finger still exposed. A moment later, she sucked in a horrified gasp. "Meg, did you see that?"

"See what?" Meg glanced around.

"The passenger in the blue pickup turned around and gave me the finger!"

Meg did a double take. Inconsiderate driving was one thing, but that level of rudeness between men and women just didn't happen in Minnesota. She glared at the Ram in disgust. So, her Fiesta came across as a mouse, did it? Well, that monster pickup had better look out because this mouse knew how to roar.

* * * *

"Did you see that?" Jim Anderson sounded ticked.

"See what?" Denny Metz stared at the car ahead, half-listening as he mulled over the status of his love life. A bachelor's existence no longer satisfied him the way it once did. Lately he'd begun to feel bored. He needed to find someone special and settle down. He wondered about his date tonight, Leeza Frank. Could this beautiful, curvaceous blonde be the one?

"They flipped us the bird, that's what!"

Huh? Denny's gaze met Jim's straight on. "Who did?"

Jim gestured toward the Fiesta behind them. "Thelma and Louise back there—that's who!"

Denny chuckled. Those two in the rusty red Ford didn't seem the type. He didn't care for their driving skills, but that was beside the point. The driver and her friend looked more like Sunday school teachers than a couple of nutty women on the loose. "You're kidding." The serious expression crossing Jim's bearded face instantly sobered him. "I guess you're not. So then what'd you do?"

With a quick tug, Jim adjusted the bill of his Budweiser cap, his jaw set. "I gave 'em one back."

"Aw, man..." Denny intoned. "That's not cool. You shouldn't do stuff like that to chicks!"

Jim's tanned face flushed, making his short, sun-bleached hair look almost white. "Well, I didn't want to, but—hey, they started it!"

"So, what'd you do to tick 'em off in the first place?"

"Me?" Jim pointed a callused thumb at his chest, his eyes wide with righteous indignation. "I didn't do anything! I was just staring out the back window, minding my own business, when all of a sudden the curly-haired one gave me the one-finger salute." He interrupted himself with a disgusted snort. "I guess I'm not her type."

Denny couldn't resist a grin. "With a face like yours, I doubt you're any woman's type." He gestured toward the Fiesta. "She probably got offended by just looking at that mangy rug you call a beard."

Jim belted out a good-natured laugh and rubbed a calloused palm along his neatly trimmed jawbone. "She probably would have privileged you with the insult, but I happened to be looking her way. After all, you're the one driving this sled."

The Fiesta moved into the right lane, eased ahead by a car length and edged its way back into the fast lane, this time in front of the Ram.

Denny shot into the space the Ford had vacated. "Oh, no, you don't, lady. We've got to get to work." He cocked one brow. "She apparently has all day."

Traffic picked up speed. Denny inched his way past the Fiesta until he had enough room to squeeze in front of her. However, once he flipped on his signal, the Fiesta sped up, closing the gap and his hope of surpassing her in the fast lane.

"Ah-h-h!" He smacked the heel of his palm against the steering wheel. "She did that on purpose." He slowed the Ram and once again fell in behind the little red rust-bucket.

"You gonna let her get away with that?" Jim flashed Denny a conspiratorial grin.

Denny glanced at the clock on the dash and let off the gas as traffic slowed again. "We're running late as it is. I don't want to hassle her. I just want to get around her...."

The driver in the Ford tilted her side mirror upward. Wisps of chocolate hair framed a rectangular face. Smoldering, deep-set eyes reflected off the glass, locking into his gaze. He studied her for a moment. So she doesn't like the way I drive, he mused wryly. That's an interesting coincidence.

"Watch out!"

Jim's shout pierced Denny's thoughts like a shotgun blast, jump-starting him into action. One foot buried the clutch, the other floored the brake as he steered sharply toward the shoulder, but his reaction came too late. In the blink of an eye, Denny Metz's Ram kissed the back of the little red Fiesta.

31

* * * *

For a moment, Meg couldn't move, stunned by the sudden jolt of crunching metal. Time seemed to flow in slow motion as she looked around, trying to grasp what just took place.

"Are you okay?" She and Nan exclaimed at the same time.

"I'm fine," Meg replied first.

"Me, too," Nan added, though her face paled.

"Come on," Meg murmured, unbuckling her seatbelt. "Let's find out what this guy has to say for himself." She threw open the door and stepped out, literally into the middle of chaos. The accident had created a traffic jam as far as she could see.

Both doors on the pickup flew open. The driver jumped out first, slammed his door and strode toward her. Meg spun in his direction with fists clenched, ready to give this joker a piece of her mind, but one good look told her this guy definitely embodied trouble. His unruly black hair hung just a little too long, his tight, faded jeans revealed just a little too much and his musky cologne smelled just a little too good. He epitomized the definition of a mother's worst nightmare, and the way he strutted up to her proved he knew it. Oh, boy, did he know it.

He towered over her, dwarfing her five-feet-four-inches like a pro-wrestler bearing down on a girl scout. His bronzed, muscular shoulders flexed under a gray T-shirt as large hands gripped his hips. Eyes of royal blue suddenly softened, throwing her off guard.

"Are you girls all right?" His baritone voice boomed over the roar of vehicles maneuvering around them.

"Yeah, we're fine, no thanks to *you*." Meg stared up at him, feeling strangely disadvantaged by his obvious concern.

The care on his lean face turned to frustration. "Look, I'm really sorry. I tried to stop, but it all happened so fast I didn't see your brake lights until it was too late."

"What a crock of bull!" Nan said as she circled the hood of the Fiesta and stopped next to Meg. "You've been on our tail for miles!"

The passenger of the pickup, a wiry blond fellow sporting a Budweiser T-shirt and baseball cap joined the group. He confronted Nan, nose to nose, his tanned face turning a dark crimson. "Whaddya saying, that Denny did it on purpose? You're crazy, woman!" He pointed to the damage on the front-end of the Ram. "It's gonna cost him a fortune to fix this!"

Everyone gawked at the Dodge. Somewhere underneath the ailing monster, liquid made a steady drip-drip-drip on the asphalt.

"Yeah, but the damage to our vehicle is worse," Nan countered in a huff. Everyone turned and peered at the Fiesta as though viewing a corpse. The left rear quarter panel, bumper and part of the hatchback sat crumpled; the tail light was now just a memory.

Meg stared in disbelief. Her quick-starting, smooth-running Fiesta now sat in the middle of I-35W, blocking traffic and looking like the ugliest piece of modern art ever created. "My car," she whispered in shock. "Look what's happened to my car!"

"No big loss." The shorter, blond guy shrugged. "It's only a Ford, anyway."

Both women gasped in unison.

"Watch it, mister." Meg glared at him. "That's my car you're talking about!"

Denny held up his palms. "Hey, hey, everybody calm down, okay? There's no need to get upset. We can work this out—"

Meg shoved out her hand. "I'd like to see some proof of insurance."

Slipping long, tanned fingers into his back pocket, he extracted his wallet and flipped it open. He pulled out a card and offered it to her.

Meg scrutinized the card. His full name read Dennis Daniel Metz. According to his date of birth, he'd just turned twenty-seven, making him only four months older than her. The card also showed current policy dates and full coverage with a reputable company.

"I'm Meg Bristol." She handed him the card back and pointed to her left. "This is Nan O'Brien."

"I'm Denny Metz." Denny offered his hand to Nan.

"Jim Anderson, here," the blond man piped.

The July temperature climbed with the morning sun, turning the freeway into the desert at high noon. Meg slid out of her gray linen blazer, draping it over her arm. Her white silk shell and straight skirt clung to her skin. The clip she'd twisted her hair into pulled so tight it hurt. "We need to call the police," she said to Denny to keep her mind off her discomfort.

"I already did." He cocked his head to one side and squinted to block out the sun. "Rather, my OnStar™ emergency service did." He glanced down the freeway. "They should be here soon."

Jim let out a sigh that sounded almost happy. "Well, we're not going to make it to the jobsite today." At Nan's quizzical look he replied, "We're in construction. What about you?"

"We're librarians." Nan lifted her head high. "We work at the main library downtown."

Jim shot Denny a wry 'I told you so' glance.

Hmph! Meg held her head high. Working in a library happened to be a very interesting job. Of course, construction workers couldn't appreciate that. After all, beer drinking and bar brawling was better suited to their expertise!

Whatever. She turned to Denny, changing the subject. "Do you think I could get my car fixed by Monday?"

"Ah, not really," Denny said. "It takes longer than a weekend to do major body work. Only, in your case, it's going to take a miracle."

Meg blinked. "You mean...it can't be fixed?"

Jim folded his arms as he walked around the back of the car, giving the Fiesta a thorough appraisal. "Not in this life. That baby's history."

Denny frowned at Jim then turned to Meg. "What he means is the book value on the car is less than what it would cost to fix it, so you'll probably just get the cash."

Outraged, Meg glared at Denny and Jim. "What am I going to do without a vehicle?"

"What's Denny gonna do?" Jim pointed to the Ram. "The front end's a mess!"

Meg watched Denny wince as Jim gave a blow-by-blow description of the damage and her anger suddenly cooled. Did Denny really deserve all the blame? Perhaps if she'd paid closer attention to her own driving she'd have noticed the slowdown sooner, giving them both more time to stop.

Could things get much worse? The stress of not one, but two disasters back-to-back began to fray her nerves. She'd vowed not to cry, but to her dismay, her eyes began to mist.

Denny jumped to her side, steadying her with one hand on her arm, his other on the small of her back. "What's wrong?" His voice turned silky, his touch proved surprisingly gentle. He pulled her close, encouraging her to lean on him. "Are you sure you're okay?"

The tingle of his breath in her ear shifted her pulse into overdrive, triggering warning bells in her head. Then his hand slid around her waist. Oh-oh, she thought as her stomach danced the Hokey-Pokey and turned itself around. This guy really knew how to turn on the charm, and he had her so flustered she could barely think straight much less explain her problem.

She wanted to lie and swear she felt fine, but all Meg could say sounded like "N-o-o-o...."

* * * *

He'd been suckered.

The instant Meg Bristol turned those soft amber eyes on Denny he knew it was all over but the cryin'. Literally. He had no problem supervising a rowdy construction crew, but no way could he cope with a woman's tears. Watching the petite brunette at his side turn on the waterworks gave him a feeling of utter helplessness, plus a healthy dose of guilt for totaling out her wheels.

Aw, sweetheart, Denny thought miserably. Don't do this to me.

"I'm—I'm sorry," Meg said shakily, as if reading his thoughts. She slowly pulled from his grasp and wiped a tear from her eye. "I'm just having a really, really bad day."

Never mind the old clunker probably had a couple hundred thousand miles of wear on it. Just the same, he got the feeling she was holding something back. No one shed tears over something so easily replaceable.

"Don't worry, my insurance company will pay for a rental," he heard himself promise. "If you'd like, we can use my road service and set it up right now." He hesitated, almost forgetting what he'd just said. She'd done it again--turned those big golden eyes on him and nearly melted down his insides.

Getting back to business, he instructed Jim to move Meg's vehicle onto the shoulder to allow traffic to get moving again. Looking relieved, she tossed Jim the keys then grabbed her purse and followed Denny to the passenger side of his truck.

She feels light as a feather, he marveled, noting the perfect fit his hands made around her waist as he lifted her into the vehicle. For a moment, he imagined himself sliding his arms around her, pressing her soft curves against his chest.

Nice idea, Metz, but you already have a girlfriend.

He pulled away as Leeza's sexy silhouette invaded his mind. Leeza had him totally infatuated--and counting the hours until tonight.

He jumped into the truck and slammed the door. Moments later, he pulled onto the shoulder behind Jim and shut off the engine.

"Ouch!" The corner of a magazine jutted out from under the seat, jabbing Meg's ankle. Reaching down, she pulled out the glossy publication and her face turned deeper scarlet than the thong bikini on the busty cover model.

"Uh, that's Jim's," Denny blurted. He snatched the copy of Playboy from her hand and tossed it into the back seat. Oops! He didn't know if his face flushed as well, but it burned hotter than a firecracker. It was time to get busy and reserve that car. Yessiree. He pressed the blue button on the dash and connected with an advisor. Together, he and Meg reserved a Malibu and arranged its delivery.

After that, they had nothing else to do but wait for the police. Denny turned on the radio and relaxed in his seat, but became distracted by Jim sparring with Nan outside his window.

"Got a question for ya." Jim peered at Nan suspiciously, his thumbs hooked into the belt loops of his worn jeans. They stood at nearly the same height; Jim looked a blond hair taller. "What'd ya give me the finger for? I mean, what'd I do to you?"

Nan's eyes flared, their sea-green irises matching her long, flowing skirt and matching blouse. "What'd you do? You gave me one, buster!"

"Only because you did it first." Jim bared his teeth like a bulldog ready to bite. "Whaddya think--I go around flipping off chicks for the fun of it? Gimme a break, woman. I've got more class than that."

"Then prove it." Nan's wide mouth broke into a sly, triumphant smile. "Apologize."

Jim looked bewildered. "I, ah...huh?" His mouth clamped shut then opened again. He stared over his shoulder at Denny, confusion widening his deep blue eyes.

Unable to keep a straight face, Denny looked away, feigning preoccupation with the music. After a moment, he glanced back again.

Jim turned back to Nan and adjusted his baseball cap, a sure sign of defeat. "Aw right, I'm sorry. I guess I overreacted, ya know."

Nan slung the strap of her purse over her shoulder and leaned against the truck. "Yeah, I know. You really upset me."

Jim shuffled his feet. "Huh!" He stared at the ground, looking like a scolded child.

Nan slid closer. "That doesn't mean we can't be friends."

Jim's head bobbed up like a marionette's, exposing a toothy smile. "Really?"

Denny rolled his eyes. What a wimp. That dumb Swede put on a tough act, but he'd humble himself anytime he thought it could help him get a date.

A siren announced an officer's arrival followed by a tow truck for Denny's vehicle. For the next thirty minutes, Denny and Meg completed the necessary paperwork while Jim and Nan arranged for rides home. Then Denny and Meg followed the tow truck in her car to a body shop in Forest Bend. Once there, he called his insurance company and reported his auto claim.

An hour or so later he'd concluded his business and felt free to leave, but something made him pause. He glanced across the dingy waiting room where Meg sat on the edge of her chair, thumbing through a tattered People magazine and waiting for the adjuster to arrive to get her settlement. She looked frustrated and tired. Denny gazed into her soft, amber eyes and his heart skipped a beat.

Aw, why not.... With a sigh of resignation, he picked a spot on the sagging plaid sofa and stretched out. "Might as well get comfortable," he said with an encouraging smile. "This could take awhile."

He pulled out his iPhone and dialed Leeza's number. After four rings, her call went to voicemail. His disappointment gave way to anticipation once he began to talk.

"Hi. It's Denny. Sorry I missed you. I just called to let you know I...ah...." He glanced at Meg then shifted his gaze to the floor. "I had an accident this morning so my truck's in the shop. I'm not sure what time I'll pick you up tonight, but I'll let you know when I'm on my way."

"You don't have to stick around on my account," Meg said as he shoved the phone back into his pocket. "I wouldn't want you to miss your date."

"Well, I'd like to hear what the adjuster has to say about my pickup, anyway," he said in a persuasive tone. The body shop's manager would have routinely called him and discussed the estimate, but she didn't need to know that. "Who knows, maybe we'll luck out and be next on his schedule."

Unfortunately, Denny's luck had nothing to do with it. He and Meg waited all morning, drinking old coffee, taking turns reading sections of the newspaper and watching game shows on a fuzzy television screen. Hours passed. Meg looked hot and uncomfortable in her designer suit, not to mention bored. Even so, he gave her credit for hanging in there.

Not many girls would have withstood the grungy conditions, or the lusty looks from the guys in the shop--another reason why he'd stayed. By four o'clock, a portly, balding man wearing navy Dockers and a striped polo shirt sauntered into the body shop. It took him only twenty minutes to survey the damage to Denny's truck, authorize the repair and scribble out a check to Meg for her Fiesta.

Meg gave Denny a ride home in her rented white Malibu, even though the trip took her at least twenty minutes out of her way. "Thanks for sticking around," she said as he opened the door and stuck one leg out.

A warm, satisfied feeling enveloped him. "Hey, it's no problem." He smiled and took her hand, gently squeezing it. "I guess I've developed a soft spot for librarians."

He'd meant his answer to be lighthearted and teasing, though once said, it sounded straight from the heart. Their gazes held, and for a moment, he almost regretted having other plans for tonight. "You, ah..." he slowly released her hand, "...take care now."

"You, too," she replied, sounding equally bewildered.

Denny paused for a heartbeat then climbed out of the car and shut the door.

He responded to her wave as she pulled away, wondering why such a pretty girl like her didn't have guys lined up, waiting to get a date. Obviously, she didn't have a boyfriend or she would have called the lucky guy this morning on the freeway. Too bad. A girl as sweet and feminine as Meg needed a man around to do things for her, like change her oil and take her out to dinner. He watched her drive out of sight, realizing how much she'd affected him in their short time together. He did have a soft spot for librarians now and always would.

Then he thought of Leeza and bolted into the four-plex, taking three stairs at a time. Inside his apartment, he checked his phone again before heading into the shower. No texts or messages... He called Leeza and got her voicemail a second time. He jammed the phone back in his pocket and paced his apartment. Where could she be? Why hadn't she tried to call him back? He tried to call her house, couldn't reach anyone until six-thirty. Her mother answered.

"Hello, Mrs. Frank, is Leeza home?" He knew he sounded anxious, but couldn't help it.

"Leeza?" Mrs. Frank echoed in a nasal voice. "Why, no. She's gone out for the evening."

"But...." Stunned, he raked his free hand through his thick hair. How could that be? "She's supposed to go out with me, Denny Metz."

"I don't know anything about that," Mrs. Frank said. "Some nice fellow picked her up about an hour and a half ago and she said she'd be out late, but she didn't say where they were going."

That would have been about the time he sat in Meg's Malibu, fondling her hand. A few highly descriptive words raced through Denny's mind, skidding to a halt on the tip of his tongue. Instead, he politely muttered good-bye to Mrs. Frank and hung up, then made a fist to take his displeasure out on the wall. Luckily, he came to his senses before making contact.

He flopped onto the sofa and stared out his picture window at the park across the street, feeling worse than when he saw the damage to his truck. Well, so much for the perfect night with the woman of his dreams. His gut twisted. "I'd sure like to get my hands on the guy who got lucky with my date," he growled. The idea had merit, though sitting in jail for assault didn't

He pulled out his phone and dialed Jim, but the call went straight to voicemail. He sighed. Now what? He refused to sit around this dump and mope. Suddenly an idea popped into his head, and the more Denny considered it the more his mood brightened. Why not? On the way down to the parking lot, he searched his pockets for the scrap of paper containing her address and phone number, his spirits soaring like a rocket. A half-hour later, he bounded across her porch and knocked on her door. It opened a crack, and Meg Bristol gingerly peered out.

"Hey, there, Meg." He leaned one hand against the frame and flashed his sexiest grin. "How'd you like to go out?"

* * * *

Meg peeked through the slim opening of her front door. "You want to go out with me?"

Denny stood on her porch wearing a black leather jacket, tight jeans and an irresistible grin. One hand rested against the frame, the other gripped a silver helmet tucked under his arm. "Why not? I can't imagine a better way to spend Friday night than with my favorite librarian."

Something didn't jive here. A couple hours ago, his night had been booked solid. She studied him warily. "What happened to your date?"

"She's, uh, busy." He gave a careless shrug. "No big deal. We're just friends."

That's not the impression I got this morning, Meg thought, remembering the voice message he left for the female in question. The dreamy glow in his eyes, the purr in his voice had described a man in love. What did he want with Meg? The answer seemed obvious. She smiled with cool politeness. "Thanks for the offer Denny, but I don't think so."

His deep, throaty laugh echoed through the opening. "Sure you do. It's eighty degrees out here and there isn't a cloud in the sky. What a waste to sit at home on such a gorgeous night."

She didn't intend to sit at home, but he didn't need to know that. As soon as she got rid of him, she planned to meet up with Nan and drive over to a certain local hangout to look for Tom and his...er, new fiancée. And when she found them...well, she had plenty to say. She took a deep breath. "Actually, I'm kind of busy, so--" She started to push the door shut, but it banged against his outstretched boot.

"So, that's all the more reason to take some time out, have a little fun. After what you've been through today, you deserve it. Besides," his eyes twinkled, his voice mellowed to a sexy, tantalizing drawl as he leaned toward her, "I want to make it up to you for totaling out your wheels."

He sounded so convincing Meg waffled a moment then shook her head. She had no desire to be this bad boy's temporary squeeze toy, even if he did radiate enough charm to fill the Target Center Arena. "You've already done more than enough for me. Thanks for the offer, but I'm not in the mood for partying." She stared at him. "Or anything else you have in mind."

"I figured we'd take a ride over to Forest Bend and do some car shopping," Denny countered smoothly.

Oh-h-h, she thought, surprised. Then...is that all? She bit back a silly impulse to ask where he'd planned to take his date. Dinner? A movie? Probably both, she reasoned with a sniff then reminded herself she wasn't interested in him, anyway. "You're asking me to go shopping?"

"Sure, why not? Dealers are open until nine."

"Since I have the rental, I don't think it's urgent to find one today. Anyway, I can't afford a new vehicle. I plan on asking my dad to help me check out some used car ads on Monday night."

He leaned closer, slipping his fingers around the edge of the door. The pungent scent of leather mixed with Polo Sport wafted through the opening. "Why wait until then?"

"My parents are at the cabin this weekend." Oops! She grimaced, realizing she'd just helped his cause.

His fingers slid up the door, touching hers. "Great. Then going with me will give you a head start."

Tiny sparks skittered across her hand, short-circuiting her thoughts. "Um...that's not necessary." She pulled her hand away and tucked it behind her back. My, but it suddenly grew warm in here, in spite of the air-conditioning.

He eased the door open wide enough to expose her face. "Aw, come on, Meg. You need a good car and I know auto mechanics better than most people do. Besides, your free use of the rental probably runs out in a couple days."

So soon? She hadn't considered that. She also had no idea if her dad, a portrait photographer, would be available on such short notice. He often scheduled evening appointments. "I don't know...."

"It's my bike, isn't it?" Denny shifted the helmet under his arm. "You're afraid of motorcycles."

Meg averted her gaze to the driveway where a black Honda Gold Wing posed strong and proud. Just like its owner. She met Denny's curious gaze. "It's not the motorcycle," she said truthfully. "It's me."

"You?" He pushed the door open all the way. "Why?"

"For one thing, I don't know you well enough to go out with you. Besides, you already have a girlfriend." She placed her hands on her hips, sensitive to the subject matter. "It wouldn't be fair to her."

Denny chuckled, raising his free hand in a gesture of a truce. "Hey, I'm only asking for a couple hours, not the rest of your life." He pulled open the door and strolled into the house, his gaze scanning her compact, but cozy living room. "And for the record, I'm not cheating on anybody. Like I said, she and I are just friends." His deep blue eyes twinkled with anticipation. "Come on, Meg. Let's go."

"It's been a long, frustrating day and I—"

"Don't worry. I'll have you back home by sunset."

She sighed. "Yeah, but--"

"The Malibu costs at least two hundred a week, you know, and that doesn't include all those extra charges and taxes."

"Two hundred a week?" Meg swallowed hard. She couldn't afford that and make her house payment, too. "Well...well..." She glanced around, thinking furiously. "I guess an hour or two would be all right."

Denny displayed a confident smile. "Great. But you'd better change." His gaze tumbled down her long yellow sundress. "You can't wear that on a motorcycle. Your, ah, skirt will be flying up around your neck."

"I'll throw on a pair of jeans," Meg said as she backed into her bedroom. "Be with you in a minute." She slammed the door and made a beeline for the closet. The sooner they got going, the sooner she'd get back home to change again and go pick up Nan. Pulling out a stack of denims, she dumped them on the bed. Not this one, she thought, dropping the first pair on the floor, then another, and another until she'd discarded them all.

"Nice little place you've got here," Denny remarked from the living room. "I like those big oaks in the front yard."

"I bought it on a contract for deed from my grandmother's estate," Meg said in a loud voice, tripping over the scattered clothes. "I love it here, but it's costing a lot to bring everything up to code."

"Did the furniture come with it, too? I haven't seen this corduroy stuff since grade school."

"Yeah, I bought it from the estate for a dollar. It's so outdated no one else in the family wanted it, and at that price I couldn't afford to turn it down." She raided the closet again, tossing clothes in the air like a juggler. Three drawers and a clothesbasket later Meg found the perfect pair of jeans and a black, rhinestone-studded Bebe T-shirt. By the time she finished dressing, her room looked like someone had broken in and vandalized it.

"Hey, you!" Denny sounded annoyed. "What are you doing?"

Meg poked her head out of the bedroom to tell him to cool his jets but ended up laughing instead. Across the room, Denny sat on a small, avocado sofa, wearing jeans and a red polo shirt. His jacket and helmet lay in a pile on the floor next to him. Mopsy, a fluffy white cat, sprawled at his feet, rolling on her back and exposing a round, pink tummy.

Denny frowned at the wiggling fur ball. "What does it want?"

"She wants you to tickle her with your toes."

He stared at Meg as though she'd suggested something obscene. "Uh-uh. I don't like cats and they don't like me."

"Well, don't tell her that. You'll hurt her feelings."

Meg shut the door again and stood at the mirror. Errant wisps of chocolate hair framed her face. What little makeup she wore emphasized her wide, amber eyes and dark lashes. In spite of it all, she looked vibrant, content, and she suddenly knew why. That good-looking, smooth-talking hotshot had worked his magic on her.

And I sucked it up like a fourteen-year-old experiencing her first crush on a handsome boy. The realization caught her by surprise.

That's it, I'm not going.

She yanked the back of her T-shirt out of her pants then caught her reflection in the mirror. "Yes, you are," she lectured the girl staring back at her. "If that rental has a time limit on it then you need to find another car as soon as possible." Stuffing the shirt back into her pants again, she thought about riding with Denny on his bike and imagined her body tucked tightly behind him...with some of her most intimate parts pushed up against him. The thought sent a shiver straight through the parts in question.

"Oh no, I'm not." She wrenched the shirt back out, spied the Malibu's keys on the dresser and shook her head. "Get serious, girl. You have to buy another car and he's offering to help. A couple hours with this guy isn't going to change your life."

With a sigh of resignation, she pulled her hair into a ponytail, applied a couple swipes of mascara and some lip-gloss. Taking a deep breath, she swung open her bedroom door. "Okay, I'm--"

Meg couldn't believe her eyes. Denny lay sprawled on the sofa, stiff as a cadaver with his legs outstretched and both arms spread along the backrest. Even his eyes looked frozen--wide open. In the center of his chest, Mopsy sat curled into a fluffy white mound, watching him with adoring eyes and purring faster than a drum roll.

How sweet, Meg thought, and wondered if she'd misjudged him. Any guy who had a soft spot for her cat couldn't be all bad.

* * * *

Denny cranked the throttle and the bike roared onto the freeway. They had exactly ninety minutes until closing time, not nearly enough to check out the half-dozen used car lots along dealer's row in Forest Bend. Even so, he meant to cover as much ground tonight as possible.

Meg sat behind him, rigid as a post, wearing a dark leather jacket and his spare helmet. For someone who swore she held no fear of motorcycles, she sure seemed nervous.

He couldn't help but stare when she walked out of her bedroom wearing skin-tight jeans and that sparkly T-shirt. He definitely liked what he saw and meant to compliment her, though he never got the opportunity. Having a ten-pound cat pounce on his chest at the same time stole his thunder, not to mention his breath!

Up ahead, the Forest Bend overpass loomed across the horizon. He signaled and exited the freeway, taking the service road to Chick's Auto Mall.

The "Mall" consisted of an asphalt lot, a dozen rows of late model cars and a small, white trailer used for an office. Denny drove up and parked the bike. Once their feet touched solid ground, he helped Meg slip out of her jacket before peeling off his own and stuffing them both into the saddlebags.

They wandered through the lot, gazing at cars of all sizes, shapes and colors.

"See anything you like?" Denny paused as a sudden sneeze overtook him. He looked down and saw frizzy white hairs decorating the front of his shirt.

"Definitely!" Sounding smitten, Meg hurried over to a fiery-red Ford. "Wow. What a cool car."

"You've got that right." Denny slipped his hands into his pockets and followed her. "It's a Mustang." He peered through the driver's side window. "It's got a lot of nice options. H-m-m-m...it's a five-speed, too."

At that moment, the infamous Chick himself decided to make an appearance. He stepped out of the trailer and moseyed toward them wearing a suit and a tie the color of dirty motor oil. "Evenin', folks," he said in a raspy voice.

Looking like the backside of fifty, he sported thinning hair and a blunt-featured face. A slight paunch bulged atop his silver dollar belt buckle, probably from munching on too many jelly doughnuts in his spare time.

"Evening," Denny and Meg replied simultaneously.

Chick nodded toward the Ford. "Just got 'er in this mornin'. She's fully loaded--cruise, tilt, CD player and power everything. Give ya a good deal."

"We'll see," Denny countered gruffly, shifting into his bargaining mode. Used-car lots in Minnesota were dime a dozen and most went out of business almost as fast as they started up. Chick reputedly stayed afloat because he knew how to talk people out of their money. Only this time he'd met his match. Denny stood ramrod straight and stared Chick in the eye. "What's your asking price?"

"Fifteen Thousand."

"Too much." Denny grunted out the words and circled the car, examining it as though it was a piece of junk.

Chick never missed a beat. Instead, he lifted the hood. "She's pretty clean. Got a V-6 with low miles." He produced a set of keys attached to a cardboard tag and unlocked the door. "Go ahead, little lady. Start 'er up." He opened the door and offered Meg the keys. She slid into the white velour seat, fitting as though it had been custom made for her. The car started at the turn of the ignition, humming softly.

Chick grinned. "They call this here color 'lipstick red.' You like it?"

"Do I ever." Meg glanced longingly around the car's plush interior. "It's too expensive for my budget, though." She looked up at him with disappointment. "I've got house payments."

Chick grinned triumphantly, as though Meg had begged him to sell it to her. He turned to Denny. "She likes it. C'mon, let's go up to the shack and work out the financing."

Denny cocked his ear to listen to the engine. "We're not ready to make any deals yet. Sounds like it's missing once in a while."

Chick shook his head. "Had my best mechanic check her out." He leaned over the engine to listen. "Said them fuel injectors are like new. Matter of fact," Chick straightened and shut the hood, "he talked about picking up this one for himself."

Denny knelt, pointing to a dark spot under the car. "Look at that." He took a sample, rubbing the oily substance between his fingers. The spot could have been there for a week, but he wouldn't admit that in a million years. What, and lose his edge in this deal?

"It's too thick to be fresh," Chick argued, calling his bluff. "Probably came from the station wagon that I sold last Thursday."

Chick walked around the hood, stood next to the open car door and stared down at Meg. "You look good in this car. You like lookin' good in this car?" He turned to Denny. "She likes lookin' good in this car. I'll take fourteen-nine for it."

"Only a hundred bucks off?" Denny threw his hands in the air, pretending to be insulted. "This thing has dents! Scratches! Dings on the doors! She's probably going to have to repaint it. We'll give you twelve."

Chick shook his head, countering with an incredulous laugh. "C'mon, man. I gotta make some money on this deal. You're trying to bust my bank. Fourteen-eight."

Denny shoved his hands on his hips. "The car already has thirty thousand miles on it. Pretty soon it's going to need new brakes and tranny maintenance. I'll give you twelve-five."

Meg turned off the car and slid out. Chick zeroed in on her by planting his face squarely in front of hers. "You want this car, don't you?"

Meg started to reply, but before she could speak, Denny eased himself between them and slid his arm around her. "Don't answer him," he whispered in her ear. Coconut scented shampoo filled his head and for a moment, he forgot all about the Mustang. His arm innately tightened around her waist, pulling her close.

Her lips parted slightly as she gazed into his eyes.

Denny swallowed hard, knowing he should pay attention to Chick, but somehow he just couldn't let the moment slip away.

Chick slapped his hand on Denny's shoulder, forcing him back to reality. "See, she wants this car, and we both know that what the little lady wants, the little lady must get, right? I'll sacrifice it for fourteen-seven."

Denny felt like telling Chick that the little lady wanted to see his lights punched out, but flashed his best killer smile instead. "Thirteen thousand or no deal."

Chick grimaced and emitted a groan, as though he'd just received a beating. "Fourteen-five. That's the best I can go."

"We'll think about it." Denny turned his back on Chick. "Come on, little lady." He strolled toward his motorcycle with Meg still at his side. He sniffled. Some of that cat hair seemed to have gotten up his nose.

Meg stared up at him. "What was that all about?"

Denny grinned with satisfaction. "About the most fun I've had in a long time." He let go of his grip on her and opened a saddlebag. "C'mon," he said as he pulled out her jacket. "Let's go find the next dealer and do it again."

* * * *

The evening sun hovered over the horizon like a fireball, painting the sky with streaks of crimson and gold as Meg and Denny walked across the parking lot of the third dealership they'd canvassed tonight.

Denny glanced back at the rows of used cars. "So, did you see anything that you'd like to take a second look at tomorrow?"

"I want to test drive that red Mustang at Chick's Auto Mall," Meg said wistfully and kicked at a pebble with her boot. Everything about that car--the 'Lipstick Red' color, the style, the excitement she felt sitting behind the wheel of such a powerful vehicle--gave it an irresistibility she couldn't resist. She'd never owned anything so sexy, or impractical in her life, but she didn't care. It was time for a change. She sighed. "I just don't know if I can afford it."

Denny paused, digging into his pocket for his keys. "I'll give Chick a call tomorrow morning and see what he's willing to realistically take for it. I've dealt with him before and I'm willing to bet he'll drop the price by a grand. How much do you have for a down payment?"

She held up her thumb and forefinger together, forming a big zero. "I'm going to use the money the adjuster gave me for auto insurance and ask my dad to loan me the down payment." Her hand dropped to her side. "He's pretty cool about helping out in an emergency. Last month he installed a new water heater for me and replaced a spring in the garage door. I guess it all depends on what he thinks of the vehicle."

"I wouldn't worry about it," Denny said softly. "If he knows anything about cars, he'll like it as much as you do. Have him take it for a test drive. I'm sure if it handles the road as good as it looks, getting the down payment out of him won't be a problem."

What a sweet thing to say. He sounded so sincere it made her regret the way she'd acted when he first offered to take her car shopping. Tom would have never gone to such trouble for her.

They reached Denny's motorcycle and began to open up the saddlebags. Meg paused, looking up. "Thank you for going out of your way to help me find another car. You didn't have to do that, but I really appreciated it."

"It's no trouble." He grinned. "I think we make a good team. Don't you?"

She nodded. "I learned more about cars and the art of making a deal in one night than I have in my entire life."

Denny reached out and brushed a tendril from her face as he gazed into her eyes. "Yeah, well, I had more fun tonight than I've ever had on a first date in my entire life."

Did he say first date? A couple hours ago, she would have vehemently opposed it, but now the idea didn't seem so far-fetched....

A sudden blare disrupted the moment. Meg blinked, trying to get her bearings when she realized the noise came from her own phone. Oh! She scrambled to answer it on the second ring. "Hello?"

"Hey, it's me, Nan." A cacophony of guitars and voices in the background nearly drowned out her voice. "I've got some fantastic news for you."

"Why haven't you been paying attention to your phone? I've been trying to reach you all night." Meg turned her back on Denny for privacy and walked away from the bike. "Where are you?"

"I'm at Northern Lights Bar and Grill with, um...Jim."

"Jim?" Meg stopped pacing, confused. What happened to Nan's plans to meet up with her tonight? "Jim who?"

"Jim Anderson," Nan replied, sounding a tad sheepish. "You remember him. He's that friend of Denny What's-his-name."

Yeah, she remembered him, the huffy little jerk with the big mouth. Meg didn't know whether to laugh or stay ticked off. "I thought you didn't like how rude he acted this morning."

"He's making it up to me." Nan let the sentence trail off, giving Meg the distinct feeling that she and Jim were gazing at each other, savoring the moment in their own little world. Well, so much for Nan's fantastic news.

"But that's not what I called about," Nan added, as though reading her mind. The noise suddenly sounded muffled as though Nan had covered her mouth with her hand. "He's here, with her."

Meg opened her mouth to speak, but ironically couldn't think of a thing to say. On one hand, she felt duty-bound to tell Tom Duffey's fiancée about his cheating, lying ways. On the other hand, she didn't relish the idea of breaking the news to the poor girl in front of his closest friends. Her business with Tom and company didn't concern them.

"How soon can you get over here? He just ordered a round of drinks, but I don't know how long he plans to stick around. If you want to catch up with him, you'd better hurry."

Meg cut a sideways glance at Denny as she debated what to do. He stood casually zipping his jacket, but when he glanced back at her, his furrowed brows showed concern.

As if sensing Meg's reluctance, Nan said, "It's now or never."

Meg visualized Tom 'showing off' the future Mrs. Duffey and clenched her fist. "I'll be right there."

She shoved the phone in her pocket and walked back to the bike. "That was Nan. Did you know that Jim asked her out on a date tonight? And she agreed?"

His jaw dropped.

"Yeah, me neither. They're at Northern Lights Bar and Grill. Are you familiar with the place?"

"Sure." Denny paused, a flash of emotion widening his eyes as though the subject hit upon a sensitive spot. "I know one of the bartenders."

"Would you mind if we stopped by there on the way home?" She couldn't wait to see Tom's face when she walked in with Denny at her side.

"Not at all." Denny grabbed her helmet and handed it to her with a wry smile. "This I've got to see."

* * * *

The parking lot of Northern Lights Bar and Grill looked like any one of the used car lots they'd inspected tonight. Rows and rows of vehicles surrounded the square, windowless building, situated on a service road next to the freeway. A neon sign flashing "Northern Lights" in rainbow colors lit up the parking lot. Denny and Meg squeezed the bike onto a narrow strip of blacktop between two pickup trucks and stowed their gear.

Nan and Jim stood just inside the door, smiling like infatuated newlyweds, their fingers tightly entwined. Jim let go of her hand and looped his arm around her shoulders. Well, well, they certainly did make up!

"Anderson, you mangy hound," Denny said good-naturedly as he held the door for Meg. "You didn't tell me you were coming here tonight. What's up?" The two men grinned at each other for a few moments as something personal silently passed between them.

Nan left Jim's side and grabbed Meg by the arm. "We'll be right back," she yelled to the guys as she pulled Meg through the crowd toward the ladies' room. Just before they reached the door marked

"Ladies," she veered sharply to the left, leading Meg into another section of the bar, a quieter area where they could talk.

Nan pulled up short and whirled around, turning her back to the crowd. "Don't look now, but they're directly behind me."

Instantly, Meg leaned to the left and stared past Nan's shoulder through the wide doorway to a spot directly across the bar. She swallowed hard, taking in the scene with disbelief. Her sandy-haired ex-boyfriend sat at a table wearing his favorite khakis and dark green blazer, laughing and conversing with another couple as though he didn't possess a care in the world. Tom's apparent better half sat on his left wearing a black designer suit and enough dazzling jewelry to require an armed guard. Her thick dark hair, swept into a French roll at her nape, looked sophisticated and professionally styled, but so retro....

"Okay, then look." Nan rolled her eyes. "I wanted to explain something before you went steamrolling over there. Right after I talked to you, I ran into—"

"Th-that woman," Meg blurted. "Is she his new fiancée?"

"Yes." Nan folded her arms, her long copper curls bouncing as she nodded. "That's what I want to talk to you about. She's—"

"She's at least ten years older than him and dresses like she's going to a funeral." Meg stared some more, fuming. "I can't believe he dumped me for someone who could pass for his...his...old maid aunt. What does she have that I don't?"

"She's loaded." Nan rubbed two fingers against her thumb, symbolizing lots of cash. "I heard she's got tons of money and investments, including this bar." Nan glanced back at the happy duo engrossed in conversation with the other couple sitting at their table, a blonde and a muscular guy wearing jeans and a navy T-shirt. "Grace owns a realty company and a large portfolio of rental property. The couple sitting with her is house-hunting."

A cash cow named Grace, huh? Meg bit her lip. "How did you find out her name? Did Tom introduce you?"

Nan replied with a matter-of-fact look. "She's my landlord."

"What?"

Meg's astonished yelp caused the woman sitting across from Grace to glance her way. Embarrassed, Meg clapped her hand over her mouth as the sexy, longhaired blonde wearing a pink, scoop-neck blouse gazed at her with curiosity. The woman said something to Grace and simultaneously everyone at the table, including Tom, turned their attention on Meg.

Her palms glistened with sweat under the scrutiny of the curious onlookers. Tom, however, regarded her with a blank stare, as thought he didn't know her. His phony act angered her, but at the same time, it made her angry with herself for blindly falling for him. The realization flooded her with regret.

Suddenly a long, sinewy arm encircled her waist, pulling her close.

"If you're looking to even the score, you'd better come up with something more shocking than just staring a hole though the guy," Denny murmured, arching one brow.

His comment touched a nerve. Or was it his honesty?

"You think I'm not doing enough to get even?" She glared at him, her face a mere inch from his. "Okay, hotshot. Then kiss me." He

It happened so fast Meg didn't have time to consider the consequences, much less change her mind. Her heart didn't even bother to try. He gripped her chin in the palm of his hand, tipped her head back and crushed his mouth against hers. The moment their lips collided, the commotion in the room seemed to fade away. Her senses shifted into overdrive, compelling her to lean forward. Denny wrapped his arms around her waist, pulling her even closer. The musky scent of his cologne filled her head, the pounding of his heart vibrated under her palms as they spread across his chest. She couldn't breathe. She didn't care. She didn't know a simple kiss could feel so amazing.

The encounter ended all too soon, but rather than pull away, Denny rested his forehead against hers and grinned. "I'll bet that got everyone's attention."

"Wow," Meg said, catching her breath. "Mine, too." No one had ever kissed her like that....

"Come on," he said in a husky voice, sounding shaken. He took one look at the people at Tom's table and scowled. "Let's get out of here." He grabbed her hand and led her through the crowd, stopping only to tell Jim and Nan to meet them next to Jim's car in fifteen minutes.

Meg drew in a breath of fresh air once they stepped outside into the warm July night. "Oh, look," she said in awe and pointed toward the night sky. "There's the big dipper."

They ambled across the parking lot, holding hands and taking in the celestial show. "I like looking at the stars, especially though a telescope,"

Denny remarked. "Astronomy is cool." He motioned toward the bar. "But not as interesting as what just happened back there."

They burst out laughing.

"How did you know?" Meg sobered as they approached a dark blue Chevrolet. "About the situation with Tom, I mean."

Denny stopped and clasped her hands in his. "Jim spilled the whole story as soon as you walked away."

She sighed and shook her head. She should have known better than to tell someone who couldn't keep a secret. "That Nan is such a busybody."

"So is Jim," Denny replied with a snort. "That's why they're just right for each other." He pulled her into his arms. "Listen, I'm sorry that jerk sitting with Grace McGuire broke your heart, but as far as I'm concerned, you're better off without him."

She groaned. "You mean, you know her, too?"

He shrugged. "I ought to, Grace is my landlord. She's always made it clear she wants to be more, but I don't date women old enough to have been my babysitter." He placed his hands on her waist and lifted her up, setting her on the trunk of the Chevrolet. "Forget him, honey. He's a gold digger. She's a control freak with a fetish for younger men. They deserve each other." Denny rested his hand on the nape of her neck, steadily drawing her closer. "Keep in mind--when one door closes another always opens. That goes for me, too."

Curious, Meg sat up straight. "What do you mean?"

"Remember that couple sitting with Grace? The blonde is Leeza Frank, one of the bartenders here. She's the girl I had a date with tonight, but she stood me up." He laughed, his blue eyes crinkling. "At first, it pretty much ruined my day, but you know what? She did me favor because if she'd have kept her commitment, you and I wouldn't have become friends." A soft breeze ruffled his dark, wavy hair. "I'd much rather be here with you, even if I am allergic to your cat."

Laughing, Meg slid her arms around his neck. "Prove it, hotshot."

He reached up and pulled the ponytail holder out of her hair, sending it tumbling about her shoulders. One dark brow lifted in approval as he flashed a lopsided grin. "We both know that what the little lady wants, the little lady must get," he said, quoting Chick. And then he kissed her.

The End

52

About the Author

Denise Meinstad, also known as Denise Devine, has had a passion for books since the second grade when she discovered 'Little House on the Prairie' by Laura Ingalls Wilder. She wrote her first book, a mystery, at age thirteen and has been writing ever since. She joined Romance Writers of America (RWA) in 1991 and has won or placed in numerous contests. In 2008, her contemporary inspirational romance, This Time Forever, was a finalist in RWA's Golden Heart Contest. Denise lives on six wooded acres in East Bethel, Minnesota, with her husband, Steve, and her two problem (feline) children, Mocha and Lambchop. She loves to read, write, study and travel.

Shadow Trail
by
LuAnn Nies

Crystal Harrington swore she had the worst luck ever. Not only had she gotten stuck with the ugly purple snowmobile, the one with non-functioning hand warmers on the handlebars, she'd also been selected to carry the tampons and matches from the survival kit. If that wasn't bad enough, the man her friend Melissa had fixed her up with for this supposedly romantic weekend decided to back out.

"You know what, Melissa?" Crystal stopped and placed a hand on her friend's arm as they reached the main doors leading to the Northern Lights Lodge parking lot. "It's okay with me if I don't snowmobile today." *Or any other day for that matter.* Spending the holiday weekend alone in the north woods, in the middle of February, wasn't Crystal's idea of a romantic weekend. Besides, she didn't want to be remembered as the only one who couldn't get a date for Valentine's Day.

"Crystal, we all want you to stay for the weekend," Melissa pleaded, grasping both of Crystal's hands in hers. "It won't be the same without you."

Crystal chuckled. "No, it would be better."

She'd only agreed to come this weekend because Melissa insisted it was time she extended her boundaries. It had been two years since her last romance blew up in her face when she hadn't leaped at the chance to go bungee jumping or skydiving. This weekend was supposed to be about her loosening up and trying something new.

Soon the rest of the group chimed in, convincing Crystal to at least stay for the day. Tomorrow morning she'd pack up and head back to the Twin Cities - leaving romance to the lovers.

She flipped her head forward, used a Scrunchy to place her unruly auburn curls in a Pebbles style ponytail, then donned her helmet and goggles. It wasn't long before she and the six couples were suited up and heading out across a frozen lake.

Now that looks like a romantic spot, Crystal sighed, admiring a little cabin nestled among assorted pines and birch trees. Throw in a cozy fire and a handsome woodsman and she'd have it made.

Crystal would have rather stayed out in the open, which made it easier to keep an eye on Melissa up ahead of her, but her friend's sled shot up a narrow trail and disappeared into a dense growth of trees. Maneuvering her sled onto the trail, Crystal blinked as she was suddenly engulfed in darkness. Within seconds, her eyes adjusted as she bumped along the twisting, narrow trail where pines, oaks, and birch trees shot skyward. She giggled. This must be what a bug feels like to be lost in a lush green shag carpet.

Her sled bounced and bucked along, jerking from one side of the rough trail to the other. As she wrestled for control of the handlebars, barely missing the rocks and trees that lined the trail, a scene from her past flashed before her eyes of a night she spent in the back seat of Danny Larson's car.

Crystal fell behind, slowed by trees, rocks, dips, and turns. When she came to an open area, she accelerated and caught up to the group. By now, they had removed their helmets and coats. They had divided into pairs, some had their heads together talking, and others stood holding hands. It was obvious by their expressions some craved privacy. Superstitious, Crystal knew she was the unlucky number thirteen, and wished she hadn't agreed to come along.

Glancing around, she found they'd stopped in a swampy area where cattails and tree stumps covered the frozen ground. Had it been summer, Crystal could have pictured a moose and calf standing up to their knees in water munching on the lush vegetation.

The sound of engines roaring to life pulled Crystal out of her daydream. She frowned. Oh, I wish I'd see some wild life. I'm sure the snowmobiles have scared everything away.

They rode for several more hours, jolting across lakes and fields and following winding trails through the woods. Thankfully, the group always stopped and waited for her to catch up. Melissa would turn, give Crystal the thumbs up sign and Crystal always returned the gesture.

Later in the day, the group stopped to check their map. Crystal removed her gloves and helmet and checked her watch; it was 2:00 pm and she agreed with her stomach—it was time to eat. *Damn, I should have stuck a cereal bar or something in my pocket.*

"How are you doing?" Melissa asked. She'd placed her helmet and gloves on the seat of her sled. She ran her fingers through her short blond hair as she strolled toward Crystal.

Crystal couldn't help but smile at her tall, slender friend. Melissa had managed, as usual, to look sexy even in her cumbersome snowmobile suit. She floated gracefully over the snow in Frankenstein boots.

"I'm fine," Crystal replied, but hoped her friend couldn't detect that she felt out of place being the only one without a partner. "I'm getting a little hungry, though."

"Yeah, me too. I think Mister Know-It-All," Melissa tilted her head toward Charles, or Chaz as he liked to be called, "Took the wrong trail. They're trying to figure out which one will get us back to the lodge the quickest."

Crystal glanced at the strange smoky sage-green color of the sky and knew it wouldn't be long before it started to snow. She'd call him King Chaz if he'd get them back to the lodge before dark.

The lead driver folded and returned his map to a secret compartment on his sled. His confident smile was all the reassurance she needed. She didn't care what the rest of the group had planned for the night; all she wanted was a good meal, a couple Ibuprofens, a hot bath and a warm bed.

When snow started to fall gently, she felt as if she were in a living Christmas card. But the beautiful scenery soon vanished and it became much harder to keep her eye on Melissa when the trail turned back into the dense woods.

Crystal came to a fork in the trail and stopped. She couldn't see Melissa or any of the other riders. She ripped off her helmet and searched both trails for fresh tracks. The snow had covered any evidence of the other sleds. "Which way did they go?" Her breath puffed out in a cloud when she spoke. She shivered. "Damn it! This isn't fun anymore!" She glanced around and strained to listen for familiar sounds. It would soon be dark. She looked up through the snowflakes and watched the treetops dance in the eerie silence.

She glanced to the right and then to the left, both trails led into the unknown. "Crap!" Should I just stay here? How long would it be before they realize I'm missing and come looking for me? Sighing, she recalled the way the couples had played grab-ass all day. "They'll pair off as soon as they get back to the lodge. They'll think I went straight to my room. It could be days before any of them come up for air long enough and realize I'm missing!"

Her stomach twisted into painful knots. If she waited, she'd be a snowmobilesicle when they found her. She couldn't just sit here and do nothing, though. "Which way should I go?" she said, straining to see through the nickel size snowflakes. "What if I go the wrong way and run out of gas?" She glanced down at the sled, "How much gas do I have left?" Closing her eyes, she released a long breath. "Lord, give me a sign, anything to show me the right way to go."

Hoping to see or hear something, Crystal waited, quietly listening, while her gaze swept the forest. However, what she saw paralyzed her with fear. There to her left not more than thirty feet away in the middle of the trail stood the silhouette of a large wolf. How long had he been watching her? Was he planning to take her home to meet the family? Was this her sign?

When he tilted his head back and howled, Crystal slipped on her helmet, turned her sled in the opposite direction, and squeezed down on the throttle. She shot down the trail, her heart slamming against her ribs. All thoughts of hunger replaced with fear and adrenalin.

She wouldn't look back. Just concentrate on not crashing! She cut a sharp curve and ducked under a low hanging branch, then stood on the metal running boards for the dips and swells and prayed she wouldn't fall off. The huge snowflakes made visibility impossible. She didn't know where she was going, but she wasn't going to be late getting there.

She came to a steep hill, gripped the seat cushion with her knees, and squeezed the throttle. She shot up the incline, missed the curve, and sailed off the trail. The engine roared as the sled soared through the air. It hit the ground and Crystal flew over the windshield, landing several feet from the sled.

* * * *

Rick Saunders poured himself another cup of coffee then stared through the window at the heavily falling snow. Though the temperature had risen, the wet heavy snow had a way of making it feel colder than what registered on the thermometer. He took a sip from his cup and the lethal brew burned all the way down his throat - just the way he liked it. It was a good night to bank up the fire, settle into his oversized leather chair, and get caught up on some reading.

He chuckled. Who was he kidding? Being a Ranger on the Minnesota Canadian border for the last eighteen years had taught him that the average person didn't have enough sense to check the forecast before venturing out. Whether on snowmobile, snowshoes, or cross-country skis, it was always the same. As he watched menacing clouds swallow everything in darkness he knew it wasn't going to be a quiet night.

When his phone rang five minutes later, Rick had already changed into his heavy clothes and filled his thermos.

"Hello?"

"Rick? Tom."

"Hey, Tom. What'cha got for me tonight?" Rick glanced out the window for him.

"Well, we got a report from the Northern Lights Lodge that a party of thirteen went out earlier on snowmobiles, but only twelve made it back as the storm rolled in."

"Do they know what section they were in when they last saw the guy?" Rick walked to the huge map on the wall. He located the Northern Lights Lodge and placed a red tipped pin by its name.

"They're pretty sure they were in the northeast corner of section E. They'd just stopped to check their map when they saw the clouds rolling in."

"Lucky number thirteen," He grumbled under his breath as he slipped his coveralls over his shoulders.

"Rick?"

"Yeah?" He reached for his hat and gloves.

"It's a woman." The line went silent.

He froze and his heart sank to the pit of his stomach. "What did you say?" His gaze shot to the window again. Was she out there?

Tom hesitated, "It's a woman, Rick, lost and alone."

Rick's gaze searched the darkness. His words came short and sharp. "I don't like this."

"I know you don't. I've split the trails between four of my guys. They're headed in your direction. They'll be on channel eighty as always. Rick? Rick?"

"What?" He snapped.

"Let us know when you find her."

"What makes you think I'll find this one?" Alive. The black tar he called coffee burned as badly coming back up as it had going down.

* * * *

Crystal found herself thigh deep in snow. Every step she took forced her to sit down and pull her other foot out of the snow to take another step. She knew she needed to get up the embankment and back on the trail; no one would ever find her down over the edge. She glanced over her shoulder; she could hardly see the snowmobile. Her helmet hung on the only handlebar that stuck up out of the snow, a trophy to the wilderness and the end of another noisy intruder.

She glanced up and focused on a large rock on the edge of the trail. "All I have to do is keep an eye glued to that rock, climb up to it, and then sit on the trail and wait. Someone will come along and find me. No sweat..." If she kept telling herself that, it might come true.

By the time Crystal trudged through the snow to the bottom of the bank, she could hardly see her target above her. Out of breath and tired, she didn't dare stop until she'd made it up to the trail. Making her way toward a tree, she brushed the snow away from one of the low branches. Placing her boot on the low branch, she reached up and grabbed another overhead. Pulling herself up, she uncovered more trees and a couple rocks and continued her climb. It was a slow process.

Although her arms and legs ached with fatigue and her lungs burned from the cold, she'd made progress. She shook her head like a wet mutt and blew at the damp hair in her face. Placing her foot on a rock, she reached for another limb. Her boot slipped and she slid down the embankment landing on her back in the snow.

Crystal lay there and glanced up the embankment. I definitely have the worst luck. She wanted to both laugh and cry. Sitting up, she worked her way back to the first foothold she'd found. "You can do this!" She gave herself a mental shake. "You have to do this." She started the slow, agonizing climb back up. After several minutes, she reached the edge. Digging her hands into the deep snow, she pulled herself back onto the trail. With her bare face resting on the snow-covered ground, she laid across the trail.

She'd made it. Her chest heaved as she drew the freezing air into her burning lungs. She was exhausted and her whole body ached, but she crawled across the trail and leaned against a large pine tree. After a few moments, her sweaty body cooled and the cold night air seeped through her damp clothes into her bones.

Reaching into her pockets, she pulled out one of the two tampons and a box of matches. I can build a fire, she thought with a light heart, then remembered that you were supposed to dip the tampon into the gas tank and the fuel would help light the damp wood. Closing her eyes, she tilted her head back against the tree. "There's no way I'm crawling back down there to dip this stupid tampon into the gas tank and then crawl all the way back up."

She glanced at the ground beside her and, with a shaky hand, reached for a broken tree branch. "I can make a fire without gas." Encouraged, she crawled around on her hands and knees, dug through the snow, and gathered a small pile of twigs and pinecones. Satisfied, she sat back against the tree and froze. Not more than ten feet away, in the middle of the trail, a wolf stood watching her. His head and back covered in snow. Was it the same wolf? Had he followed her?

He took a hesitant step toward her, stopped, and then as before tilted his head toward the sky and howled. In the eerie silence, she heard another wolf reply from her other side.

"Holy crap!" She focused on the wolf as she ripped off her gloves. With frozen fingers, she opened the tampon. Wolves are afraid of fire, right? Reaching for the largest stick, she tied the tampon to the end and lit it with a match. Holding the makeshift torch in one hand, she used her other hand to rake more twigs and pinecones into her small pile.

As Crystal reached into her pocket for the other tampon, she heard a noise and turned to her left. There in the middle of the trail stood a man-- at least she hoped it was a man. For all she could tell, it could have been Sasquatch. Its face covered in dark hair, its body covered in furs.

She waved her measly torch from the wolf toward the man. In a gentle voice he asked, "Are you all right, lady?"

She must be dreaming. Crystal peered into the darkness behind him. Where did he come from?

"It's all right." He took a step toward her. "You're safe now."

She shook her head, turned, and pointed her torch down the trail. But when she opened her mouth, only one word came out, "Wolf!"

Rick glanced in the direction she pointed and saw Shadow standing in the middle of the trail. He approached the shivering woman slowly, not wanting to spook her further. About five feet away he squatted down to her level. "It's all right, his name is Shadow." When her brows dipped in a questioning frown, he added, "He won't hurt you. He helped me find you." Rick stretched out a hand toward the wide-eyed woman who still held some sort of torch as a weapon toward him. "You're safe now. Are you hurt?" Her eyes still locked on his, she shook her head.

"My name is Rick, I'm a state ranger. What's yours?"

Her dark chocolate eyes blinked a couple of times before she answered, "Crystal."

"Can I have your torch, Crystal?" When she handed her weapon to him, he sighed with relief. "Can you stand?"

She nodded.

Rick stood and helped her to her feet. When she swayed, he pulled her tight to his side. She stood a foot shorter than him, and fit perfectly under his arm. She turned her face toward his, and asked, "Where did you come from?"

He tilted his head to his right. "The trail opens just around this curve. I've got a snowmobile there. I'll take you back to the ranger station."

"Oh? How far is it back to the lodge?"

He grinned. "About seventy-three miles. Are you up for that?"

She winced. "Is there food at the ranger station?"

"I'm sure I can rustle you up something." Rick glanced around. "By the way, where's your sled?"

Crystal raked her teeth over her lower lip and with a demure finger pointed to the edge of the trail. "Down there!"

Rick's brows shot up and he shook his head. "I'll give the Lodge the GPS coordinates. They can come and pull it out later."

Ranger Rick! Crystal chuckled to herself, as he led her to something that resembled a dogsled hooked to the back of his snowmobile. He wrapped her in blankets and furs and settled her into the dogsled.

"How's that?"

His smile softened his hard features and she sensed he was a gentle man. Big, but gentle.

"I need to call in and let the search party know you're all right. They'll notify your friends then we'll be off. It's not far."

Crystal smiled. "I'm fine. Thanks." She tied the straps of the white fur he'd wrapped around her head and snuggled down into their soft warmth. The clouds had drifted away and the moon cast a soft glow across the snow. Mesmerized, she watched as stars appeared one by one overhead. Breathtaking.

He started the sled, gave her a final glance, and then started off.

Rick's concentration continuously shifted from the trail to the woman reclining under a pile of furs on the tow-sled behind him. He wondered if she knew how lucky she was that Shadow found her so quickly. He shivered to think what could have happened otherwise.

Pulling into the yard, he drove up to the cabin's side door. Leaving the engine running, he walked back to the tow-sled to remove the stack of furs covering Crystal. Crystal, the name fit the winter woodland fairy he discovered. Then his gut twisted as the picture of her, cold and frightened and brandishing some kind of torch, flashed in his mind.

"Are we here?" Her soft voice wafted up through the furs.

"We're at the ranger station. How are you doing?"

She giggled. "I think I fell asleep."

He helped her from the sled. Once on her feet, she smiled and turned her heart-shaped face up to him. Wild curls spilled out from under her fur hat and the light of the moon reflected off her big brown eyes. Rick swallowed hard, fighting the urge to pull her into his arms and kiss her. *She's been scared enough for one day, you bonehead*, he thought, wanting to kick himself.

Crystal glanced into his intense eyes. He studied her as if he were trying to read her thoughts. "Are we going to go in?"

Abruptly, he released his hold on her. "You go ahead. I'll put the sleds away and be right in."

She nodded and stumbled through the snow toward the steps of the cabin. What had just happened? One moment he'd been concerned for her and she'd thought for sure he was going to kiss her, then like the snap of a finger his expression changed and a look of disappointment crossed his face. She shook her head as she opened an old wooden door and stepped into the cabin.

A small kitchen with a single sink and four-burner stove sat directly to her right. A round oak pedestal table and four chairs were on the other side of a chipped and stained linoleum topped counter. The table held stacks of charts, maps, and miscellaneous papers. The humble and homey area smelled of bacon grease, coffee and fresh bread. Her stomach growled.

Stripping down to her street clothes, she hung her jacket and snow-pants on a primitive wooden coat rack. Beyond that, a large map covered the wall. Divided into sections, the map showed trails crisscrossing through lakes, swamps, and over roads.

She moved to the end of the room and peered into what appeared to be a living room. A low light in the corner and the dim glow from the embers in the fireplace made it feel cozy and intimate. A brown leather couch appeared inviting. If she hadn't been so hungry, she could have curled right up and gone to sleep.

The back door opened and the ranger stomped in, shedding snow. Crystal watched him peel off his heavy outerwear and hang them on the wooden pegs next to hers. Then he turned toward her, his gaze washing over her as they sized each other up. The guy seemed quite tall, his shoulder length hair dark and wavy. She had to admit she liked his thick beard and mustache.

He looked away first and crossed to a five-foot tall fridge in the corner. Pulling the door open, he bent and peered in. "I'm afraid I don't have anything fancy..."

Crystal moved to stand by the counter and drummed her fingers on the counter top. "I'm not fussy! Right now I could eat an elephant!" Her stomach growled for effect.

At the sound, he looked up. "I finished off the elephant hot-dish last week." One corner of his mouth pulled into a slight grin. "How does moose stew sound?"

She returned his smile. "At this point, I'll eat anything that's hot."

He pulled a covered, metal saucepan from the fridge and placed it on the stove, then opened a drawer and retrieved a broken wooden spoon.

"I didn't think this was what a ranger station would look like." She glanced around the room, her arms swinging slightly at her sides.

"Well, this is what this one looks like," Rick said, pulling two bowls from an upper cupboard.

"It looks like someone's cabin."

"It is. It's my cabin. Have a seat," he said, nodding toward the table.

Crystal settled into one of the wooden chairs. A strange looking radio, which sat on a small table against the wall, caught her attention. She'd never seen anything like it. A microphone was attached with a curly black cord, numbers flashed, and a row of red lights blinked in rapid sequence across the front. Her fingers itched to twist the knobs to find out what they did. She glanced over her shoulder toward the stove, only to find Rick standing behind her, one brow raised. She smiled and reached for one of the two glasses of wine he held.

"Thank you." She knew she blushed at being caught ogling his radio. He didn't comment, just set the other glass on the table. He retrieved two bowls of the hearty stew, a loaf of fresh bread and a small crock of butter.

For several minutes, they dined in silence. When Rick finished, he took his bowl to the sink then returned with the bottle of wine and refilled their glasses. "Would you like more stew?"

She glanced up. "Oh. No, thank you. It was really good, but I'm full."

He watched as her dainty hand reached for her glass. He never would have guessed this pint-sized, centerfold was buried under that over-sized snowmobile suit. There was so much he wanted to know about her, besides what he needed for his report.

"So tell me, what happened out there?"

She leaned back in her chair, folded her hands on her lap, and a demure expression crossed her face. "I've been on a snowmobile once before when I was ten." She blushed. "I really enjoyed it, but at the time my cousin had been driving. I simply enjoyed the scenery."

She took a nervous sip of the wine and licked her lips. "Today wasn't very enjoyable though. I felt like all I was doing was racing to keep up with the group."

Then she frowned and he wanted to pull her onto his lap, comfort her, and kiss those full lips.

"Then the snowflakes doubled in size, which made it harder to see, and I fell behind." She wiped her hands across her jeans then tucked them under her thighs. "Then I came to a spot where the trail split in two directions and I didn't know which way to go."

"How did you end up so far off the trail?"

"I saw your friend, Shadow, standing on the trail." Her hands waved through the air. "So naturally I went in the opposite direction."

"Naturally!" *Man, she's cute.* Every expression followed by a wild hand gesture.

"You said he was tame. Is he part dog?"

Rick chuckled. "As far as I know, he's all wolf and there's nothing tame about him."

"But you said he wouldn't hurt me, that he helped you find me."

Could her eyes get any bigger? "That's his job. Well, at least he thinks it's his job. When I get a report that someone is lost, Shadow always seems to know right where they are. I've learned to trust him. He leads me to them every time."

"Where did he come from?"

"I'm not sure. He just showed up one day." *And if I knew then what I know now, I would have gotten to that poor woman in time.*

A frown marred his face. He stood, took her bowl, and walked to the sink.

There it was again. Snap! He'd changed right before her eyes. A chill seemed to fill the room. Crystal shivered. She ran her hands up and down her arms.

When he turned around, his face held no expression and she shivered again.

His brows pulled together. "Are you still cold?"

"I'm thawing out, but slowly."

"It can get pretty chilly up here if you're not used to it." He walked into the next room; she heard what sounded like logs being added to the fire. He returned with a brown and cream-colored afghan and draped it around her shoulders. A hint of pine and wood smoke brushed her cheek.

"Thanks." His strong hands lingered on her shoulders for a few seconds. She took another sip from her wineglass. "It's not that I don't like winter, it's just that my idea of a romantic weekend in the north woods would include a good looking, willing man." She spied him from the corner of her eye, grinned and added, "A cabin in the woods, a bear rug in front of a roaring fire." She pulled the afghan together with one hand and wiggled the fingers on her other hand. "A few candles and a couple bottles of wine."

Rick's brows shot up. In a sarcastic tone he replied, "Nope. Doesn't sound like you're asking too much to me." They both laughed. He strode to the table and leaned on the back of his chair. "Was that what this weekend was supposed to be... a romantic getaway?"

"Yeah, but as you've probably already figured out, I don't have the best of luck." She grinned, but the humor she'd heard in his voice and seen in his eyes just seconds ago vanished, and that irritating sober expression of his reappeared. The muscles in his jaw bulged as he clenched his teeth.

What made this man tick? How she'd love to find out.

Suddenly uncomfortable, Rick set his glass down and crossed the room. He needed to put some distance between him and the auburn haired beauty, before he embarrassed himself. "There's a bathroom down the hall," he called over his shoulder, as he walked to his bedroom. He pulled a t-shirt from a drawer and returned to the kitchen.

She was still seated at the table, a puzzled look on her face. He tossed her the shirt. "The bathroom is through there." He pointed to a doorway behind him. "You'll find everything you need in the closet. Take as long as you like."

"Thanks. Do you mind if I have another glass of wine?" She stood and placed her empty glass on the counter. A spark of mischief lit her dark brown eyes as her full lips formed a pouty-smile.

Rick's heart slammed against his chest. He reached for the wine bottle. His hand shook slightly as he filled her glass.

"Thanks. A long hot bath is just what I need."

Crystal raked her teeth over her lower lip to refrain from smiling at the bewildered expression on his face. She handed him the afghan, retrieved the T-shirt, then turned and headed for the small bathroom.

A deep tub dominated the room. Cedar boards lined the walls, filling the room with a pleasant clean scent. She turned on the hot water and opened the closet to grab a towel. Her hand shot to her mouth to stifle a sudden burst of laugher. "Everything I need, ha."

On the shelf above sixteen rolls of white bathroom tissue, lined up like little soldiers, she saw three bottles of generic shampoo, seven bars of Irish Spring, two bottles of Cornhuskers hand conditioner, one can of deodorant, an antique can of shaving cream, and one new toothbrush. "Looks like Ranger Rick doesn't get a lot of overnighters." The notion that he didn't have someone special in his life made her heart flutter. She grinned.

Water rushed up and over her shoulders as she sank down into the deep tub. Steam rose and filled the room like a heavy fog. "Heaven," she sighed. Closing her eyes, she relaxed and let the heat of the water soothe her sore muscles as her mind filled with thoughts of her mysterious rescuer.

Rick walked into the bedroom to grab a pillow and blanket. *It's not like I've never slept on the couch before.* Glancing toward the pine-log bed, he wondered how long had it been since a woman slept in his bed.

"Don't go there, man," he said shaking his head. "You could at least change the sheets for her."

That accomplished, he turned and caught his reflection in the mirror. He looked like a hermit. His beard and mustache needed a trim and his hair was longer than it had ever been before. He headed for the kitchen and frantically dug in the drawers for the electric clippers.

He plugged the clippers into an outlet under the hallway mirror, then yanked the garbage can out from under the sink. Placing the garbage can under the mirror, Rick preceded to shorten his beard and clean up his mustache. Changing the setting, he shortened his black curls in hopes of looking more presentable and not like a wild animal.

He washed up and changed his shirt, then studied himself in the mirror. Although he looked more civilized, he was still the same man. Yes, he admitted he was attracted to Crystal, but she lived in a different world. And hadn't history already proven that pursuing a relationship with a woman like her would never work out?

Rick wandered into the living room, placed another log on the fire, and then sought solace in the worn leather chair.

He felt fortunate, though. Not everyone could say that they liked their job and where they lived. And not everyone could stand on their deck at night and watch the phenomenal northern lights dance across the sky. He smiled. *I'd love to see the expression on Crystal's face the first time she witnessed the northern lights from here.*

Crystal slipped the faded gray t-shirt over her head. The sleeves rested at her elbows and the hem fell mere inches above her knees. Walking into the cozy living room, she found Rick reclining in front of a roaring fire. When she entered the room, he attempted to stand.

"No." She raised her hands. "Please stay seated." She felt his gaze upon her as she strolled to the couch. Settled on the far end of the couch, she pulled the afghan across her bare legs. When she glanced up, he averted his stare to the fire.

She studied him. He'd trimmed his beard and mustache, and his thick curly hair appeared shorter. He'd changed his shirt and a hint of Irish Spring mingled in the air with the pine smoke. The warmth of the room and the dim light from the fire mixed with the events of the day caused several wide yawns to escape Crystal. But her eyes widened when Rick abruptly stood.

"It's late. I'll show you where you can sleep."

When he walked out of the room, she stood and followed. He switched on a light in a room down the hall from the bathroom. The room was sparse but clean, and the sheets and blankets had been pulled back, inviting her to crawl in.

"I'll sleep on the couch," he said, then turned and started toward the door.

"I hate to take your bed." She fidgeted with the hem of the t-shirt. "I'd be glad to sleep on the couch."

With a frown etched across his face, he studied her for a second. Turned and then pulled the door closed behind him, leaving her alone in the room.

Crystal shivered at the sudden chill in the room. She dove under the covers, switched off the lamp, and snuggled beneath the blankets. Within moments, she drifted off to sleep.

Rick rolled over for the hundredth time seeking a comfortable position. Glancing at the clock over the fireplace he noted it was only ten minutes later than the last time he looked. Had he gotten any sleep?

Throwing the blanket aside, he rose, shuffled to the fireplace, and tossed in another log. He made his way to the kitchen and started a pot of coffee.

Crystal awoke to the smell of coffee and bacon frying. She stretched and groaned when she glanced at the clock radio next to the bed.

"It's five fifteen!" Closing her eyes, she grumbled, "So much for spending the weekend relaxing in bed..." Reluctantly, she dressed and on stiff legs stumbled into the kitchen. She drew in a deep breath. Rick stood in front of the stove, the snap on his jeans hung open, and his bare chest covered in dark curls and lean muscles appeared broader than it had before. Her fingers curled and she held them tight to her side to keep from reaching out and sliding them over his bare skin.

He's drop-dead-gorgeous.

"Did I wake you?" He turned down the burner, retrieved a t-shirt from the end of the counter, and slipped it over his head.

Crystal yawned to hide her disappointment. "I smelled coffee."

One corner of his mouth hiked up in a slight grin as he reached in the cupboard for a cup and filled it. "How did you sleep?" He handed her the cup.

"I slept fine." Taking the cup of liquid energy, she perched on the edge of a chair. "How was the couch?"

He frowned. "Not as comfortable as it looks."

"Sorry." She combed her wild hair with her fingers. "You should have slept in the bed." When he froze, one brow raised, she stammered, "I mean *I* should have slept on the couch. I just snuggled up in a little ball and fell right to sleep." She tried averting her gaze, but saw him grin and knew she was blushing.

He dished up two plates of bacon and scrambled eggs and walked to the table. "After we eat, I'll drive you back down to the lodge."

They ate in silence, and when he'd finished, he took his plate to the sink then disappeared into the bedroom. Several minutes later, he returned and slipped on his boots and coat.

"I'll go out and start the truck, give it some time to warm up."

Crystal nodded. She didn't want to leave, she was very attracted to this rugged ranger, but his mixed signals and the fact that he kept her at arm's length puzzled her. She wanted to spend some time getting to know him. She had never been so attracted to a man before. There was something about him that called out to her. She didn't want to walk away not knowing if he was someone special.

Rick opened the door and a rush of cool air burst in. He stopped in mid-step. "What the—"

Crystal jumped to her feet. "What's the matter?" She rushed to the door.

Rick's gaze met hers. "I think you have an admirer."

Puzzled, she moved closer. "What are you talking about?" She peered over his shoulder. "What is that?"

Rick grinned. "It's a rabbit."

Crystal wrapped her arms around herself. "Where did it come from?"

"My guess, Shadow left it for you."

"But why would he do that?"

"I think he likes you." With a straight face he asked, "What would you like me to do with it?"

She took a step back. "I don't want it!" She closed the door, stood on her tiptoes and peered through the window.

Rick chuckled, picked up the gesture-of-affection and carried it away.

* * * *

The pickup lumbered down the two-lane, snow-covered road.

Crystal hadn't spoken since they left the cabin; she just huddled against the door and stared out the side window. He wondered what she was thinking. Hell, he wanted to know everything about her. What it would feel like to run his fingers through her tumbled curls, what she'd feel like in his arms, and what it would feel like to kiss those ripe, pouty lips.

He glanced at her again. "So, how do you like your rabbit?"

With a puzzled look on her face, she asked, "What do you mean?"

"Your rabbit?" He fought to hide a grin. "How do you like it fixed? In a hot-dish, stew, or roasted?"

Her eyes widened in horror. "Gross!"

"What?" He said innocently. "Rabbit's good. Tastes like chicken."

Her brows pulled together; her lips snarled. "I'm never eating chicken again."

Rick grinned. "You were willing to eat elephant last night, and ended up eating moose."

"But a bunny?" She pulled a face that made him laugh. "I don't think I could eat a bunny." She shivered and shoved her hands deep into the pockets of her jacket.

Rick shook his head in mock disgust. "Shadow's going to be disappointed." The silence returned and Rick wished he'd met Crystal under different circumstances and that they didn't live at opposite ends of the state.

"Here we are, like I promised." Rick pulled up in front of the lodge's main doors.

Crystal noted he left the engine running. Although he'd kept his distance and their conversations casual, there were still subtle signals reinforcing her suspicions that he was interested in her.

"Thanks again for risking your life to find me." She smiled and placed her hand on top of his. Their eyes met and his darkened. The muscles in his jaw jumped, and she knew she hadn't misread him.

"Your friends will be relieved that you're back safe and sound." He pulled his hand out from under hers and placed it on the back of the seat.

"I suppose they will." She played with the zipper on her jacket. "Would you like to stay and meet them? Have lunch and dinner with us? I owe you a couple of meals."

He didn't reply just stared out the windshield. What was he thinking? Crystal watched and waited for joking Rick to return. Then he turned and it looked as if he was going to say something, when the passenger's side door opened, and Melissa wrapped her arms around Crystal.

"Oh, I'm so happy you're safe. We were all so worried about you. Are you hurt?"

"I'm fine," she replied between gasps for air.

"All the guy would tell us was that you were fine and were going to stay overnight at a ranger station. I'm so sorry. How can I make it up to you?"

Crystal returned Melissa's hug and whispered in her ear, "Disappear for a minute."

Melissa released her, stepped back, and glanced around Crystal to see Rick. "Hi!" She smiled. "Are you the ranger who found my friend?"

Rick nodded and held out his right hand. "State Ranger, Rick Saunders."

After Melissa shook Rick's hand, Crystal gave Melissa a dirty look, which she ignored.

"It's nice to meet you, Ranger Saunders. Thank you for finding Crystal and taking good care of her."

Crystal flashed Melissa another glare and bared her teeth.

"I'll wait for you inside." Melissa grinned and closed the door.

Crystal turned to Rick and smiled. "Within five minutes, the whole lodge will know I'm back."

"Well, I'd better let you get to your friends." He drummed his fingers on the steering wheel.

This was it, she thought. He's going to let me walk right out of his life. "Alright." She glanced out the windshield. "I guess that's it then." She turned toward him. "Thanks for everything. Take care."

"Yeah, you too," he muttered.

Crystal opened the door and jumped out. "Good-bye, Rick."

"Bye, Crystal."

When he shifted into drive, Crystal slammed the door and watched him drive back to the highway and out of her life.

"What happened?" Melissa reappeared. "What's the matter?"

Crystal wrapped her arms around herself, feeling forlorn. "I thought my luck had changed. I guess I was wrong."

Hours later, Rick slouched in the brown leather chair. He hadn't turned a page in the book he held for several minutes. Unable to concentrate, he closed and tossed the book on the cluttered table next to the chair. "You're a bonehead, Saunders," he said, leaning his head back and closing his eyes. He'd called himself every name he could dream up on his drive home. He couldn't believe he'd just taken off like that, left her standing there.

He rose, walked to the window, and looked out. The land, which had once meant everything to him, appeared cold and strangely empty. Cold and empty like his home, like his arms, and like his heart.

Should he go back? Would she even talk to him after the way he treated her? Maybe he should call the lodge and see if she would even speak to him.

"The only way it's going to work is if I move to the cities." He slid his hands deep into his front jeans pockets. Could he do it? Could he leave his job and all of this? "Yes, if it meant a chance with Crystal."

He heard a knock at the door. He crossed the dark living room, switched on the kitchen light, and pulled the door open. Crystal faced him across the threshold. She smiled, then sucked her lower lip between her teeth. An overnight bag hung from one shoulder, a purse over the other, and she held a grocery bag.

"You wouldn't deprive a woman of her romantic weekend would you?" she asked, her cheeks turning pink.

"It depends," he said, grinning. "What's in the bag?"

Her eyes sparked with mischief. "Steaks. I'm not taking any chances." She grinned. "At least not with my food."

Rick plucked the bag from her hands and set it on the counter. Then he pulled her into his arms and kissed her.

The End

About the Author

LuAnn Nies is a member of Romance Writers of America and Northern Lights Writers. She currently writes contemporary romance and contemporary western romance, but loves to read spicy historicals.

Counting the Days
by
Diane Pearson

Monday, April 6

Dear Mickey,

Wow! What a delightful surprise! The birthday card and your note brought back so many happy memories it made me cry. Can you believe how fast three years go by?

Sorry I didn't write after we moved to northern Minnesota. I never dreamed I'd be living up here this long. I thought for sure we'd get back to the Twin Cities a few months after Rob's parents died. But I was wrong. Now he says with this shaky economy, he'll never find a buyer. Sometimes I feel stuck here.

Hearing from you brightened my day.

One thing is for sure; I could never handle the hurricanes that you have to put up with where you live. Thinking about the ocean and big waves makes me nauseous. I guess it all goes back to the time after finals when we partied on Lake Minnetonka and I fell out of the boat. You came to the hospital and brought me that bouquet of red and white carnations. You made me feel extra special. That was when carnations became my favorite flower; and they still are. One good thing is the nightmares about drowning have stopped. That's a good thing, yes?

Last summer, Rob demanded I take swimming lessons. I've tried twice and now that spring is here again, he says he expects me to make progress. Well, I have improved; but he doesn't see it. I float and thrash around in the water doing my version of the dog paddle. It's not pretty

73

and now I don't get panic attacks when I'm near the water. But mostly, I'm more comfortable near the lake as long as it's calm or frozen over to a good twelve inches.

Gosh, it's so good to remember all the fun we had. I miss dressing up and you taking me to salsa at the pavilion. Now that you've mentioned it, I had forgotten about my purple stilettos and little black dress that you favored. They're packed away some place—not sure where. Up here the fashion is jeans, flannel shirts, and boots.

Sorry I can't give you a cell phone number. Since there is no signal up here, I've cancelled my phone. For now I have to stick with snail mail.

We have a landline, but Rob doesn't like me to use it. According to him, the phone is only for business and emergencies. Besides, I'd feel uncomfortable talking to you if he's around. Maybe when the library gets hooked up to the Internet we can e-mail. Don't know when that will happen; the city council has been talking about it for over a year. Gosh, I miss my computer. So many clients from the Twin Cities are asking for Internet access, I hope Rob will change his mind and get a Wi Fi hookup. He says it's too damn expensive and that the clients come for the rustic experience. Well, there is rustic and then there is, the dark ages. But he doesn't care what I think.

The mailman is due any minute, so I'll sign off for now. I promise to write more real soon.

Sincerely,

Mary Eden
From the "rustic" Northern Lights Lodge

* * * *

Monday, April 20

Dear Mickey,

Aha, you got back to me first. Yes, there are public phones in town but they all seem to be too much out in the open. I'm afraid someone will see me and tease Rob. You can call me a chicken. It's best not to raise questions. It's ironic, but secrets leak out faster up here without the benefit of modern technology.

Rob saw your envelope and asked who M Swan was and I told him that you were a high school friend and that our mothers were close friends. I didn't tell him about college. He didn't seem to want to hear any details, which was fine with me.

Anyway you asked what I did for fun. Does cleaning count? Rob says I don't need to clean the cabins. He says I shouldn't be so picky and that the guests aren't that fussy. Besides it gives a bad impression with me doing the work that he has a hired staff for. He keeps harping about staying out of the maids' way. Well the two young girls are only part time and I doubt he's paying them a huge amount. When I told him I wanted to help out and maybe he could pay me, he yelled at me to stay out of his business. Then he stormed out saying, "I can take care of my own damn family."

I feel so stifled, useless.

You asked about my painting. I haven't done anything since moving up here. Some day I'll get back to it, but really, I can't seem to get in the mood. And canvases and oils are expensive. Rob says there really isn't money for "frivolousity". That was his word.

Anyway I think I'll go for a walk. That's another thing I enjoy doing around here, as long as it isn't hunting season. Maybe I'll take shooting lessons. Then I can conquer my fear of guns. Don't you think? I've mastered the water—sort of. Firearms could be next. Besides a girl just might need to protect herself someday. Right?

The mailman's coming, gotta go. It's best if I don't leave my outgoing mail laying around for Rob to see.

Until next time,

Mary Eden

* * * *

Tuesday, May 12

Dear Mickey,

Sorry I haven't written lately but I've been busy. Several weeks ago while hiking, I stumbled upon an old shack up over the hill less than a quarter of a mile away. I guess it was used as a trapper's shelter. The stream that ran by it dried up years ago and one of the windows was broken out, but the roof and walls look solid. You'd be so proud of me. This time I didn't give up the argument and Rob finally agreed to let me clean it up. As long as I don't spend his money on it and not count on him to help. Anyway, I didn't want his help. He acted is if I wouldn't make anything of the dilapidated shack. We'll see. I intend to turn it into an art studio. <grin>

So now I have a project and am totally excited. I hear the mail truck coming.

Bye,

Mary Eden

* * * *

Monday, May 18

Mickey,

I'm really down. Sorry to dump on you, but you're the only person who understands me. The forest fire up in Canada has scared off a client. Even though the fire is over seventy-five miles away the client cancelled for all of next week. It's bad because they had the whole resort booked. Rob was furious. The reports are that the fire should be contained by the weekend and is not expected to come anywhere near this far south. The client still says they are not coming.

And worse is I think Rob has started drinking again. It's so sad because he'd been doing so well ever since our engagement.

Sorry I'm in such a pissy mood. I'm going to do some serious scrubbing to clear my head.

So much for living in paradise,

Mary E

* * * *

Monday, June 15

Oh, my dear Mickey!

You really shouldn't have. The check is way too generous. I promise to pay you back as soon as I can. Once I get the studio set up, and create some paintings to sell, I'll pay you back.

Best friends forever,

Mary

* * * *

Sunday, June 28

Hey you,

Guess what I stumbled on? I overheard some guys talking at the gas station about the recycling depot behind the post office. I checked it out and wow! I found paint: daffodil yellow and an odd green, which I like. Best thing is I found a window, well, actually two. I'll replace the broken one and add the other. It'll bring more light in. Tommy, Rob's maintenance man has agreed to help me install them on his next day off so I certainly won't have to bother Rob. He hasn't been himself lately. His drinking is beginning to scare me.

I don't understand why he can't see the positive in things. He thinks I'm wasting my time on the shack even though it hasn't cost him a dime. This negative side of him makes me uncomfortable. At least I have a project that excites me and of course your letters. I look forward to each one.

Your friend,

Mary

* * *

Thursday, July 2

Dear Mick,

Things are taking great shape. I'm very pleased with my progress. Kinda looks homey if I do say so myself. Rob should be happy now that I'm not lending a "helping hand" to his staff. But he's not. With the big weekend coming up, I expect his mood to improve.

You have a great holiday.

* * * *

77

Monday, July 6

Sorry, I didn't finish this and mail it sooner. I'm better today. The swelling has gone down and the bruises don't hurt as long as I don't press on them. Rob keeps apologizing for his flare up. I'm staying out of his way.

It happened Saturday night an hour before sunset. He came up to the shack, for what I don't know. In all the time I've been up here working, he has never come by. So why last night I have no clue. At first I thought he was coming by out of curiosity. Maybe he was, but we never got that far because when he saw the brass lockset I installed he scudded into an intense rage. He demanded to know what secrets I was hiding. He screamed at me as to why I needed to lock him out. He didn't give me the chance to tell him it was something I found at the recycling center. And it looks nice with the dark wood. He demanded I get a key made and threw ten dollars at me.

I'm now sleeping on the couch.

I don't understand why having a lock is such a problem. Am I wrong?

Anyway, I'm glad we've reconnected. Your letters keep me sane.

Got to sign off and get back to the lodge for the mailman.

You take care, by the way here's a key for you.

Mary

* * * *

Thursday, July 23

Great news, Mickey,

I've taken on a new adventure. Hadn't planned on it; it just fell in my lap. It started with a retired couple from Duluth who came for a weekend of fishing. Anyway they had the most gorgeous dogs—husky and wolf mixes. Lobo and I bonded right away. Maybe it was because Lobo growled every time Rob came near me. Molly, on the other hand, curled in a ball in the sun and didn't seem to favor anyone.

It turns out that that couple wanted to scale down their dog breeding business and asked if I might be interested taking the dogs. After three days with Lobo, I couldn't resist. The best thing was that the man said I could try it out for the summer. He did warn me that Lobo has a mean streak in his lineage, but he's so darned gentle that I'm sure it won't be a problem. The man gave me some books and lent me his kennels until I got fencing installed on the south side of my studio.

Things are really improving around here. Lobo makes me laugh which feels very good.

Also, my guardian angel must be looking out for me because I found the fencing I needed at the recycling center. Somehow, I seem to be forgetting to get a key made. <Teehee>

And to top that, I sold three paintings so I have extra money for wood for a large doghouse.

By the end of next week I should have everything done. I am absolutely in love again. Lobo and I are pals. Molly on the other hand is … cold. Kind of like Rob who hasn't spoken to me for the past two days. At least he isn't complaining and yelling. Don't know which I dislike more.

With the dogs here, I sometimes wonder if Rob is jealous of Lobo or if he misses Max his German Shepherd that died of old age last winter. Bye for now,

Mary

* * * *

Friday, July 31

Mickey,

I love it here. I sold another picture, this time to a guest. Now Rob says I can hang pictures for sale in the dining room. To start paying back your loan, I'm sending you a check, my first one from my own account, MEden Enterprises. Yep! I'm in business.

You are my best friend,

Mary Eden, businesswoman extraordinaire (hopefully)

* * *

Monday, August 3

My dear Mickey,

So you're not taking the money back. Now I don't know what to say other than thank you dear friend.

I am so excited you're planning a trip to Minnesota. I didn't know the resort had a website. Rob doesn't tell me much. I gave up a long time ago trying to discuss business with him.

Well if there is a web site, Internet access should be next. Yes? Heck, in a few years if things go as planned, I expect my business will be able to afford the expense.

By the way, when you make your reservation, request cabin 8. You will have a good view and access to the lake, and it is on the far end of the resort and closest to the shack.

I can hardly wait to show you the tricks the dogs have learned. Molly is mostly uninterested and only learned two. But, oh my gosh, Lobo is a genius. He is so smart and he still growls whenever Rob comes near. It's kind of funny and I have to stifle my giggles because it makes Rob mad.

Looking forward to tripping down memory lane with you.
Love,

Mary

* * * *

Monday, August 10

My dearest Mickey,

I'm counting the days until you come. I've asked Chef Brian—the best cook on the planet to cook something special when you're here. I found the box with my purple heels and can still squeeze into them. I told Rob that I wanted to dress up for one special night with my special friend. He got all tense until I told him he didn't have to dress up, only me. I also told him it was my small gesture to close the past. I can't believe he bought my lie. We are going to have such a good time.

I can hardly wait to show you the latest trick I've taught Lobo. Now I have to tie a red bandana around the gate hook so he knows he's not supposed to open the gate and get out. That is one very smart dog.
Lots of love,

Mary

* * * *

Tuesday, Sept 1

My dearest,

How can I tell you how much you have done for me?

Your visit went all too fast!!!!

For the first time in three years, I feel alive, renewed. I have a new passion thanks to you. The flowers you brought still look good next to my easel. Carnations do last a long time.

I'm smiling broadly. I can still feel your caress, your gentle touch. Nobody satisfies me like you do. And the mere memory of your breath feathering across my breasts makes me want you more. Until next time,

Always yours,

Mary

* * * *

Monday, October 26

My Dearest Michelle,

Sorry I haven't answered your last letters. I've been busy. The insurance agent just left.

"I'm so sorry for your loss, Mrs. Eden. Such an unfortunate accident," she said handing me a check for one and a half million dollars. "Your husband was very generous man." What could I say? So I just looked at her.

"The money is a small consolation," I said leaning over to stroke Lobo's head hoping she couldn't read the truth on my face.

"If you need anything more, please call me," she said as she drove away.

It was surreal because the sheriff said the same thing when he brought Lobo back. It's too bad Molly had to be euthanized. The sheriff said the autopsy showed Rob did not die from the massive puncture wounds that Molly inflicted as he first thought. He died from natural causes, a heart attack exacerbated by alcohol intoxication.

The staff was touched when I had them plant a tree along with his ashes on the far edge of the resort. It's in a spot on the other side of the lodge and where I can't see it from the shack.

Next week I meet with the accountant who said the business was not operating at a loss as Rob has always led me to believe. He'll fill me in on the details later.

Also sometime within the next ten days a satellite dish will be installed. I've made a donation to the library so they can get a computer and connect to our dish. By the way, the accountant said we could write off the donation as a business expense and he is willing to show me other ways we can improve the profit margin. He bought one of my paintings for two thousand dollars. Can you believe that?

I miss you so much. I love you!

I count the days until you come back, all my love,

M E

The End

About the Author

Diane Pearson writes mystery and romance spiced with the ridiculous.
At the age of twelve, Diane wanted to be Nancy Drew and solve crimes. As time passed, she took a different path through stints in dentistry, sales, and computer software support.
Writing and reading mysteries and romance has always been a part of her adult life. She is a member of the Twin Cities Chapter of Sisters in Crime, Romance Writers of America, and the Northern Lights Writers.

Love, Fish and Fangs
by
Edna Curry

Late Friday afternoon, Bob and Jody Miller and their ten-year-old son, David, drove about two hours south from their home in a Minneapolis suburb to Whitewater State Park.

David bounced excitedly in the back seat of the car. "The newsman said the north lights will be out tonight, Dad. Can we go see them?"

"Northern Lights, David," his mother corrected.

Bob laughed. "Sure, son, we should be able to see them from the park if the weather cooperates."

"What do you mean, if the weather cooperates?"

"If it's not too cloudy. Clouds sometimes get in the way so you can't see them."

"In any case, I hear the trout are biting this week," Bob assured David as they arrived at the park. They enjoyed primitive tent camping and a weekend away from Bob's police work in the crowded city so they could enjoy nature was a treat.

Yellow dust swirled behind them as they drove along the graveled road that wound along the creek at the bottom of the wooded valley. A few campers were already set up in little clearings in the trees off the sides of the road. Bob pulled in at a nice spot beside the rapids.

Jody made coffee on the camp stove while Bob and David set up their tent. When they'd finished, David asked, "Can I explore, Dad?"

"Sure. Don't go far." They went down to the creek, finding several places shallow enough to wade across its rocky bed. Bob worked his fly rod in a deeper pool, hoping to catch enough trout for supper. Jody spread a blanket on the grass nearby and relaxed, enjoying the sunshine and the graceful picture Bob's tall, slim figure made.

Suddenly they heard an angry shout. David came running toward them through the trees around the bend. He slid in close to his father and glanced fearfully over his shoulder.

"I wasn't doing nothing, honest, Dad. I only walked by them and the man just got mad and yelled at me to go away."

"Who, son?"

"That guy by the tent back there. He was just kissing her. I didn't do nothing to them at all!"

"Oh," said Bob, sending Jody a grin. "That explains it. Most people don't like to be watched when they're kissing. Leave them alone and forget it, son."

"But she was always so nice to me before. Maybe she didn't remember me," said David, sniffling. He wiped his drippy nose on his shirtsleeve.

Jody handed him a tissue and asked, "You know the lady? Who was it?"

"Mrs. Wanderford, on my paper route. You know, the lady in the green house on Willow Street, where the road makes an s-curve at the bottom of the hill."

Jody frowned, concentrating. "I don't think I've met them. They're new in Circletop Drive, aren't they, Bob?"

Bob nodded, keeping his eyes on his fishing line. "He's in construction. I've seen him at the golf club several times. Hey, I've got another fish! That should be enough for supper."

By dark they'd cooked supper, eaten and watched the Northern Lights for a while.

"Oh, they're pretty," David exclaimed. "Look how the colors move up and down. How do they do that, Dad?"

"Nobody knows for sure. Some think it's light reflecting off the ice cap near the north pole. Others say it has something to do with sunspots."

Then some clouds moved in and hid the light show. Disappointed, they went into their tent to sleep, snuggling into their sleeping bags against the night's chill.

* * * *

The next morning the sun shone so brightly the water sparkled over the red and yellow rocks and sand. They sat on campstools enjoying bacon, eggs and coffee that seemed extra flavorful in the crisp, fresh air.

Then the peaceful summer morning was shattered by screams and shouts from around the bend upstream.

As they ran towards the sounds, they saw that a crowd had already gathered near a tent. "Anybody have service on their cell phone?" a man asked. "Mine doesn't work." "Mine either. Somebody drive for help." Moments later, a car raced off down the road toward the park headquarters.

"Keep back! The man in the tent is dead, and there's a rattlesnake still in there," one of the men told them. "Someone went for the police."

Bob ran back to the car and returned with his gun. He approached the tent cautiously, and shot the snake. "Keep a sharp eye out for its mate," he warned the others. "They usually travel in pairs."

One of the park rangers arrived with the local police. David was disappointed at having to go back to their own camp. "He's the man who yelled at me yesterday," he said.

"You didn't see the man." Jody had purposely kept him back.

"No, but that was the tent they were standing beside."

"Hmm. There was no woman with him now," Bob said. "Did you see Mrs. Wanderford today?"

"No, but that was the tent," David insisted.

"You must have been mistaken, David. The dead man wasn't Mr. Wanderford, and the letters on his car license plates show it was from this area, not Minneapolis."

Jody shuddered. "What a horrible accident."

"The local police have jurisdiction here. They'll handle it."

After they returned home, Bob searched the newspaper for more information, but found only a small paragraph about the snake-bite death, buried on an inside page. The dead man was John Silks, who had worked for a large computer firm in Rochester, loved to fish on weekends, and was single. An ordinary obituary.

Still, something seemed wrong to Bob. David was not an overly-imaginative boy. He seldom made things up. And he had been so positive of his identification of Mrs. Wanderford.

A couple of weeks later, as Bob pulled his car into his driveway one night, David came riding up to him excitedly on his bike.

"Hey, Dad. Guess what Kenny and I just saw?"

"Careful, there, pal. Wait until I stop!" Bob got out of his car and tousled his young son's hair. "Now, what's all the excitement?"

"We saw real, live rattlesnakes, Dad! Mr. Wanderford showed them to us. He's got them in cages in his basement. He catches them with a special long stick and milks them for their serum for some lab downtown."

"Is that so?" Bob's eyes narrowed as he frowned thoughtfully.

"Isn't that something, Dad? Mr. Wanderford says they're not dangerous if you know how to handle them right."

A snake expert! And David had said that Mrs. Wanderford was the woman the dead man had been kissing the afternoon before he died. What if it had been no accident? What if she had recognized David? Bob felt the hair on his neck prickle with fear for his son.

He snapped, "You stay away from them, you hear?"

David stared at his dad, surprised by his sudden, sharp command. "Okay, Dad," he muttered. "Gee, I wouldn't get close enough for them to bite me."

"Just do as I say!"

The next day Bob told his friend Lt. Walker of Homicide about the incident and Mr. Wanderford's snake-milking sideline. "I know the case is outside our jurisdiction," he said, "and the cops down there have ruled it an accident. But I can't help feeling that there is something fishy going on, pardon the pun. A snake expert's wife making love to a man who dies from a rattlesnake bite is a pretty suspicious combination."

"Suspicion isn't good enough. We have only David's word that the Wanderfords were anywhere near Whitewater that day."

"Then I'll find more."

But after a week, Bob had found nothing. No one else remembered seeing the Wanderfords at Whitewater Park. Bob could make no provable connection between the dead John Silks and Mrs. Wanderford.

Was David wrong? Had the lady been someone else who only resembled Mrs. Wanderford? And was the fact that Mr. Wanderford milked rattlesnakes only a coincidence? Instinct told Bob the odds were against it. He didn't like coincidences. In his experience, they were usually more than that and had some connection. Bob insisted David 'forget' to collect payment from the Wanderfords for their newspapers, for fear seeing David would refresh her memory of where she had seen him last. If Mrs. Wanderford knew that it was murder, and thought David could connect her to the dead man...

On the other hand, Mr. Wanderford must be unaware that David knew, or he would never have shown off his rattlesnakes to the boys, Bob reasoned.

Weeks passed. They heard that Mr. Wanderford had been very ill, hospitalized for several days with an intestinal ailment. After he recovered, a for-sale sign appeared on their well-manicured lawn and Bob heard he had sold his business and they were moving back west.

Bob fumed when he met Lt. Walker for lunch that day. "They're leaving and he's getting away with murder. I just know it."

"Whoa! You don't know anything of the kind. And even if he is, we can do nothing without proof."

"I know. But it burns me up!"

"When are they leaving?"

"Next week. There's a neighborhood farewell party at their house tonight. Everyone in the area got invitations."

"So are you going, Bob?"

"Of course. I wouldn't miss a last chance to get into that house to look around."

The afternoon proved a busy one, so Bob and Jody arrived very late at the Wanderford's house.

As they approached, they saw the flashing lights of an ambulance parked in the driveway. A stretcher was being loaded into it.

"It's Elaine Wanderford!" Several of their neighbors began explaining at once. "She went to the basement after more liquor, and some of the snakes had gotten loose and bit her on the leg."

The ambulance screamed away. Harry Wanderford did not go with it. The crowd all milled back into the house, half-subdued, half excited by the incident.

"She'll be all right," Harry said, making light of the incident as he poured more cocktails and handed the hors d'oeuvre tray to a neighbor to pass.

"I gave her an injection of the Antivenin that I always keep handy. I've been bitten several times myself, and recovered okay. Not much fun at the time, though," he assured them with a grin.

Bob took the cocktail, heat rising in his face. Another snake incident couldn't be an accident—just the thought of it made his stomach churn with anger and frustration. His gut told him this was no accident, it was attempted murder. He couldn't let Mr. Wanderford get away with this again.

"Such a terrible accident, wasn't it?" May Knight, another neighbor, gushed at his elbow. "But then, she was drinking quite a bit tonight, so I suppose she didn't notice that the snakes were loose. Such horrible things to keep in one's home, don't you think? I'd be frightened to death." She patted her perfectly groomed gray hair with a pudgy, jeweled hand.

"Yes, of course," Bob managed and went to look for Jody among the chattering, dancing groups of guests.

"Accident, indeed!" he muttered to himself.

He spotted Jody's bright red dress and blonde curls across the room, and began to weave his way through the crowd to her. But a fat, bald man who had had too many cocktails bumped into him, knocking Bob against the wall. Bob's cocktail glass smashed, cutting his hand.

Blood dripped from the wound. "Damn," Bob said, and began hunting for a bathroom instead of Jody.

He found it three doors down the hall, and began washing off the blood. Then he looked behind the fancy mirrors for a medicine cabinet. He found the Band-Aids, and helped himself to one. When he tossed the wrapper in the wastebasket, he saw a hypodermic syringe, still wet. Probably the one Harry had used on Elaine tonight. Bob stared at the bit of fluid remaining in the syringe.

Then he pulled out his handkerchief, carefully picked up the syringe, wrapped it in the handkerchief and slipped it into the inside pocket of his jacket. The horrible truth of the new situation was clear to him now.

He pulled out his cell phone and phoned the hospital and Lt. Walker, then went out to his car. He grimly returned to the party, keeping one eye on Harry, who was still playing the role of benevolent host.

It was getting late and the guests were beginning to leave when the hospital called. When Harry answered, he told them Elaine Wanderford was not all right. She was dead.

Harry sat with his head in his hands, the picture of a loving, grieving husband. The guests all gathered about him, murmuring sympathetically.

All except Bob. He took a pair of handcuffs out of his pocket and grimly snapped them on Harry before he could lower his arms.

"You're under arrest for murder," Bob said, and began to read him his rights.

"Murder!" Everyone gasped in dismay and surprise. Harry was too surprised to react immediately.

"But...it was an accident," Harry stammered. "I was up here. A rattlesnake bit her."

"Yes, just like the snake that bit John Silks in Whitewater State Park last month!"

Harry's jaw dropped. He gasped, "How did you know about that?"

"We were there, too. My son saw your wife kissing him."

This reminder was too much. His face red, Harry exploded, "Yes, kissing him. Meeting her lover behind my back. I got suspicious of too many 'visits' to her girlfriend and followed her. She never went to her girlfriend's house. Instead, she met him in the state park. I saw them at his tent through my field glasses. He deserved to die."

Bob could only shake his head.

"And she did, too," Harry snarled, shaking handcuffed fists. "That was no illness that put me in the hospital last week. She tried to poison me! That's when I knew it was all over. There was no going back to a happy home life. At first, I thought she believed her boyfriend was accidentally bitten. She never let on she knew. Acted nice as pie. Then whammo! She fed me poison. So I had to get rid of her! She might have succeeded next time."

Bob nodded grimly. "So you released the snakes in the basement, knowing she'd go down there after more liquor tonight after you deliberately 'forgot to bring it up'. Then you made a big pretense of taking care of her by calling an ambulance and giving her antivenin."

"I did give her a shot. All of you here saw me do that! You can testify to it." He looked around hopefully at his neighbors, who stood by uncertainly. A couple reluctantly nodded, others looked shocked and uncertain. Jody stood nearby, wide eyed and listening.

Bob nodded. "Yes, you gave her an injection. Only it wasn't antivenin you gave her, was it? I found the syringe in the bathroom. The lab reports should be interesting. It was a big dose of snake venom, right into the blood stream to make sure that nothing the doctors could do would save her! And she'd been drinking, to make matters worse. But then, you knew that that old wives tale about liquor being good for snake-bite isn't true, didn't you?"

Harry's shoulders sagged and he suddenly seemed to age ten years before their eyes. Lt. Walker strode in followed by two other officers. Seeing Mr. Wanderford already in handcuffs, they whipped out notebooks and began asking questions of all the guests.

"This time it's in our district," Bob said, satisfaction in his voice.
"Yes, it is," Lt. Walker agreed. "I'll need your statement, too, Bob."
"With pleasure."

The End

About the Author

Edna Curry lives with her husband in the scenic St. Croix River Valley in Minnesota where she sets most of her stories. She will have 5 new novels out in 2011: Double Trouble, Dead in Bed, I'll Always Find You, Never Love a Logger and My Sister's Keeper. Check out her website for details about her current novels and about her backlist titles of novels, short stories and articles once again available on many e-book sales sites.
http://www.ednacurry.com ,
http://www.facebook.com/profile.php?id=613178895

Heal My Heart
by
Shirley Olson

June knew she needed to escape tonight. She couldn't take her stepdad's abuse any longer. If only she'd been brave enough, strong enough, to stop him years earlier! But now she was finally ready, pushed to the limits of endurance. Fully dressed, she crawled into bed with an old wooden baseball bat concealed at her side, the one Frank sometimes used to beat her mother. It would be justice, long denied, she reminded herself.

Now that it was time, she had to force herself to lie still. Her heart thudded so loud it seemed to echo inside her head, almost deafening her, as she waited for the monster's arrival.

Suddenly the door creaked open and he stumbled in, reeking like a brewery. June closed her eyes, unable to watch, as Frank fumbled to unzip his pants. He mumbled curses at his uncooperative clothing until June heard the rustle of his pants dropping to the floor and felt the side of the bed sag. She had to act. It was now or never.

As her stepfather continued to crawl onto the bed, June lifted the bat, scrambled to her knees and struck him on the head with all the force of seven years of pent up anger and hatred.

If the angle hadn't been so awkward, she probably would have crushed his skull. As it was, blood spurted from the wound as he groaned and collapsed, rolling off the bed and crumpling to the floor.

June hopped over his limp body, not bothering to check to see if he was dead or alive. Just tugging his billfold from the pocket of his discarded pants made her skin crawl. She was in the act of opening the wallet when she thought she heard a faint moan. Panting in terror, she yanked out all the cash before throwing the billfold in his direction, snatching up her purse and backpack and rushing from the room.

Flying past her mother, sprawled in an unlovely heap and passed out on the couch, June cried, "You deserve each other, you drunken pigs!"

Then she fled out of the prison that had held her captive since she was ten years old and her mother married Frank.

Sprinting through eerily dark Rochester city blocks, June finally spied a city bus. The driver must have seen her frantic gestures because he stopped right in front of her. She lunged up the steps, jammed in the required fare and hurried to the back of the nearly deserted bus. She'd studied the routes and knew that this particular one would take her directly to the Greyhound depot. She had no clue as to where she was going. She just knew she had to get away as fast and as far as possible.

Running shaking fingers through her hair, June couldn't stop peering through the back window. She licked her lips, terrified that Frank would suddenly appear, cursing and yelling, to drag her back to the hellhole from which she'd just escaped. Taking a deep breath, she tried to calm her racing heartbeat.

Time seemed to stretch in an endless loop until at last the bus pulled into the depot. June bolted down the steps and into the building. In her rush, she slammed into a man, who grunted and stepped back.

"Oh, I'm-m so sorry. Are you okay?" Licking her lips, June yanked her jacket tight around her shivering body.

"I'm fine. What's the big hurry, young lady?" Both the stranger's smile and voice were gentle as he stooped to help her gather up her purse and backpack.

Unaccustomed to this type of response, June could only stare at him. If she'd rammed into him, Frank would have slapped her six ways to Sunday—

But Frank wouldn't be knocking her around again. *Don't show any weakness.* "Hey, I'm sorry. Guess I was in a hurry to get to the ticket booth. My first time on a bus trip and I'm a little excited."

"Well, let's stroll over there together, shall we? It's not my first bus trip so I can answer any questions you might have before my bus leaves."

June lagged behind him, just close enough to hear him tell the ticket master, "Good evening, I'm Bill Anderson, and I'd I like a ticket for Duluth, please."

After completing the transaction, he walked away and sat down on a chair against the wall.

June stepped up to the ticket booth and drew a deep breath. *Look confident.* "My name's Jane Anderson. Ticket to Duluth, please."

"So you and your dad are travelling together, huh?"

After checking to make sure Bill was out of earshot, June nodded. She counted out the cash, trying to look like an independent young woman and hoping the clerk didn't think it odd that her father hadn't also paid for her ticket.

But apparently the guy didn't think he earned his salary asking questions and he just handed over her receipt and a ticket.

June felt relieved at how crowded the terminal was at this hour, as she needed to blend in. After her pretence at the ticket booth, she decided that she'd better sit as close to her "dad" as possible. The only remaining seat in the row was to the man's right.

As she approached with some hesitation, he smiled that kind smile again, one that seemed to draw her towards him. "My name's Bill Anderson. You're welcome to sit here if you like. Are you also going to Duluth?" She held up her ticket and he nodded. "Since we appear to be traveling companions, may I ask your name?"

After she sank down and tugged her jacket more closely around her shoulders again, he held out his hand.

June gave it a quick, light clasp. "I'm er, I mean, call me Jane." She groaned inwardly, wishing she'd thought fast enough to come up with a better name. No way would she share her last name. After all, he was a man and, in her limited experience, they were all the same. Users and abusers.

She found her gaze straying to the front doors. Would the bus to Duluth ever get here?

Folding her hands in her lap, she stole another glance at Bill's face. Laugh lines crinkled around his eyes. His body was tall and strong looking but he didn't appear to be a threat. June shuddered, wishing she could confide in him. She desperately needed someone to trust, to confide in.

Her legs kept quivering, shaky as cooked noodles. The adrenaline surge of her escape had faded; she felt sick to her stomach, the beginnings of a headache pounding at her temples. Over and over, her mind kept repeating, "Help me make it out of here. Please."

Bill remarked, "You look pretty young to be traveling alone. Will someone be waiting for you when you get to Duluth?"

"Uh, yeah." *Why didn't I come up with a good cover story!* June straightened, trying to look as mature as possible. "I plan on meeting up with my sister. I'm eighteen, plenty old enough to travel on my own," she lied, hoping to prevent him from asking any more inconvenient questions.

"Since we're both going to Duluth, we can be travel buddies, if that's okay. You look like you could use a friend. When we get there, I can wait with you if your sister's late in picking you up."

June stared at him, uncertain of this guy's angle. Was he coming on to her like creepy Frank? Pretending to be the Sir Galahad, a knight in shining armor- type, to women?

Aloud, she said, "I appreciate having a 'travel buddy' but you won't have to stay with me. I'm not a kid and my sister will be there on time."

They sat in silence, June unable to keep her gaze from darting to the doorway, expecting at any moment to see Frank, his head a bloody mess, storm into the depot to drag her back home.

Seemingly unaware of her terror, Bill yawned. "I think I'll take a catnap. Wake me when the bus comes, travel buddy."

Relieved that she didn't have to answer any more questions, June sighed and tried to quiet the tremors that kept running through her body. But as Bill dozed off, she felt alone, still a prisoner of the black thoughts and terrors that had made up her life until now.

Suddenly a policeman appeared and glanced around the huge room. People ignored him, rolling luggage in their wake or hauling backpacks. A baby wailed and June knew just how it felt.

The cop headed straight for June. Her thoughts spun in circles. *What shall I do? Did my mom call and report me for hitting Frank? Maybe he'll take me home. I can't go back there! What if he drags me off to jail?*

Her mind in agonized turmoil, June could still smell the tang of blood. The horrific thought that she might have stains on her clothing had her peering down at her jeans and jacket in a frantic check for spots.

She snatched up a folded newspaper lying on a nearby bench to shield herself but it was too late to hide. The police officer stopped in front of her. She smelled tobacco on his uniform, either he smoked or rode in a car with someone who did.

Her heart pounded so loud she thought he would hear it. *Now I'm a goner.*

"Are you traveling with anyone?"

Right now June hated the fact that she looked like she was fifteen. But she was very thankful that one, she'd met Bill Anderson and two, he appeared to be a sound sleeper. "Oh, yes. I'm with my dad."

"Okay, as long as you're safe. We always like to make sure that kids are safe." The cop nodded. "Have a nice trip."

Looking for runaways. Wait, I'm a runaway! Whew. How many more lies do I have to come up with before I get out of town? At least I won't be going to jail tonight.

Suddenly June realized the magnitude of what she'd done. *I may have killed a man! Killed Frank!* But then she told herself with fierce conviction, "If he's dead, he deserved it!"

She felt a bead of sweat running down her back as the headache returned with a vengeance. Rocking in her seat, June glared at the huge clock on the wall, begging the hands to move faster.

Finally, the announcement she'd been waiting for: "The bus for Duluth will be arriving at Gate 10 in fifteen minutes."

June sighed. Only fifteen more minutes of this torture. Once on the bus, she knew she'd feel much safer, as if her journey had finally started.

Strangely enough, she also felt the pangs of loneliness and hoped that she could sit close to Bill when they got on the bus.

The announcement that their bus was pulling in had people all around getting to their feet and grabbing hand luggage. She poked Bill in the shoulder. "Our bus just pulled up to the station."

He appeared to wake instantly. "Thanks." Bill stretched like a big cat, tiger-sized. "That nap felt good. I've had a busy couple of days and not much sleep."

Bill only had a small carryon and took charge of her backpack. June couldn't help but feel a huge sense of relief. She was finally leaving her terrible life behind, but her memories still had to come with her. And what was she going to do when she got to Duluth?

This sudden thought made her weep as she automatically sat down next to Bill. The only bright spot appeared to be finding Bill, someone who didn't want to hurt her, who said lame things like his suggestion that they be 'travel buddies' but carried her backpack and offered to wait with her, if necessary.

Somehow she felt a bond, that she could trust him. He didn't seem like the rest of the men she had known, the ones her mother used to bring home.

She blotted her tears with the sleeve of her jacket and pretended to gaze out into the darkness but saw Bill's reflection, his head turned towards her.

Bill asked, "Why so sad? Anything a travel buddy can help with?"

June blurted out, "No, no. I'm just tired. And I'm not exactly sure what will happen when I get to Duluth since I don't know my sister's new name."

She clapped her hand over her mouth. *Idiot!!!!!!!*

Almost afraid to look at her companion, June shuddered but Bill said nothing.

Then the dam burst and June confessed, "She doesn't know I'm coming. She sent a postcard saying she was getting married but I haven't heard from her since. I guess I just realized how big Duluth must be and that it might be tough to find her. I'm sorry. I can't seem to stop crying lately. But I'll be okay." June wasn't sure why she was spilling her guts to this stranger. But she somehow felt that he wouldn't hurt her.

Bill remained silent for another moment before saying, "Don't apologize, Jane. It sounds like you need a friend and I'd like to help, if I can. Do you have a place to stay in Duluth?"

"I'm going to be at a hotel for a day or so."June sniffed back more tears. She didn't know why she'd suddenly turned into a weeping willow tonight, she should be happy. But freedom felt scarier than she'd anticipated.

"Okay, but if you aren't able to locate your sister, give me a call. Here's my card with my cell phone number. I'd like to hear from you."

June fumbled to tuck his card into her purse. "If I had a father, I would have liked him to be just like you. I've never known my real father. He left us when I was a baby." June didn't know why she couldn't stop talking about herself, but she'd needed to someone to listen to her for such a long time.

Bill frowned. "A disappearing father--that's tough. Any other brothers or sisters? Your mother, did she remarry?"

"Only the one sister, she left home when she couldn't stand it any more. My mother remarried and he's a real creep. Mom's judgment isn't the greatest—I mean, she likes the bottle too much. Frank being such a jerk is the reason my sister left home. Now it's my turn to get out of there."

"I'm sorry about your family. I hope and pray that your mother gets the help she needs. You can pretend I'm your father, if that will help you until you find your real one."

Bill started to pat her arm but she stiffened and pulled away. June couldn't bear for a man to touch her, although, she sensed that this one was different, that he wouldn't harm her. All she could do rely on was her instincts, all she had in the world.

They talked until June finally dozed off. On awaking, she suddenly became nauseated and rushed to the tiny bathroom in the rear of the bus. Retching into the sink, she felt like she was going to lose her whole insides. *Oh, no, what if I have the flu? Maybe it's just nerves. This is not the best time to get sick.*

Looking at her reflection in the mirror, June could see that all color had drained from her face. When she returned to her seat, she hoped Bill wouldn't notice that she'd been ill. She was just glad to be able to collapse into her seat.

"Are you okay?"

Bill's worried tone made her believe her instincts were right; he was a good man and she could trust him. "I'll be okay, just a little sick to my stomach. I think it's just a touch of nerves or the flu." She tried to laugh. "Or it might be the excitement of going to see my sister."

After a few minutes, Bill said, "If you aren't feeling any better when we get to Duluth, I know a good doctor who likes to help people. A young woman like you shouldn't be so pale. And I couldn't help but notice the shadows under your eyes. I'm just concerned that there may be more going on with you than you think. Would it be okay if when we get to Minneapolis that I call her and see if she can squeeze in an appointment for you?"

June had a suspicion of what might wrong with her but she couldn't tell a complete stranger. She didn't want to even think it could be a possibility. However, she needed to see someone sooner or later so she sighed and nodded.

Arriving in Minneapolis around eight in the morning, they found themselves with a layover of several hours. They wandered into a small diner and ordered breakfast. After finishing his meal, Bill pulled out his cell phone and called to make the appointment. June picked at her scrambled eggs; she had no appetite but knew she needed to eat to keep up her strength.

Closing the phone, Bill slipped it back into his pocket. "I was able to get you in to see Dr. Andres on Thursday. That'll give you a few days to settle in. Her office is next to the hotels, near the bus station. You won't have any trouble finding her." He handed June another one of his business cards on which he'd printed the doctor's name, address and telephone number.

June stuck it in her purse, along with the other card. "I'm sure I'll be okay."

"If you feel better later and you decide don't need the appointment, just call and cancel. She'll understand."

Resting awhile before boarding the next bus, June enjoyed Bill's companionship. She respected that he never once made any advances toward her, that he treated her how she dreamed a father would treat his beloved daughter. June realized she really would like to find her father, but had no idea how to begin such a search.

"Okay, your turn. Tell me about your family. Are you married and do you have any children?" June asked.

"I was married and had two small children. But my job kept me away for too many hours and one day I came home to find out that my wife had run off with someone else." Moisture sparkled in Bill's eyes. "My youngest was only three years old."

"Did you ever try and find your children?"

"Yes, but my wife changed her name and kept moving around. I suspect she was living with different men so her name was never on a lease. But I wanted my kids back--I never gave up the search."

His eyes brightened as he continued, "Recently, however, I was finally reunited my oldest daughter. She and I now have a wonderful relationship. I'd love it if you could meet her sometime. You remind me of her a little bit."

"Wow! Our stories are quite similar," June said as her heart thumped with a strange excitement. *His daughter was three when he lost her, the same age as I was when my father left.*

The bus arrived in Duluth late in the afternoon. Bill shook her hand and told her to remember to call him if she couldn't get in touch with her sister.

"Don't forget to keep that doctor's appointment," he reminded her before leaving. As Bill vanished into the crowd of people at the bus depot, June sighed. Now she was alone again.

She decided to find a room and rest before figuring out her next step. As she walked to the phones lined up against the outer wall, she grabbed a newspaper from the stand and tucked it in her small bag. If she couldn't locate Tara right away, she'd need to find a job.

June also realized she was hungry, so she found a quiet corner at a nearby deli. The scent of freshly baked buns made her stomach gurgle. She ordered a sandwich and a soft drink. As she waited for her food, she pulled out the card Bill had given her and for the first time, saw that Bill was actually a detective with the Duluth police department.

Her pulse rate jumped. *I'm glad I didn't know what he does for a living when we were on the bus! If he finds out what I did, I'll go to jail. But I'll bet if Bill ever had to arrest me, it would be the nicest and kindest arrest in the history of police work.*

As June gobbled down her sandwich, she pulled out the paper she had tucked in her bag. Her heart almost stopped when she read the front-page headlines. "Vicious Attack in Rochester". The story reported that a young woman attempted to kill her stepfather after stealing an undisclosed amount of money. A picture of June at the age of ten seemed to jump out at her from the page. People were instructed to contact the Rochester police department if they saw June.

The good news is that my family wasn't much for taking pictures. But even this old photo looks too much like me for comfort. There's a chance I'll be recognized. I have to do something to disguise myself.

June's hands shook as she folded up the paper, dug a scarf from her purse and used it to conceal her dark hair. Head down, she hurried the three blocks to the hotel.

Registering under the name of Jane Nelson, she paid cash for two nights. After receiving her key, she hurried to her room. Safely behind a locked door, she sat down and continued reading the story, as her whole body shook.

Apparently, Frank was still alive. *I couldn't even kill him. He must have called the police as soon as he came to. How I hate that filthy pig! I won't be safe ever again—he'll never stop looking for me.* June couldn't rid herself of the heaviness of the constant fear and hatred towards Frank.

June stripped down, stepped into the shower, and scrubbed hard and long to wash the dirty old man's thoughts off of her. She hated him so much that it consumed her, burning like a fever in her soul.

After coming out of the shower wrapped in a towel, she flopped down on the bed, hid her head under the pillow and sobbed until she finally fell asleep, although past nightmares returned.

The next morning when June awoke, she decided the first thing she needed to do was to find a beauty salon and disguise herself to make it more difficult for Frank to trace her. Whenever she thought about him, her heart seethed with that terrible *wanting to kill*-hatred.

June called the front desk. "Is there's a beauty salon close by?"

"Yes, 'The Best Hair Salon' is located in the mall, about five blocks away, right on Second Street."

The front desk clerk also gave her the phone number and June managed to get a ten o'clock appointment. She tied the blue scarf over her hair again and stopped at the front desk on her way out. "If I stay for a week, would I get a cheaper rate?"

"Yes, the weekly rate would be $300 for five days, today through Saturday at noon."

She paid for the week and then hurried the five blocks down the hill to the salon.

After signing in as "Jane", June didn't have to wait long before a young woman with swirling dark red hair sauntered over. "I'm Angie and I'll be your hairdresser. What can I do for you today, Jane?"

June said, "I'd like a complete makeover—new hairdo, hair color, hair cut—the works."

"You have such beautiful long black hair, are you sure you want this cut?" Angie ran her fingers through June's hair. "It's going to be such a huge change."

"Yes, I decided I'd like to be a blonde." June wasn't sure about cutting her hair, as she loved wearing it long, but she felt she had no choice.

"Blondes have more fun, right?" Angie giggled.

"No, I just want a change. And I could use a job." *Here I go, blurting out whatever's on my mind!* It was as if someone had unlocked her tongue.

"What kind of job are you looking for? Interested in waitress or hostess work? I noticed an advertisement for a waitress at a place called the Watering Hole. I've never been there, but I think it's a bar-restaurant. You'd have to be eighteen but you look like you're not older than fifteen."

"I'm old enough," June said, mentally adding, *old enough to be on my own.*

"If you aren't, you'll look eighteen when we finish with you here." Angie had such a sweet smile and treated her so nice that June felt at ease and tried her best to forget her problems.

When Angie finally finished, she gave June a mirror. "You look absolutely lovely."

June hardly recognized herself. Her white-blond hair hugged her head like a cap and the new hairstyle made her appear much older. "You did a great job. Thanks!"

"I have an hour off for a break. How about we go for lunch? I'll introduce you to my friend next door. He had a job open a week ago which he just filled, but maybe he'll keep you in mind if there's another job opening soon."

Hesitant but feeling good about her make-over and more confident she wouldn't be recognized, June smiled. "I appreciate this, Angie. Besides being a great with hair, you're great with people, too."

Angie chuckled. "You can't have enough girlfriends, that's my motto."

June had never had a girlfriend, only a sister that she missed so much she could hardly bear the pain in her heart. Angie's smile made her feel as if she was on the verge of a new life.

Angie yelled to her partner, "I'm taking a break! Back in an hour," and off they went next door to the Grizzly Bear Night Club, which was just opening for the day.

As they entered, a man came over and hugged Angie. "Who's your pretty friend?"

"This is Jane and she could be your new waitress or hostess if you hire her. Jane, meet Jim, the Grizzly Bear's manager."

"Nice to meet you, Jane. I wish I could hire you, as I know any friend of Angie's would be an asset. One of my girls told me she may be leaving next week, so if you're still available, you could join our little family here."

June's heart thumped when Jim smiled, his deep blue eyes made her stomach flip, as if he could see right inside her soul. He had wheat blond hair and a muscular body, which looked like he worked out. She guessed him to be about twenty-three or four.

"I hope there's an opening soon because I need a job. I'll start looking around other places but if you can hire me, I'd be thrilled." June glanced at her surroundings. The restaurant had the rustic warmth of northern Minnesota with a back patio overlooking the sparkling waters of Lake Superior. "I really think I'd like working here," June told him with sincerity.

"Why don't you join us for lunch, if you have a break?" Angie asked Jim. "We'd like to try your roast beef specialty."

"Sure, it'll be fun getting to know your friend better."

Jim led them to the patio where they enjoyed a wonderful meal. June almost forgot to eat as Jim kept looking over at her with a special gleam in his eyes. He gave her a lot of attention, which unsettled her. June thought that he was coming on pretty strong and her heart raced every time he looked at her. Suspecting he was Angie's boyfriend, however, she felt awkward and was unable to relax.

As they walked away from the club, June asked, "Are you and Jim a couple?"

"No, we're just good friends. Actually, we're cousins. I'm happily married to a wonderful man," Angie said, laughing.

Relieved, but hesitant, June decided that Jim's attentions were non-threatening and a compliment and she hoped to hear from him again. When he shook her hand as they left, a tingle had danced up her spine. It was an exciting sensation, one she'd never felt before. *And one I could get to like!*

Returning to her hotel room, June checked the help wanted section of the paper but there didn't to seem many jobs for seventeen year old runaways. She knew she had to find her sister before her money ran out, but the article in the paper had shaken what little confidence she possessed.

I don't have a driver's license and if I give my social security number, the police might find me. My only option seems to be a waitressing or dishwashing job at a place where they pay cash to avoid paying the government. Maybe I could clean houses or something.

June decided she had to stockpile as much money as possible to give her time to find her sister. Remembering Angie's mention of seeing an ad at the Watering Hole,

June looked up the number and called the restaurant. A gruff voice answered and she tried to sound confident. "I'm interested in the hostess job you have listed. I've had some experience." Experience in what, June avoided saying, but she hoped she could learn on the job.

"Come in before four o'clock tomorrow, when we open. We're looking for an evening hostess. We'll check you out."

"I'll be there, right at four tomorrow. Thank you."

That night June slept better than the previous night. It was actually a relief to know that she wasn't a killer.

June woke up early and struggled with a bout of nausea again. When it passed, she crawled into bed and fell asleep again. This time when she awoke, she felt somewhat better and decided to walk to Wal-Mart to buy a new outfit for her interview.

She found a dark blue pantsuit that made her look older, a pair of comfortable walking shoes and a few other necessities. After paying her bill, she realized that she had better get a job soon as her money was going fast.

On her way back to the hotel, June realized the exercise and excitement of possibilities had given her back her appetite. She was starving and decided to stop in and ask Angie if she would like to have a bite to eat with her. Secretly, June hoped to see Jim again.

Wow, he's such a hunk! Wait, what am I thinking? I can't have a relationship with anyone until I settle my big problem—Frank! But a girl can still dream, can't I?

Luck was with her and Angie said, "I'll be happy to have lunch with you. The special on Tuesdays at the Grizzly Bear is a unique type of pasta. You don't even have to be Italian to love it. I sure do. I'll be ready to go in just a minute."

As the two walked into the Grizzly Bear, Jim came strolling up to them with a big smile on his face. "Jane, I was hoping to see you again. I even have a little time before I start slaving away. Would you mind if I join you two?"

"I'd like that." June's heart did a flip-flop as he led the two of them to a booth. She decided to sit back and thoroughly enjoy this time and the changes in her life.

After finishing lunch, Angie left for the salon. June found herself alone with Jim.

They talked for a few minutes until Jim suddenly took her hands in his large warm ones. "Jane? I'd like to get to know you better. Would you like to go out with me one night this week?"

His unexpected invitation stunned June. She'd never had a date, and this man gave her feelings which she had never experienced before. What should she do? She was both frightened and, at the same time, excited. She really liked Jim but was afraid. She certainly couldn't tell him that she had been hurt by someone whom she hated with all her might, and that she'd almost killed the guy.

June wasn't sure if she could handle a date. Then inspiration came and she replied, "I'd like to, Jim, but perhaps we can make it a double date with Angie and her husband."

"Great idea. I'll talk to Angie this afternoon. Okay, today is Tuesday, maybe we could make arrangements to go out tomorrow evening around seven. I can pick you up at your place."

"I'm staying at the Day's Inn on Third Street for now so you could pick me up there." June wasn't sure what she was getting into, but she felt that if she looked into his blue eyes another minute she'd drown in them. He was so gorgeous and sweet.

When Jim's hand brushed against hers, thrills shivered along her spine again, along with the ever present fear. Should she keep the date? How would she handle herself if he tried to kiss her?

"I'll be looking forward to tomorrow evening. See you then, Jane."

She hurried home and when it was time to leave for her appointment, she changed into her business outfit, using darker lipstick than usual, along with eye shadow. Looking in the mirror, she decided she looked much older. After drawing a deep breath for courage, she walked back over to the restaurant for her four o'clock interview.

As June entered the Best Watering Hole, her confidence vanished as she was taken aback by the stale cooking odors and dusty carpet, not at all what she expected.

The burly manager called her into his office and, after looking her up and down, said, "Yes, you're exactly what I'm looking for. We need young gals like you working here. When can you start?"

June recoiled when he held out his large hand toward her. She felt numb—he didn't even ask her age. His expression raised gooseflesh on her arms and he reminded her so much of Frank that she wanted to gag. However, she didn't know how long it would take to find her sister and she had a feeling that she could tell this guy her name was Jane Doe and he wouldn't care.

I can take care of myself, I've done it all my life. I can handle this jerk. Aloud, June asked, "When can I start? I'd like to begin working as soon as possible."

"Call me Clint, baby. Okay, come in on Friday, we'll have uniforms ready for you. The main thing to remember is you can make good tips if you keep the drinks coming fast and you're nice to the boss."

June shuddered inwardly. The smells of food prepared in too much grease brought back the nausea and she had to bite down hard on her lower lip.

Clint grabbed her arm. "Are you local? Cause if you're from out of town, you'll need a working card from the federal office downtown. Let's see, you can start working next Monday. Size eight?"

She tugged free of his grasp. "What?"

"Your uniform size—eight?" He clicked his tongue. "I got an eye for women, honey."

June scowled. She had no intention of getting a card and had a feeling he wouldn't care. "Fine. I'll be here to pick up the uniforms on Friday."

She fled into the fresh, sharp air and hurried to the hotel. On the way, she told herself that if she came back to this bar, she'd voluntarily put herself in a situation which could lead to the same problem she'd experienced at home. But nothing would ever be as bad as home, sweet home. Surely the bar had some type of bouncer to keep her from getting pawed by sloppy drunks and the worst danger was probably a few fanny pinches from Clint.

June reminded herself that she was a survivor, that she'd been through her own private war and lived to tell about it. If only she could escape from the burning hatred that haunted her thoughts and dreams.

The only solution to avoiding Clint was to buckle down and find her sister before her money ran out. If worse came to worse, perhaps she could work for a month or so and tap dance around her boss long enough to build up some cash reserves.

That evening, June took advantage of the unusually balmy weather for October and sat outside the hotel, surveying the beautiful city of Duluth overlooking Lake Superior.

Someone up above seemed to be throwing a party to celebrate

June's freedom and the wonder of meeting Jim. She watched the northern lights dance in the sky with the reflection of stars bursting out all over.

She reflected on all the good things which had happened this week. June was starting to feel a little better about herself and her future. She'd found three new friends, Angie, Bill and Jim. Especially Jim.

June gave a gurgle of pleasure as she remembered his broad shoulders and booming laugh. Every time she thought about him, her heart seemed to skip a beat. She sensed that he liked her, that he liked her a lot. Maybe she wasn't such a bad person after all, although that was hard to believe after all the stuff hammered into her head ever since she could remember.

Suddenly June saw the shadow of a man coming up the hill toward her. Fearing the worst, she started to get up to rush to her room when she heard someone call out, "Jane, is that you?"

Startled, June recognized Jim's voice and gave a relieved sigh. "Yes, I'm enjoying this beautiful night. We won't have too many nice evenings like this before the blustery winter nights are upon us."

Jim sat down beside her and June felt the trembling began again. He was so gorgeous and sweet. If she wasn't so frightened of her future and so scarred by her stepfather, she suspected she could learn to love this man. But how could June have any type of a relationship with a nice guy? Any man of decency would be disgusted by her past and run the other direction.

Jim broke into her thoughts. "I was walking home from work and then I noticed someone sitting here all alone. I remembered you were staying her and hoped it was you. May I share your view of the northern lights?"

Leaning closer, June inhaled the scent of Jim's aftershave and the atmosphere of the Grizzly Bear Club. "I'd love the company. I just came out here to look at the city and the lights sparkling on the lake."

They sat and talked for a long time—of what, June didn't remember the next morning as it seemed like a beautiful dream.

Finally Jim sighed and stood up. "It's getting late; I'd better get going and finish my homework. I take classes at the University in the mornings."

"Oh! Lucky you." June imagined the joy of sitting in the classroom without a nightmare waiting at home. "Maybe someday I'll be able to go back to school. I've always thought that I'd like to be a nurse."

"Wow! Great minds think alike. I'm going to become e a doctor, but I've many years of school left. Medical school isn't cheap but I'm fortunate to have a job that gives me hours in the late evening. I'll be looking forward to seeing you again tomorrow."

June smiled up at him. "I can't wait!"

"Good night." Jim brushed his fingers against June's face, cupped her chin in his strong hands and leaned close to kiss her, but she shrank back. She wasn't ready for such intimacy yet.

Instead, she held out her hand to him and as he took it, that tingle raced up and down her spine again.

She shivered as Jim laughed and kissed the palm of her hand. "Sleep well, Jane," he murmured.

She watched him walk away until he was swallowed up by the darkness.

That night June couldn't get to sleep right away. Her thoughts were all of Jim. He was a nice guy, so different from Frank, from the boys at school who tried to take advantage of her. This was the first time that she'd ever looked at someone and thought he might be one she could happily spend the rest of her life loving.

You just met the guy, she told herself over and over. It's only a date, you're not getting married tomorrow!

June woke up feeling queasy again the next morning. She skipped breakfast and worked on a plan to find her sister. Frank had tried to prevent Tara from dating but June remembered that her sister had managed to sneak out to see a couple of guys. Unfortunately, June couldn't remember their last names but she started combing through the phone book, hoping a name would jog her memory.

Although she had a tight budget, the urge to make tonight's date special with a new dress overwhelmed her. She could put up with Clint for a couple days, just to look good for Jim.

At the mall, June found a simple dress on clearance whose color matched her eyes. Back at the hotel, she fidgeted around, unable to concentrate on television because her mind was full of images of Jim. She couldn't wait to see him again.

After showering and fixing her hair, she slipped into her new dress and carefully applied makeup. Setting down her blush brush, she looked at her reflection in the mirror and was satisfied that she looked as attractive as possible.

Then the doubts crept in. She couldn't shake the cloud of anxiety that enveloped her, triggering memories of her stepfather's pawing hands and the smell of alcohol choking her throat.

Around seven, a knock on the door meant Jim was right on time. Seeing him standing there, handsome as ever, she admired his sharply creased pants and crisp white shirt. His clear blue eyes sparkled as he grinned at her, starting her heart to flutter as if it was going to jump out of her chest. Oh, he was a hunk! June started to believe that she may be falling in love, whatever that meant. As their eyes met, she could almost feel that he was looking right inside her. June couldn't help but be frightened of this sensation but wanted to hang on to it as long as possible.

"You look absolutely wonderful tonight," Jim said, as he slipped his arm around her waist. She surprised herself when she didn't shy away from him, but instead stayed within his light embrace.

He led her outside to his car. "We'll be picking up Angie and her husband near the restaurant. You'll like Sam. He's a great guy and really funny. I hope you like Thai food, there's a place downtown that serves huge portions and we need to fatten you up, little girl. How does that sound?"

June would eat wood chips in this man's company. "Sounds wonderful. I haven't seen anything of Duluth except for the mall, your club and Angie's shop." She didn't mention the Watering Hole.

That evening was the most enjoyable time June had ever experienced. If she died tonight, they could put on her tombstone that she'd been on the best date ever!

But the feeling that things were going too good to last crept in, overshadowing her joy. How could she even think of becoming involved with such a nice guy, her with her filthy secrets and a pain filled past. June decided to treasure every moment with Jim and not worry about the future.

They dropped off Angie and Sam before returning to the hotel. When Jim walked June up to the front door of the hotel, he paused to take her chin in his hand, tilt up her face and kiss her gently on the lips. She wasn't able to stop him this time—and she didn't want to stop him.

After the kiss ended, June said breathlessly, "Thank you for a fantastic evening."

"You're like the northern lights, June. You light up my dark evenings with your color and gorgeous blue eyes. May I come in for awhile?"

June wanted to prolong the evening in the worst way, but she knew she couldn't. She wasn't ready yet. "I would love for you to come in, but not tonight. Bless you, Jim, for giving me such a wonderful time." Then she'd hurried down the hall and into her room, fumbling with the lock on the door, hoping to dream of him.

* * * *

The next morning June woke, after a restless sleep. Her doctor's appointment loomed at one o'clock but she couldn't stop smiling. Surely the doctor would tell her that she just needed to rest, that she was run down and hit hard by a bug that was going around.

While filling out the necessary paperwork at the doctor's office, June explained to the friendly receptionist that she didn't have insurance.

"Dr. Andres will see you anyway, honey, don't worry."

June decided put down her name as Jane Nelson and changed her birth date by a year to make herself eighteen. She filled in her medical history as best as she could but realized she had no idea what to put down for her family history. That made her sad and brought back the ache of loneliness.

After June finished the paperwork, a nurse took her to an office. "Put on this gown. I'm going to take your blood pressure, temperature and weight and Dr. Angela Andres will be in soon."

Dr. Andres proved to be a plump woman with a riot of brown curls and warm dark eyes. She immediately gave June, shivering in her skimpy gown, a quick smile. "Let me get you a blanket to wrap around your little self. It's too chilly to be wearing just that scrap of fabric."

June huddled in the blanket, grateful for its warmth, while Dr. Andres glanced through the chart and read her symptoms.

"So you've had this nausea for nearly a month?"

"Off and on. I thought maybe it was just a touch of flu but it doesn't seem to go away. I've also had a lot on my mind, so maybe it's from worrying too much."

Dr. Andres peered into June's eyes, ears and throat and a few other places. When she'd finished the exam, she sat down on the stool again and gave June a grave stare.. "Do you currently have a boyfriend, Jane? How long have you been sexually active?"

Flabbergasted, June could only stammer that she didn't have a boyfriend.

The doctor frowned."But you had a boyfriend within the past several months, didn't you?"

June could only shake her head. Here it comes, she thought. The bad news to punish me for meeting Jim.

"I'm afraid you're about two and a half months pregnant."

June suddenly felt faint. Tears stung her eyes. "No, I can't be! This is a nightmare!"

Dr. Andres closed the chart and let June cry for a few minutes. Then she said, "Well, you do have choices. Either you carry the baby and keep it or put it up for adoption. Or if this won't work for your situation, you could elect to end the pregnancy. You need to talk with someone so they can help you make up your mind. Do you want me to call anyone? Your parents, perhaps?"

Hands pressed against her abdomen, June shrieked in fury and anguish. "Don't even think about calling them—my stepdad's the one who got me pregnant and my mother never did a thing to try to stop him. I hate him, I hate him, I hate him!"

Dr. Andres rose and came over to give June a hug which had her break down in convulsive sobs.

She could hardly hear the doctor's calm voice when she said, "We need to report your situation to the authorities as a sexual assault. I'm assuming this wasn't consensual?"

"No way! He forced me to do it—he's been touching me for years. When he first moved in, he told me that if I told anyone, he'd hurt my sister. After she left, he's been threatening to kill me."

"Oh, Jane---"

"You don't understand, he's been doing this to me since I was ten years old! I'm only seventeen." June's nose started running and she twisted her hands in her lap. "When I tried to tell my mom what was happening, she called me a liar and ordered me to get out of her sight. But I escaped and now I'm afraid he's going to track me down and make me pay."

The doctor placed her arm around June and gave her a comforting squeeze. "Do you have a safe place to stay? I won't call your mother if you truly believe she might put you in danger, but I do need to contact Social Services."

June lunged to her feet. "No! I'm almost eighteen, I don't want anyone poking around into my life, talking to my mother. She'll tell Frank where I am—can't you see that my mother won't protect me against Frank! I'll die before I go back to that house."

The doctor handed June a box of tissues. "Blow your nose and stop being so dramatic, my dear child."

She waited until June had been reduced to sniffles and hiccups before saying, "I'd like you to give me permission to tell Bill Anderson what you just told me. He's in a position to get people working to make your life better and your stepfather's much worse.

"Now, if you agree, I'll call Bill, give him your phone number and bring him up to speed. He seemed quite worried about you and I understand you only met on that bus ride. He told me you needed someone to feed you about fifty good meals and that you had enough bags under your eyes for an entire family vacation."

June gave a damp giggle and another hiccup. "I could be in big trouble. I hit my stepfather with a baseball bat in order to get away."

"Well, I hope you swung for the fences, dear. You can trust Bill to do his best to get you put right."

June nodded and managed a half smile.

"Good," the doctor said. "In the meantime I'm here to help you as much as possible. I'll have to contact Social Services but you're old enough to make some decisions about your future. I'm also going to give you a number for a counselor. I recommend you try to get an appointment set up as soon as possible. Things seem hopeless right now, but there are lots of folks on your side, Jane."

June left the doctor's office in a daze. This was the absolute worst. She thought about killing herself but decided that she should live, just to spite Frank. Her hatred for her stepfather consumed her--if Frank would have been within arm's reach, she would have attacked him without hesitation. She didn't know it was possible to hate someone so much.

Her mind swirled with tormented thoughts. A glimpse of freedom and choices had just been snatched away by this news. How could she raise a child alone? Or even stand to feel it growing inside her, an ever present reminder of Frank's thick, gross hands touching her, his beery breath in her face.

Would she ever be able to get a job and keep it? What about Jim? He'd never want her when he found out her condition and how it happened. What was she going to do? Maybe she should run away again.

Shoulders shaking with sobs, she walked back to the hotel, her thoughts racing. Suddenly she noticed a sign above a stone building which read: "Need help with an unwanted pregnancy? We have the solution."

Desperate and completely defeated, filled with the awful thoughts of wanting to hurt something or someone, June snatched up a rock and fired it at the building. She hurled three more stones but the violent action didn't make her feel any better.

Then June realized that maybe the solution did lie in the building before her. She hesitated, but quickly made up her mind to explore her options. All her options.

The outer clinic space contained several young women sitting thumbing through magazines or staring at the wall. One held her cell phone close to her face, her finger darting as she sent a text message.

All sat isolated, not making eye contact with each other. The odor of some type of anesthetic stung June's nose and she placed a protective hand over her stomach.

Although still in shock, she suddenly asked herself, what if I stood here with my sister, or with Angie, could I still go through with this? She hesitated, thoughts of having to confess her secret to Jim, his horror at seeing her grow fat with Frank's child, tormenting her. Then she sighed. No matter how this baby got started within her, it was still life.

What if Jim stood beside her right now? Would he urge her to go ahead with the procedure or to wait and consider more options? Then June thought about Bill and the kindness in his eyes.

Shaking her head, June turned and left. The baby was innocent, unlike disgusting Frank. "God, if you exist, please help me. I hurt so bad inside and I don't know who to talk to or what to do."

A woman standing near the clinic walked over and handed June a pamphlet. "I'm from an anti-abortion group. I understand what you're going through. Maybe this will help." She turned and walked away without another word.

June stopped and studied the pamphlet. A paragraph caught her attention: "If you're pregnant with an unwanted child, we can help. We don't ask you to do anything that will harm you or your baby. You have choices! We offer Christian-based love and understanding to help you get through your situation. Call our crisis nursery."

The address shown was in Duluth. The words, "We can help" gave her a feeling of hope.

After reading more of the pamphlet, June decided that she should take the time to check out the crisis nursery.

Back at the hotel, she collapsed on her bed and worried about her dilemma. *Now I can't get involved with Jim. No matter what I do, he's gonna hate me forever. Why did this have to happen?* June cried herself to sleep.

Suddenly she was startled awake by the sharp ringing of the phone. She winced at every movement, her body stiff from her uncomfortable sleeping position. June rolled over and grabbed the phone from the nightstand. The little clock indicated it was just past six o'clock in the evening.

The sound of Bill's voice brought some relief. *I hope he has good news. I don't think I can handle any more bad news.*

Remembering her condition, June felt even more tears burn her already sore and swollen eyes.

Bill said, "Glad I caught you in. You're going to have to get a cell phone, young lady, so we can keep in touch. Now, I've got something important to talk to you about so I need to know where you're staying. Are you up for company? You don't sound real perky."

June wondered how much the doctor had told Bill—had he recognized her picture from the paper and linked a young runaway from Rochester together with the attack on Frank?

Right at this minute, prison might almost be a relief. Then she wouldn't have to make any decisions and she wouldn't have to explain to Jim why she couldn't see him any more.

Her voice hoarse, June said, "I'm okay. I'm at the Day's Inn on Second Street near the bus depot."

"Let's grab a cup of coffee or a burger at the restaurant. I'll be there in a few minutes."

"You might not recognize me, Bill. I've changed." *Let's see if the great detective recognizes me as a blonde!*

June washed up and put on her jeans and a clean tee-shirt. She didn't even have the energy to add makeup. She found Bill in the lobby and smiled at him. "Hi Bill."

"Wow! And here I was expecting a cute brunette, not a blonde bombshell. You definitely look older. Let's sit closer to the back where we can have more privacy."

"I decided that I needed a new look because I wanted to be a new person, have a new life. But that's all over now." June forced herself into the booth, scared of what she was going to hear. "You might as well give me the bad news first."

"Guess your life has been full of bad news, hasn't it, June." Bill sat across from her. "I went back to Rochester to check out the story in the paper. I knew you must be in some kind of trouble, a young girl catching a bus so late at night, constantly looking around as if the Hound of the Baskerville was on your trail..."

He chuckled at her puzzled expression. "A Sherlock Holmes tale about a giant hound. Anyway, Dr. Andres called this afternoon and said you wanted me to do a little spadework on your behalf, to see where you stood with regard to what happened with your stepfather."

Bill asked the waitress strolling by to bring him a cup of coffee and told her that June needed a large glass of milk, a bowl of soup and a piece of pie. "Need to feed her up," he explained to the bored looking young woman.

"Where was I?" He added some creamer to his coffee and gave it a brisk stir. "To set your mind at ease, your stepdad only had a mild concession and needed about ten stitches. Head wounds bleed but they aren't usually serious."

After a sip of coffee, he continued. "The good news is Frank isn't in any position to press charges against you. The bad news, he went out and got hammered and then decided to hammer on your mother."

June gasped and Frank reached across the table to take her hand. "I apologize, that was a rough way to break it to you. Your mother's in the County Hospital in Minneapolis. A neighbor called the ambulance for your mom but Frank had already left the house."

He patted her hand. "I visited your mother and talked for a moment. Her face is so swollen that you probably won't recognize her and she's got some other injuries, but the doctor thinks she'll recover. Her nurse said she's been restless, begging them to find you and your sister. She seems to want your forgiveness for not protecting you from Frank."

June sniffed and grabbed a paper napkin to use as a tissue. "I don't know that I can forgive her. How can you not protect your own kids against a monster! When I think about what that creep did to me and Tara--"

"Tara?"Bill looked long and hard at June. "Your sister's name is Tara and she's going to be twenty in March. Your birthday is in August."

June sat for a moment, speechless, before demanding, "How do you know that? Did my mother tell you?"

"No, I still remember the birthdays for both my girls."

June felt as though the booth shifted beneath her and grabbed the edge of the table to keep from falling over into a heap.

"When we met, I was in Rochester looking for you, June. Tara had described Frank, said he kept changing his last name and moving you girls and your mother around, at least while Tara lived there. But the last known address was in Rochester so I thought I'd start there. Who knew I'd actually end up sitting next to my own daughter on a bus and not recognize her. If the guys at the station ever found out, they'd never let me hear the end of it."

"You were looking for me?" June could hardly take it in. "Wait, you called me June, not Jane earlier. So you knew!"

"The newspaper article gave the runaway's name as June and I immediately recognized your mother. When we met, I kept thinking there was something familiar about your face, so I stopped by Tara's to look again at the few photos she'd brought with her. I realized then you were the girl on the bus. Remember, I last saw you as a three year old. You know, when you told that story about your dad leaving you, it ripped my heart out because I was afraid my daughters believed I abandoned them."

Bill rubbed his thumb at a spot on the table. "I couldn't wait to find you again, June. But I had to make sure before letting you know my identity. You've gotten so thin and pale, you don't look anything like that chubby little girl I remember. But I never stopped searching for you, sweetheart."

June's head buzzed and her heart thudded in her chest as she suffered from emotional overload. Bill was her dad? He knew where Tara was living! She couldn't seem to wrap her mind around all this information.

"You were married to my mom." June shook her head. "She told us you left because you didn't want kids. Don't get me wrong, I'm happy you're my dad, really happy, but I don't know if I can handle much more. My mother could have died and I'm pregnant by someone I hate with all my being. Now the father I thought had abandoned me is sitting across the table. How much more can I take?" June placed her hands over her face and wept.

Bill slid in next to June and put his arms around her. "I can't imagine what you're going through but I'm so happy I've got my daughter back that this tough detective might cry! I'll never let my guys know that I'm such a marshmallow. Now, we'll get Frank, and I promise you, he'll go to jail for a long time for what he's done to you, your sister and your mother. She also was his victim, although that may be hard for you to understand right now."

The waitress dropped off their orders, giving June a curious look but not saying anything.

"Try to eat what you can, June, you need your strength. When I talked to your mother, she said she just wants you to forgive her."

"I suppose I should see her, but I'm afraid to go to Minneapolis. I'm so angry at my mom and Frank, so angry I could kill him right now."

"I wouldn't exactly shake the guy's hand," Bill muttered before saying, "I'll protect you but I can't force you to see your mother. I'm here for you, no matter what you decide to do about the baby or your mother, June. Remember that."

She took a sip of milk. "I do want to see Mom, I guess."

"The doctor assured me that she's going to make it but she'll be in the hospital for close to a week, with broken ribs and facial injuries."

"Frank probably used the same bat on her that he used on me," June murmured. Nauseated, she pushed the bowl of soup away.

"No, eat. We'll order something else if you like but you need the calories. Tell you what, we'll still be travel buddies but perhaps we can also be 'forgiveness' buddies, and help each other to get over the anger we feel toward your mother. After you eat something, I'll take you to see your sister. And tomorrow we'll go down to Minneapolis and visit your mother."

June felt the tears again, but this time they were happy ones. "I want to see Tara again."

"She's married and they bought a house not too far from here. Maybe you can stay with Tara and her husband until you get on your feet. I've only got a small apartment but you're also welcome to live with me."

June was in awe with what Bill was saying; she still couldn't believe the news, but she was starting to like it—like it a lot. "I'm so happy, Bill, I mean, Dad."

"You can call me whatever you like, honey."

"Speaking of babies, what about—" June gestured at her tummy.

"I'm going to get you to meet with a counselor but I don't want you to act in haste. There are so many couples that would love a baby that I hope you might consider adoption."

June nodded and picked up her spoon. Might as well start eating for two, she decided. I'm so happy to have my father back that I can deal with just about anything.

"I know that I can't kill it, even if Frank's responsible. I stopped by an abortion clinic and decided that I couldn't do it. Then on the way out a woman gave me a pamphlet about adoption. It was weird because I had just said, 'God if you are out there please help me.'"

"There is a God and He loves you very much. How do you think we ended up next to each other on that bus?"

June grinned. "I guess that was either a miracle or a mind blowing coincidence, wasn't it?"

"I believe in miracles, June. I'm looking at one right now. Finish your soup and pie and we'll go see your sister."

***

Tara and her husband were waiting at their house. June ran up to Tara and gave her a big hug, as they both said almost simultaneously, "Oh, I missed you so much!" Their dad watched them, a proud smile on his face.

Then Tara said, "I want you to meet my husband, Mike."

June turned to Mike and shook his hand, saying, "Glad to meet you. I heard Tara had gotten married. I'm happy for both of you. When was the big day?"

"Almost a year ago," Tara said. "I only sent that postcard because I was afraid to send anything with my address in case Frank decided to track me down and haul me back. I really wanted to have you as my maid of honor, June. Oh, it's so wonderful to see you again. I've been praying for your safety since I left home."

"Sounds like you should have prayed for Frank's safety," Mike put in and they all laughed.

Tara seemed thrilled to see June again and couldn't stop hugging her

117

sister. They decided that June would move into the guest room after the trip to Minneapolis. The sisters' reunion lasted until after supper and then Bill took an exhausted June back to her hotel room.

"We'll pick you up around eleven o'clock tomorrow, sweetheart. Can I pray for my girl before I leave her?"

She nodded and, safe in the circle of his arms, listened as he prayed, "Dear Heavenly Father, protect my precious daughter. Thank you for the miracle of finding her. Help her to trust in Your mercy and strength. You are her keeper and we know that you will carry her through, in the name of Jesus, Amen."

He gave her another squeeze and left.

June just stood there for a moment, in awe of all the wonders that had happened that day. After a shower, she decided to pack her few things in the morning and went to sleep almost immediately, an unfamiliar peace in her heart. Tonight her dreams were of a strong hand reaching down, pulling her out of a deep hole and taking her to a place of refuge.

The next morning June awoke realizing that she had a few things to handle before meeting up with her "real dad"—that was so nice to say. She walked out to the front desk and told the desk clerk she was planning to leave today. She then returned to her room and packed up her few belongings.

She'd decided she didn't want anything from her former home in Rochester. All new stuff, for a new life.

The phone buzzed and it was Bill. "I'll be over in just a few minutes. I picked up a cell phone for you so we can keep in touch. Anyway, we'll meet Tara and her husband for lunch before we head down to Minneapolis."

June could hardly contain herself, it felt as though bubbles zipped through her veins and she couldn't stop smiling. Grabbing her backpack and the shopping bags containing her new clothes, she headed to the lobby and checked out. After storing her stuff with the desk clerk, she walked out front to watch for Bill.

Humming, June lifted her face to the sun, enjoying the warmth. Without warning, a blow knocked her back from the sidewalk and into the wall of the hotel.

Clutching her stomach and gasping for air, she looked up to meet Frank's furious gaze.

"So you thought you'd gotten away, huh?" he spat on the ground.

"Get away from me!" she wheezed, looking around desperately for help. However, the area in front of the hotel was deserted at the moment.

"Knew you either took a bus or went to a friend and you didn't have any friends. The guy at the depot recognized the description of my runaway little girl and said he sold you a ticket to Duluth. Just had to tell him you were only fourteen and that I was worried to death about you."

June realized she was unable to run, she couldn't even catch her breath.

Frank continued to brag. "Yeah, I just had to go around to all the hotels up here and spread a few bucks to find if any little gals with long black hair checked in—paying cash. Using my money!"

Panting and gulping, June prayed for lightning to strike Frank. He was going to hit her again and she had no chance to escape. From the alcoholic mist, she deduced that he'd had a couple drinks and there was no way to talk him out of this beating.

"You hit me with a bat, so I used the same one on your mother, you little slut." He doubled up his fists and took a step closer.

June closed her eyes, unable to watch the knuckles coming towards her face.

But a thud and a grunt of pain had them flying open, in time to see Frank rolling on the ground, holding his nose, which was bleeding in a very satisfactory manner.

Bill loomed over him, rubbing his own knuckles. "Haven't had to do that in ages. Are you all right, June?"

She nodded and listened as her father pulled out his cell phone and called for someone to come to the scene and arrest Frank for assault. Wincing, June tried to straighten up but couldn't. The pain in her stomach got sharper and she sank down to the ground, her back against the wall.

"Please, help me." June whispered, her voice trembling from shock. She felt the warmth of blood trickling down her legs and realized she'd been hurt.

Bill crouched beside her, holding her hand and shouting on his phone for an ambulance.

* * * *

Dr. Andres entered the cubical and took June's hand in hers. "I'm afraid that you've lost your baby, June. Now I need to take you to

119

surgery to make sure you don't have any tissue left inside of you."

June wasn't sure if she was glad or sad, but she knew she was angry. She hated Frank even more now. All she wanted to do to destroy him like he'd destroyed her. Bill hovered nearby and kissed the top of her head before they wheeled her out for the D&C.

She ended up spending the night in the hospital and then rested at Tara's house for a couple of days before they made the trip to Minneapolis to visit their mother. .When they arrived at the hospital, the familiar scents made June press her hand protectively against her stomach before remembering that the baby was gone.

Did she really want to see her mom? She looked over at Tara, who gave her a reassuring smile in return. "Are you scared of seeing Mom again?" June asked. "Do you still harbor hard feelings like I do?"

Tara placed her arms around June. "Let's pray that God will lead you to a place of forgiveness, where you'll be able to release the burden of pain and anger. Although I understand how you feel, June, your hatred only hurts you, not Frank."

Her sister said a quick prayer, right there in the hallway, and again June felt much more peaceful.

"There must be something with this Jesus thing," she told her sister. "I sure feel better since we prayed."

Bill stayed out in the hall to let the girls see their mother alone. As the two entered the room, June gasped. Her mom appeared almost unrecognizable. Her swollen eyes looked like balloons protruding from their sockets. Bruises, bandages and tubes covered most visible areas. Even after several days in the hospital, she was still in serious condition.

Rattled, June froze, unable to move.

However, Tara walked over to the bed. "I'm sorry you've been hurt so much. I've missed you." She reached down and gave her mom a gentle hug.

One of her mother's hand raised slightly off the bed, trembling. "Sorry, Tara. So sorry." she managed.

"I forgive you, Mom." Tara turned and beckoned to her sister. "June's here too."

"June? Come here. I'm sorry, June Bug."

The familiar pet name from childhood brought June out of her paralysis and she joined Tara as they each held one of their mom's hands.

June said, "I, I—forgive you, Mom, I just wished you could have been strong enough to stand up for yourself and for us."

Their mother's battered body shuddered. "I was so stupid to let Frank control me. But I'll make this up to you." Her voice trailed away.

The nurse came in and told them that they needed to let her rest. Bill had reserved a hotel suite nearby and they stayed several days until she was released from the hospital and then admitted to a rehab program specializing in alcohol addiction.

During their time together, June said to Tara, "There must be something with this Jesus, since you and Dad have such peace. I would like this peace for myself."

"You just need to want forgiveness for your sins and ask Jesus to come into your heart. He wants to give you hope and a future, June, one where you're not weighted down with anger but totally free. If you want, we can pray right now."

After they prayed together, June felt as if she was a different person, with a sense of comfort and peace she had never felt before.

***

When they arrived back at Tara's house in Duluth, June could not believe her eyes when she saw Jim waiting beside Tara's husband.

Jim hugged her after she climbed out of the car. "I missed you, Jane or June, or whoever you are!"

Turning to her sister, June asked, "How did—"

"I didn't think you'd mind if I straightened a few things out," Tara told her. "I also said you'd be coming back today. Guess he missed you."

June looked at Jim and said, "I missed you, too!"

She suddenly realized she'd been blessed with the chance to learn to love again, now that her past was behind her. But she had to tell him about her scars and, if Jim was the one, he'd understand that what happened wasn't her fault.

"Okay if I take my girl June out for dinner?"Jim was talking to Bill but gazing down at June.

"That's a great idea," Tara said. "Have a nice time--I'll keep the front light on for you."

"Yes, Grandmaw," June retorted and the sisters laughed.

Jim took June to a romantic spot where they had a dinner and later they walked along Lake Superior enjoying the beautiful northern lights.

Although it was hard to begin, once June started talking, she couldn't stop until she got to the end of her story.

Jim said nothing, but held her hand in a warm clasp, giving her an encouraging squeeze each time she got to a difficult part.

When she finished, Jim took her into his arms. "I'm sorry for all you've suffered and if I'd been there, I'd have done more to Frank than break his nose. And if I ever see him outside a courtroom, he'll wish that he was in prison."

He gazed into her eyes. "I've fallen in love with you, June. In light of your past experiences with Frank and my feelings about this, we'll need couple's counseling but you are definitely worth it."

This time when his lips touched hers, it was with a passion it made June's head spin, in a good way!

* * * *

June stayed in Tara's guest room and, in the evenings, worked at the Grizzly Bear restaurant with Jim. Bill had promised to pay her first year's rent for an apartment of her choice as soon as she was ready to live alone. But for now, she was enjoying being with Tara. And Jim, of course.

Her mother stayed in rehab and June and Tara drove down to Minneapolis to see her as often as possible. June still struggled with forgiveness but the love she'd once felt for her mother seemed to be re-surfacing.

During the week, June also took classes towards earning her nursing degree. With counseling, she began to hope that with Jim at her side, her future could be limitless. The only dark cloud on the horizon was Frank's trial.

She still feared her stepfather but knew she had to testify, for her own sake, for Tara, for her mother and especially for the baby's sake. Frank must to go to prison for a long time or he'd hurt other girls. June still dreamed about the baby she'd lost.

On the day of the trial, walking toward the witness stand, her legs again felt like cooked noodles. But whatever happened, she and Tara and Bill would walk out together and she knew Jim waited for her in the hallway outside the court room.

As she passed Frank, he leaned toward her and said in a low, vehement tone, "When this is over, I'm going to hurt you!"

June gave him a defiant look. "When this is over, you're going to prison."

Tara had testified earlier how the two girls had tried to barricade their door at night to keep Frank from hurting them and then cried when she described how much it hurt to leave June behind.

June's own story was similar and when Frank's attorney cross-examined her, June admitted hitting him before making her escape. She managed to keep from sobbing when she told the judge about the pregnancy and the miscarriage caused by Frank's blow to her midsection.

When Frank heard the results of the DNA tests that proved the baby was his, his gaze dropped and, for the first time, June recognized that he was afraid of her testimony. That he was scared of her!

Seeing the expression of defeat on Frank's face served as June's revenge. She had beaten him. Hopefully, he would be locked up for a long time and would never hurt any woman again.

After the trial ended, Frank was found guilty and given the longest possible sentence. June was able to live with that. She knew she'd be able to let herself love and be loved for the rest of her life.

The End

About the Author

Shirley Olson is married, a mother, grandmother and a retired registered nurse. She's been writing for many years and has published two fiction books, The Truth Shall Set You Free, and Train Wreck in the Sierras, both published by Infinity, and one non-fiction book, Life after Death, published by Eloquent Books. Shirley has received awards from the American Christian Writers and Honorary Mention awards from Writers Digest contest and Midwest Senior Expo. She's a member of Northern Lights Writers, a chapter of Romance Writers of America, and also a member of the Minnesota chapter of the ACFW. She is now enjoying life to the fullest, writing, reading, and being with her extended family. Her books are presently available on the Internet in both e-book form and hard cover.

Check out her websites:
http://www.Skalpinolson.com or http://www.Truthinfiction.net

Candlelight and Silverware
by
Edna Curry

"Ow!" Carol exclaimed, pulling her hand back quickly from the spitting grease in the frying pan where she basted her husband's eggs. She turned down the gas flame to where it should have been if she'd been paying attention to her cooking instead of stewing about their argument.

"Burn it?" asked Tom, looking up from the toast he was buttering. He jumped up and held her hand under cold water at the sink. "Better?"

"Yes, nothing serious. I'm just nervous this morning." She frowned at the angry red mark on her hand, sighed, and served the eggs.

"Oh, yeah, I forgot. The Jamisons are coming to dinner tonight."

"Yes." Carol turned away to get his coffee, pursing her full lips. Forgot! After that big fight the other night when he had casually told her he had invited them to dinner? Fat chance he'd forgotten! They'd hardly spoken a loving word since.

The Jamisons were Tom's latest important clients at his advertising firm. And Tom had known Carol felt terribly inadequate beside Lori Jamison, yet he'd gone right ahead and invited them to dinner without consulting her. So inconsiderate of him.

True, he often invited clients home to dinner on short notice, but not someone like her. Lori always looked like she'd just stepped off a fashion magazine cover.

"Aw, honey, don't let it upset you. They're nice people, just like you and me," Tom pleaded, running a large hand through his dark curly hair.

All Carol's anger flashed back as she poured his coffee, then her own and sat to eat her breakfast. "Just like us? Ha! What a laugh. We hardly ever leave this Minneapolis area. We're just plain old

124

suburbanites. We go to church and school activities, shop at the local mall. They've been all over the world, visit all kinds of people--why, they're rich! Our rambler may be fairly new, but it's nothing fancy like they're probably used to. I do all my own cooking and housework while she's used to servants and everything. How will my dinner and home look to them?" She waved a hand around her nice, but nothing fancy kitchen.

Tom looked around, clearly puzzled. "We have one of the nicest homes in this neighborhood. They won't expect it to be fancy, honey. Please, I've got to run! Just relax and be yourself. I'll see you with them at seven. Aren't the kids ready yet? They'll be late for school." He shrugged into his brown coat and pulled his furry cap down around his ears. With a hurried goodbye kiss, he was gone.

Carol sighed and drank her coffee, then got up and began fixing eggs for her teenagers. "Bob, Cathy, breakfast is ready! Hurry up!"

Bob appeared, his curly brown hair so like his father's, uncombed. As usual, he wore faded Levis and carried his backpack of books under his arm. At fourteen, he was quiet and studious. Dropping the backpack onto a chair, he sat and ate quickly and noisily.

A minute later, Cathy appeared. "Ugh, eggs and toast again? Why don't we ever have anything romantic?"

"You would say it was fattening and refuse to eat it anyway. Hurry, now, you'll be late."

Tall and slim at sixteen, Cathy was at the independent, impossible age between girl and woman. Still, Carol shouldn't complain. They were good kids, usually cooperative and polite. Both did well in school and had many friends.

Five minutes later Carol found herself alone with an empty house and her thoughts. She seethed at Tom's lack of consideration for her feelings. But the invitation couldn't very well be cancelled. She went through her usual morning routine with extra care. Would her suburban Minneapolis home seem poor to the Jamisons? How would they act?

She'd met them only once, at a company dinner at a restaurant a few weeks ago. Lori had worn a fantastic low-cut evening gown and a blonde wig, though another friend had told Carol that her real hair was dark brown. She looked gorgeous.

And I felt plain and ordinary beside her. All that talk about Paris and Rome and Tokyo— whatever am I going to discuss with her tonight? I've only read about all those places!

She worried all morning as she worked. The children were going to an away football game on the bus after school, they wouldn't be home until late. So there would be just the four adults at dinner. At least that would eliminate the usual dinnertime teenage drama.

Carol wished she could have invited a few others, so she and Lori wouldn't be alone. But Tom had said no, since he and John had to work out details of their new contract after dinner.

She'd chosen a simple dinner menu– roast beef for the main course. She went over the grocery list again, making sure she hadn't forgotten anything. Oops, she hadn't made ice cubes for cocktails. She glanced at the clock as she slid the ice cube tray into the freezer. Eleven already! Where had the morning gone?

After brushing her hair and applying lipstick, Carol climbed into her red Volkswagen. She spent the next several hours getting her hair done, shopping for groceries and doing errands.

Home at last, she went through the familiar routine of preparing a company dinner. Roast in the oven, potatoes ready to put in. She'd made a dessert and rolls the day before, grateful for her habit of depending on make-aheads to take the pressure off the party day.

She always kept her silverware polished and company tablecloths clean and ready. Candles. Carol added leaves to the dining room table and began to set it. Good china, candles, centerpiece, napkins, and butter dish—better put out the butter to soften a bit. Would they like her homemade rolls? She could warm them in the microwave at the last minute.

She checked the roast. It looked fine, and the delicious aroma reminded her she had skipped lunch. She nibbled hungrily on the hors d'oeuvres as she made up a pretty tray of them, mixed a sour cream and chives topping for the potatoes, prepared a tossed salad, and put the potatoes into the oven to bake.

What else could she do? Five-thirty. How about some time for me? A leisurely soak in the tub sounded better than a shower. Maybe the hot water would relax her. She carefully covered her hairdo so the steam wouldn't ruin it, and enjoyed a soak as long as she dared. Then makeup, her favorite perfume, charm bracelet, and her best hostess outfit, a red pantsuit. She surveyed herself nervously in the mirror.

When Carol returned to the kitchen, she noticed that rain still spattered on the windows. The children hadn't come home, so their game must be on. She worried about them as she always did when they were away in bad weather.

She was putting the vegetables on to cook when the doorbell rang. Lori stood there, her hairdo blonde, unusual and perfect to the last detail. Her blue outfit looked new and expensive, but she was a bit wet. The drizzle was changing to sleet.

"Sorry to be early, dear, but the men said to come ahead and they'd be here later."

"Of course. Come in, please, Mrs. Jamison."

"Call me Lori," she laughed, shaking out her fur coat. "My, but it's cold out there!"

Carol hung up her coat in the closet. "Yes, the weather is nasty tonight."

"Mmm, smells delicious in here! Can I help with something?" Lori sounded sincere.

Carol relaxed a bit as Lori followed her to the kitchen. She opened the oven to check on the potatoes and roast. The meat thermometer read close to rare. Carol prayed the men wouldn't be late. Why had she chosen simple foods, which had to be perfect? I should have made a fancy meat mixture which wouldn't be ruined by waiting in case they were late, she thought desperately.

"What a huge roast! Is someone else coming?"

"No, but I have two teenagers. They had a game tonight, but will be home later."

"Of course. I'd forgotten your children. What can I do?"

Was she condescending? Or did she really want to help? "Everything is about done except to watch the food cook. I'll put the vegetables on. The men should be here any minute. Do you want to put these hors d'oeuvres on the coffee table in the living room? Here's a little fork for them—oh, dear, I forgot to put on the silverware!"

"I'll do it," Lori offered. "I hear John's car."

"Thanks. The silverware chest is in the top drawer of the buffet beside the table. I'll mix the drinks," Carol answered, relieved that Lori was making herself at home, and the men werc not late. She heard Tom and John's voices as they came in, and carried in the tray of drinks.

"What a night!" Tom exclaimed, kissing her lightly. Everything under control? his eyes asked her. She smiled in reassurance and handed John his cocktail.

"Lori, you look lovely as usual," Tom greeted her as the other woman joined them.

John laughed. "She always does. Is that a new outfit, dear? This gal should own a clothing store—she's always shopping!" He sat on the couch and opened the buttons of his expensive sports coat to make room for his ample middle.

"Yes, it's new," Lori admitted. "I stopped at this darling shop this afternoon and just couldn't resist it. The boutique reminded me of that cute little place in Paris where I got so many things when we lived there, remember, John?"

"Sure, I remember the bills. But at least it wasn't as expensive a place as that 'Maries' in Milan. I thought I'd go broke that summer!" He chuckled, indicating that he didn't mind and could well afford to indulge her whims.

Carol smiled, trying to ignore the sinking feeling in her stomach as she wondered how plain she must seem to them, when they could compare shops and cities all over the globe.

Carol went back to the kitchen to serve the meal. Lori followed. She seemed to really want to help and Carol began to relax as she carried in the food. Lori lit the candles.

They sat down to eat and everyone seemed to be enjoying themselves when Tom looked questioningly at her across the centerpiece. Now what? Whatever was wrong must not be something he could ask out loud. What had she done wrong? Drops of nervous perspiration slid down Carol's back and her throat tightened.

She smiled and nodded agreement to whatever John had said, hoping that was a suitable response and picked up her fork. Only it was her spoon.

And then she knew. The silverware! The knives and spoons were on the left and the forks were on the right. But how? Of course. Lori had put the silverware on. Carol wanted to laugh or cry. But Lori and John didn't seem to notice. They were eating and talking to Tom.

How could Lori not know the correct way to set a table—Lori who had raised a family herself—had eaten elegant meals in expensive restaurants all over the world? Even if she hadn't done the work herself, wouldn't a person remember where the silverware went just from picking it up to eat with it? Tom had noticed immediately, and he'd never set a table in his life.

Suddenly the nervousness left Carol. Lori might be beautiful and glamorous and experienced in some ways, but she was ignorant in others. I'm superior in some ways, too, Carol thought, her confidence returning.

"Terrific food, Carol," John was saying. "This roast is perfect. And your homemade rolls are delicious."

"Aren't they, John?" Lori said. "I never learned to bake. Never had to, I guess, or was just too busy. There was always some social event or another to get ready for or attend."

"True, Lori." John agreed amicably. "Yeah, it's a real treat to eat home cooking, Carol. Sure is nice of you to have us over."

"My pleasure!" Carol smiled and meant it. "I'll get the dessert and coffee."

After dessert, the men moved to the den while Lori and Carol put away leftovers and loaded the dishwasher.

Lori asked for the dessert recipe, so they settled in the kitchen with Carol's recipe box on the table in front of them. While Lori copied Carol's pistachio pudding cake recipe onto a fresh index card, Carol wrote down the name and number of Lori's hairdresser on another.

"And I want that recipe for Rhubarb Custard Pie next," Lori said. "I missed the tangy taste of rhubarb so much when we lived in the southeast. Do you know I tried three times but couldn't get it to grow there?"

"Really? Why not?"

"I'm not sure if it was the soil or the hot climate. I found it frozen in a large supermarket once. But my own little market didn't have it."

When her teens returned from their football game a while later, Carol looked up happily, thankful for her children's safe return from the nasty weather.

"Any food left, Mom?" Bob bounced in first. "Oh, hello. Sorry, I forgot you were having company." He stopped uncertainly, standing awkwardly on one foot as Carol introduced him to Lori.

129

"Hi." Cathy smiled, coming in after her brother. "I'm Cathy. What a lovely outfit, Mrs. Jamison."

"Thank you. How was the game?"

"Terrific. We won even though the field was kind of muddy," Bob said enthusiastically. "But it was too cloudy to see the Northern Lights tonight."

Cathy explained to Lori, "They're usually gorgeous driving out to the ball field, away from the floodlights. All red and yellow and green, dancing flares of color, you know."

"Yes, they are. I've seen them," Lori agreed.

"Can I heat up this roast beef in the microwave for a sandwich, Mom?" Bob asked from behind the refrigerator door.

"Sure, honey, and there's cake, too."

"But you just had three hamburgers at the game," Cathy exclaimed. How can you eat all that already?"

"They weren't very big hamburgers," Bob protested.

Lori laughed. "My three were the same when they were growing up. It seems so long ago now. But then, we lived in so many places, and they went off to boarding schools so young." Her voice trailed off, as she sat thinking. For a moment, her face didn't look glamorous, just tired and sad.

"Boarding schools. Why would you send your kids to boarding school?" Cathy asked in an appalled tone.

"John and I traveled so much for his business. We thought it would be better for them to be in one school, rather than having to change schools and make new friends all the time."

"Oh, yeah, Bummer. I'd hate leaving my friends and moving around, too." Cathy agreed as she grabbed a can of diet coke from the refrigerator and popped the top. She and Lori exchanged sympathetic smiles.

And in that moment, Carol stopped envying Lori and began to genuinely like her. Maybe this business association wouldn't be so bad after all. They might even become good friends.

Much later, after the Jamisons had left, Carol and Tom got ready for bed.

Tom said, "See, the dinner turned out terrific, as usual, Hon."

"Yes, it did." She folded the quilted bedspread, laid it on the cedar chest, and smiled indulgently at her husband's attempt at making up.

That's probably as good an apology as he can handle. And he's right. It turned out fine. I am a good hostess, even if I'm not a world traveler.

"You always worry for nothing." Forgive me? his eyes pleaded as he got into bed.

She cuddled up for a goodnight kiss to tell him all was well between them again.

"But what was that business with the silverware? Or was I the only one who noticed?"

"I'll explain it sometime," she murmured sleepily.

The End.

Night Magic
By
Nancy Pirri

September 1934

John Swenson slouched in his chair at O'Reilly's pub, drinking a tall mug of beer, his second of the evening. His flinty-eyed gaze swept around the pub, stopping now and again on one pretty woman then another.

"Stop staring at the ladies, John!" Helen Swenson scolded. "You're supposed to be finding a man for me."

John's laughter lifted above the raucous sound of piano music across the room. "There's no reason why we can't kill two birds with one stone, is there, sis?" he asked, one eyebrow lifted.

Helen tossed a hank of unfashionable straight blonde hair over her back. "I wouldn't need to be finding myself a man if you'd return home with me, and help out at the resort."

He gave her a long, withering look. "That resort is not my home." Changing the topic, he tilted his head to one side and stared at her. "You know, you should do something about your hair."

"What's wrong with my hair?" she blustered.

"It's long, boring and not quite the thing these days. You'd have a better chance of attracting a man if you cut and permed it. Also, it would look much better with that hat you're wearing."

"I refuse to waste a single cent on myself. You know how important the resort is to me. It's my livelihood, and I mean to make something of it."

"Sorry, Sis. With this depression, the place is losing money. People can't afford a vacation nowadays with so many out of work. Besides, why did our parents have to buy all of that land up north, nearly to the Canadian border anyway, for God's sake? I refuse to live away from civilization, and that's that. Now stop your fussing. I'll find you a nice sturdy man, one unafraid of physical labor. It just might take me some time is all," he murmured, his eyes on the waitress headed straight for their table.

"Another brew for you, sir?" she softly inquired.

With a small smile, John asked, "What's your name, darling?"

"Why…why, it's Maggie."

Helen took pity on the poor girl whose cheeks were turning pink as she grasped an empty beer mug in each hand. "We were just leaving, Maggie, so nothing more. Thank you."

"Oh, but don't leave on my account!" the waitress protested.

"I'm not, John said, his grin widening, "I'll have another brew. After the long dry spell we've had in this country, I have some catching up to do."

Helen rose from her seat. "I'll be at your house. I'm returning home in the morning."

"You just got here," he protested "What's the rush?"

"A few fishermen are coming up from Iowa and I have a cabin to clean, that's what."

"Thought you said it's been a slow season."

"For summer it was. But this early fall, I've had a few come in, like this one tomorrow."

"I'm frankly amazed, but what the heck. Make hay while you can, especially since winter will be here soon." He frowned. "Then what will you do?"

"I'll just hole up in my cabin for the entire season, same as last year."

"Fighting off bears again?"

"I hope not," she said, her voice trembling as she recalled several close encounters she'd had with roaming black bears on the resort property.

"Come home for the winter since you've no customers."

"I need to work to make the cabins more habitable, and winter is the season to do it," she said. "Remember? That's why I came down—to find someone to help me."

As she left the pub, she thought about her home, Swenson's Haven

133

Resort, in northeastern Minnesota. Beauty and isolation surrounded her at the small resort.

Her parents had purchased several acres of lakeshore property on a large Canadian border lake called Crane ten years ago. They'd started the small vacation spot in 1928, before the stock market crashed. They built three small cabins and the following year, two more. Before rough times, the cabins had always been booked with guests, from mid-May until late October; guests wanting to experience the great outdoors, including fishing, hunting, and enjoying nature at its finest.

During late fall, an array of colors called the aurora borealis, would paint the sky—a breath-taking sight unlike anything Helen had ever seen in her life. She couldn't wait to see it again.

Unfortunately, the cabins had never been insulated properly and were never meant for winter habitation, but Helen had chosen to live there year round. Insulating her cabin was necessary and she had no idea how to go about it. She'd tried using various items over the past winter, but nothing seemed to work well.

For Helen, born and raised in St. Paul—civilization, in comparison—it hadn't been easy taking on the job of resort owner after her parents died in a boating accident the previous summer. She'd felt duty-bound to quit high school in her last year to carry on her parents' dream of building a flourishing resort. John, six years older, had helped her over that first summer, driving up each weekend. But when winter struck, he'd returned to St. Paul. He'd finished college with a degree in accounting and was one of the lucky few to have found a job in his field during these depressed economic times. Running a resort was the furthest thing from his mind.

She'd moved from the family home in St. Paul, where her brother still lived, to the main cabin at the resort. She shuddered when she thought about the bears, and other critters, roaming the wilderness around her cabin. When evening arrived, she'd been afraid to go outside, the various animal sounds and noises unnerving. She made sure to complete her nightly relieving in the outdoor bathroom before dark, but kept a chamber pot under the bed for night emergencies. She'd viewed the northern lights from her cabin window, wishing it were safe to go outside.

Helen was convinced she'd learn, over time, to cohabitate with nature. She just needed a handyman who knew how to swing a hammer and pound a nail with accuracy. Knowing something about electrician's work would be a help as well. She had big plans for her resort, including building bathrooms inside each cabin, plenty of insulation installed in all of the cabins, and a new furnace so she could live in hers comfortably all year.

She strode down the street, deep in thought, not noticing the appreciative glances from the men passing by. She wore a bias-cut dress with a cowl neck that ended mid-calf, made of dark blue rayon. She was completely unaware of the pretty picture she made in the blue dress with her long blonde hair flowing down her back, a small matching blue hat perched on her head.

Pain struck her wrist then and she gasped when she glanced down and saw a hand snatch her handbag. She looked up in time to see an adolescent boy with a harried look on his face. Helen heard him mutter, "Sorry, ma'am," before he slammed his hands against her shoulders and shoved.

Twisting sideways as she fell, she landed on her side, grimacing when the outside of her leg scraped on the sidewalk. She rolled to a sitting position but dizziness overcame her and she lay down on her back, stunned, her eyes closed against the brilliant sunlight.

Then strong hands pulled her up and held her steady. Surrounded by a big man's body, her cheek pressed against scratchy wool, she shuddered against him.

"You all right, Ma'am?"

Helen tried pulling away, but he cupped the back of her head and held her pressed against him. "I can't breathe," she managed, her hands pressing against his chest.

He released her immediately with a "Sorry", and then "I'll be right back."

Helen watched him, amazed when he tore after the culprit who'd snatched her bag. She hadn't really gotten a good look at her savior, but she'd heard his low, Irish-accented melodious voice.

She leaned back against the wall of a men's haberdashery and waited as several people stopped to ask if she was all right. Heat bloomed in her cheeks at the fuss they made over her and she told them she was fine, and that someone was looking after her. Two elderly ladies, and a man stood with her as she waited for the man who'd taken off after the thief to return.

Then she groaned at the sight of the run in her silk stocking. She supposed it didn't matter for she wouldn't be returning to St. Paul soon, and she never wore dresses at the resort. The tall, muscular man appeared again and strode toward her. She was relieved to see that he had her bag in his hand. He stopped in front of her and handed over her purse with a big smile, his white, even teeth sparkling in the light of day. Then he thanked the people who'd stayed with her and they left. He handed over her purse. "Here you go."

Then, looking around a moment, he turned to her with a frown. "You walking the streets alone then?" At her slight nod, he said, "You really shouldn't. Things are hard for folks right now. And your purse was too much temptation for that boy."

Again, that silky Irish voice reached her ears and she felt her body go limp. His voice was like music to her ears, which made her wonder if he didn't make sweet music for his livelihood. Looking way up, she met his eyes, an unusual topaz-color, saw his curling hair the color of rich mahogany. She caught the worried expression on his face and set out to calm his fears, wondering at the same time why he worried about her welfare when they didn't know each other.

Self-conscious now, she straightened her hat and tucked her hair behind her ears, glancing surreptitiously at him. He was half a foot taller than she was, and built like the lumbermen she'd seen along the St. Croix River cutting down trees.

"You want to call the police and press charges?"

Her eyes widened on him as she pulled herself up straight and side-stepped away from him. "Why, I don't think so. Besides, I don't know the boy, and he's likely far away from here by now."

"I know him, but I don't know if I should give you his name or not."

"Why not?" she asked, suddenly growing angry about the assault, now that she'd recovered. "He could have really hurt me."

"Not Peter. He's got a drunkard dad, and a mom who took sick and to her bed months ago. Peter's the sole supporter of his family, which includes four younger brothers." Looking around, he leaned down and said softly, "It's hard enough for a grown man to find work, let alone a fourteen-year-old boy."

Her anger dimmed then and her heart softened as she nodded. "You're right, of course. When you speak with the boy, tell him he could have asked me for coin and I would have helped him."

The man grinned. "I certainly will tell him that." He tipped his hat then and stood there, smiling down at her until she grew uncomfortable. Then she thought about his words, 'drunken father'.

"Wait a minute. You said his father was a drunkard?" At the man's nod, she added, "But we've been in prohibition for the past several years."

"Ma'am, there's ways a man can find a drink if he needs it—craves it—like Peter's father does."

She sighed. "I suppose you're right. Well, thank you for helping me."

"You're welcome. Now how about I escort you home?"

"I don't live in St. Paul, but I'm staying at my brother's place."

"Then I'll walk you the rest of the way."

As he took her elbow and walked her down the street, heading past shops and cafes, she chattered nervously. He simply smiled, listened, and nodded now and then to something she said, but didn't talk much. In a way, his quiet manner intrigued her, especially since her brother talked incessantly. Soon she quieted as well, feeling self-conscious by his silence.

They turned on Arbor Street and she stopped at the foot of the steps leading up to a two-story brick home. She stuck out her hand. "I can't thank you enough for coming to my rescue." He took her hand and squeezed it gently, his gaze searching hers.

"No problem, Ma'am."

"Well, then, I'd better let you return to your work." She turned away and took the first two steps up when he spoke.

"Don't have any work right now."

She whirled around and took him in from head to toe. He wore dungarees, a long-sleeved chambray shirt with a flannel wool plaid jacket over it, and boots with worn toes on his feet. His newspaper boy's hat he wore tilted jauntily on his head. Suspenders held up his dungarees and Helen found herself gazing upon his broad chest and strong muscular arms beneath the long sleeves of his shirt; strong arms that could easily, she imagined, swing a hammer and pound a few nails…

"Mister….

"Riley Flaherty, ma'am."

"I'm Helen Swenson," she said with a nod, "so stop calling me ma'am. How would you like a job?"

* * * *

Riley pulled his steamer trunk from beneath his bed at the lumbermen's crew house where he'd lived for the past seven years. Everything he owned fit into that trunk, and as he folded his clothes neatly inside, excitement flared through him, which was something; he hadn't felt excited about much for a long time.

He hummed a song as he thought about the pretty Swedish girl he'd be working for—Helen Sweeney. A lovely name for a lovely young woman. He tried to imagine her living alone last year in her wilderness home and couldn't. He had been born and raised in a bustling city and wasn't so sure he could take the solitude, but he was willing to try.

She was tall for a woman, but narrowly built, sweet, and feminine. All he could think was how unprotected she was there, alone, with just a few people renting cabins over a brief time of the year. It just wasn't right for the woman to live there alone, and her brother should have put his foot down, sold the property, and made her stay in St. Paul.

He slammed the lid shut, and hoisted the trunk to his shoulder. Then he bent and picked up the handle of the case that held his prized possession, a fine fiddle, from his grandfather when Riley left home for America. Riley had had some lessons from his grandfather, and had easily learned how to play the instrument. For a short while, upon arriving in America eight years ago, he'd managed to make a living playing the instrument for coin, on the streets—to whoever paid to hear him to play. He'd even secured a month long run playing his fiddle every night in the Wabasha Street Caves in St. Paul, in one of several speakeasies built into the sandstone caves located on the south shore of the Mississippi River.

As he ran down the steps, he shouted 'goodbye' and good luck' to his fellow lumbermen, ready to embark on an exciting new life for himself. The pay from Helen would be only a third of what he'd earned as a 'jack' but it didn't matter. Other than a few personal necessities and food, he needed little.

He was a simple man who led a simple, but satisfying life. The only thing that hadn't satisfied him was being without a wife and children. While he'd listened to Helen talk about Swenson's Haven, he couldn't help imagining her in her modest cabin home, in the midst of a vast wilderness, growing flowers and vegetables, cooking, the wafting scent of freshly baked bread as he entered the kitchen. He imagined himself being married to her and sharing that modest cabin. He imagined her big and round with his child and heat suffused his face at the thought. But then the thought of living away from the bright lights of the city made him feel gloomy. He loved tipping a pint with his fellow workers in the local pubs, and had to admit he'd miss that, but then again, he'd be married to sweet Helen who he thought would be perfect for him.

Damn. He was getting way ahead of himself. He had to learn to get to know the lass first.

He sighed then as he strode toward Arbor Street. This was a business arrangement, yet he couldn't see a problem with mixing a bit of pleasure with it. Besides, he remembered her saying how she'd been lonely with no one to talk to all winter long and his smile widened. She wouldn't be alone this winter for he'd made a full year commitment to being her 'handy man'.

Riley arrived outside the Swenson family home just as Helen was struggling down the steps with a box. He dropped his steamer trunk from his shoulder and eased the box from her hands, astonished by its weight, and that this slip of a girl had managed to carry it. Frowning, he said, "This is way too heavy for you. Where do you want it?"

"Good morning, Riley," she said. "Why, in the back seat of my automobile would be fine."

Riley followed her pointing finger and his eyes widened. She owned an automobile, specifically an American-made Austin Model A coup. "You…drive?" he asked.

"Why, yes. How else would we get to the resort?"

Heat flared in his cheeks again and he murmured, "Thought we were taking a streetcar or train."

She laughed. "Where we're going, there few forms of transportation. We drive or we take a small airplane, Riley, which I refuse to do."

He stared at her a moment, taking in her long wheat-colored hair worn straight to her waist. God, how he wouldn't love to fist his hands in all of that fine stuff, he mused. His eyes slid to her surprisingly mannish attire, which looked enticing on her; a tan-colored broadcloth shirt that buttoned down the front, with matching tan-colored pants, and practical low-heeled tie shoes on her feet. She wore a red and gold plaid woolen jacket, similar to his own, and held a straw hat in her hand which she brushed against her leg as she met his gaze straight on. He liked that, how she didn't blush, and look away.

Riley heard a door slam then and a man who resembled Helen raced down the stairs. He clutched a full-length robe around him and wore a scowl on his face. Giving Riley a nod in passing, he stalked over to Helen and scowled down at her. "You really are returning to the resort, aren't you?"

"I told you that I was—it's my home now."

He sighed. "You were leaving without saying goodbye."

"It's the crack of dawn and I know how you hate rising early."

"True, but did you think I wouldn't want to say good-bye to my own sister, whom I won't see for who knows how long?"

With that, he pulled her into his arms for a big hug. She hugged him in return and Riley sighed, wiping away ill thoughts of this man being a possible beau.

John released her then and strode over to Riley. He held out his hand and Riley took it. Riley saw John sizing him up, suspicion on his face, but soon he smiled and released his hand. "You appear to be a trustworthy man, Mr. Flaherty. Take care of my sister. You hear?"

"I will, you can count on me," Riley said, his voice firm.

"Have a safe trip, you two!" John called as he raced up the steps and disappeared inside the house, slamming the door in his wake.

Riley looked at Helen and she shrugged. "He's glad I've hired you on."

"Uh, don't you think it's unusual how he seems to trust me, a stranger?

"Not at all. He checked you out, including interviewing your previous boss and friends at the lumber mill."

Riley frowned.

"You're not mad about that, are you? As you said, we are strangers and…"

"Your brother did the right thing. It's just that I'm not used to my personal life being invaded, but like I said, I can't blame him."

"Then let's get going, shall we?"

Riley watched her as she walked over to the passenger side of her car and slid inside. He caught a glimpse of a pretty, slim ankle as her pants rode up a bit, then she tucked her legs inside and closed the door. He stood indecisively, riveted in place, his cheeks heating up again.

She opened the door and stood up with a quizzical expression. "What's wrong? Did you forget something?"

"Uh, Miss Swenson? I don't know how to drive."

"Oh!" she gasped. "Sorry," she murmured, a small smile on her lips. "Didn't want to possibly chance bruising your male ego by having you ride with me rather than drive." With a shrug of her shoulders, she left the passenger door open for him and came around to the driver side. As she slid behind the wheel, she said, "None of this Miss Swenson business. It's Helen. Let's get going. It'll take us six hours to get to the resort."

He settled down in the passenger seat, and closed the door behind him. He'd wanted an automobile for the past five years, but had yet to save up enough money. Maybe she'd let him take it out on the resort property for a spin or two, he mused.

Seeming to read his mind, she said, "I'll teach you how to drive since you'll want to use to haul supplies from the storage cabin to the resort cabins you'll be working on. Really, what I should do is get us a truck, but I want to spend my money on renovating the cabins first."

"I understand, and thanks for the offer to teach me. I appreciate it."

The farther north Helen drove, the less assured Riley felt about taking the job. As they left the city behind, farmlands being harvested for crops filled the landscape. With miles in between, they passed through several small towns composed of a few shops, mercantiles, and at each place they stopped at a petroleum station and topped off the tank on Helen's automobile.

Riley thoroughly enjoyed the hustle and bustle of crowds and city life, especially after working in fair isolation, with just a few other lumbermen for companionship cutting trees in the north woods for several weeks at a time. It appeared Helen's home was in the woods and away from any sizeable city. He wondered if he could handle the peace and quiet he expected for an entire rotation of seasons. He'd signed on with her until the end of next summer, nearly a year away.

Helen played tour guide and Riley relaxed some as he listened to her talk about the crops on the farms they passed, pointed out the different types of trees and animals along the way. He looked out his passenger side window and lurched forward when she hit the brakes suddenly.

"Be very still and he'll leave the road. We don't want him to possibly charge us," she whispered.

Riley followed her gaze and swore under his breath when he saw an enormous moose standing in the middle of the road, staring at them.

After several minutes of waiting, he nudged Helen.

"Uh, maybe you should hit the horn."

"No. I've been with my brother when the very same thing happened. He sounded the horn and the moose charged us. Luckily we were able to go into reverse, and then turned and drove away—swiftly, I might add." She tilted her head to look at the moose critically, and added, "This may be the same moose. We must be in his territory."

At a loss for words, and thinking what he'd gotten himself into, he slouched down in his seat and scowled at the beast who languidly stood, watching, waiting for them to make a move, he suspected. A few minutes later he breathed a relieved sigh when the animal ambled down the road, then headed off into the forest.

"Finally!" Helen exclaimed, then put the automobile in gear again and drove away.

The weather had grown noticeably cooler, too, and he hadn't thought to pack more than a medium-weight jacket. He wasn't worried though as Helen said they would drive into the town nearest to the resort, about once a month and he could purchase winter gear there.

The sky went lower in the sky and he knew it would soon be dark.

"Almost there," Helen said.

He heard the enthusiasm in her voice and smiled. She was happy to be home, and her happiness piqued his interest.

After having headed north for several hundred miles, mostly on poorly paved roads, they took a turn east onto a rough dirt road. The automobile rumbled merrily along as she drove while Riley held onto the seat and set his teeth against the jarring motion. After another half hour, they arrived in a small clearing where he counted five small rustic cabins.

Helen parked her automobile near one cabin, jumped out of the automobile and ran around to the passenger side. "Come on!" she called as she swung open his door, "You have to see the lake. It's gorgeous at dusk."

He grinned when she pulled at his hand and he grasped hers and allowed her to pull him out of her automobile and around the log building. She stopped suddenly, before the ground headed down to the lake, and he paused beside her, following her gaze. They looked across a good-sized lake and at the sun as it just started setting. The sky had turned a purple-pink color and Riley's heart pounded wildly as he stared at the magnificent sight. He'd never seen a lake so unencumbered with lights and buildings until now, and the sight mesmerized him.

"Beautiful, isn't it?" she whispered with rightful reverence.

"Like nothing I've ever seen," he murmured.

They stood side-by-side, holding hands as they watched the sun make its final descent and disappear beneath the horizon. He stared at Helen then, saw a hank of pale hair flowing across her face and, without thought, reached out and tucked the strand behind her ear.

She turned then and faced him, her eyes sparkling still, smile in place.

"What did you think?" she asked.

He raised one eyebrow. "About what?"

"The sunset, of course."

"Beautiful." Just like you, darlin'. He saw her cheeks turn pink and then she shivered. "Later, we'll come outside and I'll show you an even more brilliant sight. Let's go inside. You're cold."

"Good idea," she said, all businesslike. She strode to the cabin right behind them, pulled on a string latch, which opened the door.

Riley frowned as he followed her inside, closed the door, then stared at the bar across it. Jamming his hands on his hips, he continued glaring at the door.

"What's wrong?"

"You don't have a lock on this door. And what good does this one bar do?"

"Don't need one. We're in the north woods."

He looked at her over his shoulder. "What does being in the woods have to do with safety?"

"We're miles away from civilization," she said as she moved to a small stove where an old tin coffeepot sat. "I don't need to lock the door."

"Don't you have paying guests up here though?"

"Just a few this late in the season. Day after tomorrow I've got some fishermen coming up from Iowa, so I need to clean the cabin they'll be using for the week. Stop fussing. If you feel so strongly about it, you can put a lock on the door." She grabbed the coffeepot.

A brisk breeze swept through the room. "And there's no insulation in here," he complained. "You're telling me you stayed up here, alone, all last winter?" At her nod, he snapped, "Good grief, woman, how did you plug the holes around the door, not to mention the holes between the logs?"

"I stuffed socks, fabric, weeds, hay—whatever I could find to close me in, that's how."

"Don't tell me you were all snug and warm. I won't believe it."

"I won't tell you, but I did survive," she said, tilting her nose in the air. Then she opened the door.

"Where are you off to?"

"I'm making coffee and the water's in the pump outside."

His arm came out and he stopped her from leaving. "I'll get it."

She relinquished the pot to him. "Alright, thanks."

Helen smiled when she heard Riley mutter softly, "First thing we'll do is install indoor plumbing." That would be fine with her. Once the snow came and temperatures dropped, she couldn't pump water any more, but had resorted last winter to bringing in pales of snow and melting it over the stove.

While she busied herself pulling a few potatoes and onions out of a bin, she frowned as she reached the bottom. A week ago, before she left for St. Paul, the bin had been filled to its limit with vegetables from her garden she'd harvested, but it was near empty now. Then she heard Riley's roar outside and she rushed to the door. Just as she reached to open it, the door slammed open and Riley raced inside, soaking wet. Whirling around, he slammed the door behind him and braced his arms and legs hard against the wooden portal.

"What happened?"

* * * *

"Bear," he gasped.

Helen raced to the window and peered between the curtains. Sure enough, there was a medium-sized black bear, headed straight for the cabin.

"Damn, he's following me." Riley glared at her. "This is why we need a lock on the door."

She scoffed, "You can't mean to tell me you think a bear will try and come inside, do you?"

Helen stilled at the sound of scratching against the wood. Her eyes widened in horror when the bar started to lift then fell down with a clap. They rushed forward, bumping into each other until Riley pushed her aside. She paused and watched him as he leaned his body weight against the door, then shrieked in dismay when the door started to open. He pressed himself firmly against it until it slammed shut once more.

"What are we going to do?" she wailed.

Riley peered around the room and his eyes lit upon a heavy wood table. "Come over here, and lean against the door."

"Me! Why, I weigh far less than you do."

He smirked. "I know that. But if we want to keep this bear out, we need to shove something heavy against the door. And the only thing I figure that will work is the table."

Without a word, Helen raced over and traded places with Riley, jamming her back against the door and digging in her heels. Thank heavens Riley moved swiftly for he managed to shove the table in front of the door before the bear made his way inside, though Helen felt the door give several times as she held her weight against the bear's strength.

They both heaved sighs of relief when they heard the bear's high-pitched complaints then silence. They straightened up, released their combined weights from the table's edge and peered out the window again. They saw the bear lumbering away and disappear into the forest.

"Okay, you were right," Helen said. "That bear's been inside the cabin before."

"How do you know?"

"Cause my vegetable bin is near empty and I'd filled it with vegetables from my garden before I left for St. Paul."

Riley frowned. "Doesn't the bin have a cover?"

"Sure, a hinged one, which I probably left wide open." She sighed, and then looked into his eyes—very blue eyes that sparkled with humor.

"You think this is funny, don't you?" she said indignantly.

"No. But you are one sweet colleen, Miss Helen," he breathed softly.

Helen widened her eyes as he leaned down to her, his gaze now focused on her lips.

He was going to kiss her. She knew she should turn away from him but she couldn't. His eyes were mesmerizing as they stayed focused on her lips. Male scents surrounded her; his tangy shaving cream, the wool scent of his shirt, a tiny waft of tobacco, though she hadn't seen him smoking, or chewing any. She remained utterly still. Just as his lips brushed hers, she stepped back and shook her head.

She reminded herself that this was a business venture, nothing more. Turned away, Helen strode to the table and shoved it, intent upon moving it back to its original place, but Riley stopped her. "We're leaving that table right where it is until I install a lock tomorrow."

She paused and swiped a lock of hair off her forehead. "I suppose you're right."

"Have bears tried coming in here in the past?"

"Inside? No, but I've seen them on the property before, this past spring. I guess they didn't realize I was here then." She gnawed on her lower lip a moment then added, "But I'm thinking it's getting closer to winter and the bears are likely looking for food before they go into hibernation."

"You're probably right. But weren't you here last autumn and winter?"

"I didn't arrive until late November, and after the first snowfall. I didn't see any bears until mid March."

"Makes sense," Riley said, giving a decisive nod. "But we're here earlier this time. I'll just feel a lot better once I insulate this place and put on a lock."

"Me too." She tilted her head and smiled at him. "Thanks for being here."

"Don't thank me yet. I'm having some doubts about signing up with you. I might just change my mind and leave you here."

Helen grinned at his scowling visage. "And I don't blame you, I guess. But then, you said you don't have any work to return home to, so why not stay? I've a feeling we've a true north woods adventure ahead of us."

"Kiddo, your sense of adventure could be the death of us," he groaned. "Not only am I picking up a lock tomorrow, but a gun wouldn't hurt."

* * * *

The next day, Helen and Riley drove to the nearest town of Orting—tiny at eighty people—to the only hardware store in the vicinity. Riley purchased a lock for the cabin's front door, and several heavy-duty woolen blankets he planned to cut into strips he'd use to insulate the cabin. He also, upon guidance from the shop keeper, bought a long-range Hauser game rifle and several boxes of ammunition.

Helen stood beside him at the store as he paid for it and shuddered. "Don't expect me to learn to use it. I hate guns!"

He slanted a smile at her. "Wasn't expecting to teach you. The kick from this gun would land you on your—"

"—you don't need to tell me," she snapped. "Do you know how to shoot it?"

He gave a brief nod, but didn't meet her eyes. She had a feeling he knew all about guns, just from how he handled it, sighted down the length of it.

Helen purchased some extra food provisions, gassed up her automobile, and headed back to the resort. While she drove she smiled, thinking how embarrassed Riley seemed last night, sharing the cabin with her. She wondered how a big, handsome man like Riley could feel self-conscious around her. Shouldn't it be the other way around? She hadn't been self-conscious or uncomfortable sharing her cabin with a virtual stranger. Her smile slipped. Maybe she should have been, but then she shrugged. She enjoyed having company in the form of Riley Flaherty and looked forward to spending a cozy winter with him. He'd insisted on taking the single bed in the small, second bedroom while Helen slept in her own big bed. Alone.

Helen hadn't much experience with men, but had been courted enough to know a good man from a bad one. Her instincts about people had always been good and she had a good feeling about Riley.

With just a few miles to home, Helen decided it was the perfect time for Riley to learn to drive. She pulled over to the side of the road and stopped the automobile. Opening her door, she jumped out, crossed the front of the automobile and stood at the passenger side.

He'd raised his eyebrows as he sat slumped in his seat. "We stopping for a reason?"

"You're going to drive. If something happened to me, you'd be stuck up here."

Eagerness crossed his face as he hopped out of the automobile and raced around to the driver's side. She settled into the passenger seat and nearly laughed aloud when she saw him clutching the wheel, his head ducking down to check out the automobile's gauges. The awed look in his eyes made her think of a child opening presents on Christmas.

"So, how come you never learned to drive?"

"Been planning on buying one the last couple of years, but have never been in a rush to since the company drives us to our cutting jobs. Haven't really had a need for one. And I've been saving my money for other more important things."

"Like what?"

"A home of my own, for one thing. I've sort of outgrown living in the bunk house with the other lumbermen. Need my own place."

She nodded. "Yes, I couldn't imagine cohabitating with several people. I enjoy my privacy and solitude—to a point."

He grinned and held onto the steering wheel. "But you let me in your door, though. Why?"

"I really do need a handyman to help me at the resort if I want to grow and succeed at my business."

"How many other men had you asked?"

"Actually, I'd come down to St. Paul to beg my brother to return with me. Other than him, you're the only one."

He frowned. "You always make it a habit to approach strange men?"

"Never. This was the first time," she laughed.

"I wouldn't advise doing so again," he warned.

"Remember? I said my brother had you investigated and deemed you safe. And now I won't have to find another handy man, will I?"

He nodded then said dryly, "Give me some pointers."

"Well, there's really little to do." She explained to him how to start the automobile, put it into gear, how to press on the pedals to go and stop it, and on the clutch to change gears. He proceeded cautiously, but not for long. Soon he drove along with ease.

Helen was amazed and impressed. It had taken her a year to learn how to drive and shift the gears without thinking about it so much—until it became second nature.

After several miles, she praised him, "You're doing great! Now, would you like me to take over for awhile?"

"No. I need more practice."

She laughed, then wondered what other talents he possessed. The man had learned to drive from the moment he started—a natural, guess you could say. She sank back in her seat and for a change enjoyed the scenery, even though the road was rough and bumpy.

Once they arrived at the resort, they unloaded their supplies. Riley started out immediately cutting the blankets into strips and pressing it between the logs where he saw daylight. Helen gathered her cleaning supplies and fresh bedding. As she headed out of the cabin, she said, "I'll be at Owl's Nest."

He looked up with a confused expression. "Owl's Nest?"

She grinned. "The cabin just up the road a bit. My parents named the cabins."

"Why Owl's Nest?"

"Cause it sits on a high hill. My fishermen will be using that cabin so I'm getting it ready."

"What's the name of this cabin?"

"Home Sweet Home."

"Ah, good name, but I didn't see any sign on the cabin saying so."

"I've been meaning to have some made—haven't had the chance yet."

"I can do that for you."

"Wonderful! There's an engraver in town that can do it. And he thankfully doesn't charge a fortune."

"No charge since I can make the signs and do the engraving too."

"Oh, you know how to engrave?"

"Sure do. Even have my own wood tools."

She grinned. "I just had a feeling you'd be a good handyman, but engraving is an art. You are multi-talented, Riley."

"Thanks," he murmured, not meeting her eyes.

Her grin widened when she saw his cheeks and neck turn pink. Apparently, the man wasn't used to compliments. She made up her mind then to pay him as many as she could. Then guilt plagued her; she'd hired him for much less, she was certain, than what he'd been paid as a lumberman. She prayed he'd stay the one full year to which he committed.

She went around back of the cabin, and returned pulling an old wagon behind her. She entered her cabin again and picked up soap and vinegar she'd wrapped in towels and carried them to the wagon.

"Let me help you," Riley said from the open door.

"Thanks," she murmured, grateful for his assistance.

He left the house with his arms piled high with bedding and plopped them into the wagon. "You sure you can handle that load?"

"Sure. No problem."

"I'll go with you," he insisted.

"No, I'm fine on my own. Besides, winter will be setting in soon so it's important that you get that chinking done. It'll take you awhile."

"All right, but don't be afraid to call me for help if you need it."

"Okay." She turned away, pulled on the handle and trudged up the road. She reached a dirt drive and turned right, walking toward the Owl's Nest, tucked neatly into the woods. As she neared the front door she frowned when she saw the door wide open and flapping in the breeze.

She paused a distance away and looked keenly around the cabin, but saw no sign of human or animal. Maybe the latch had broken after the last patrons left at the end of summer. She hadn't been in any of the cabins for over a month and decided she'd better check the other three as well once she'd cleaned this one.

Cautiously, broom in hand, she moved toward the front door. She peeked inside then jerked back when she saw movement close to the ground. Gulping down the growing lump in her throat she gathered her courage, took another step and peered inside. The cabin's first room was the kitchen-living area.

A large furry animal appeared, and she shrieked to the heavens as he ran toward her. She propelled backwards, stumbling to get away from the fleeing animal. The thing rushed up and past her, bumping hard against her pants leg and prickly pain seared her skin. The air around her reeked of an ammonia-scent and she realized what her fury friend was a skunk!

* * * *

She heard pounding, running footsteps behind her and she whirled around to see Riley. The first thing that entered her mind was how swiftly he ran for a big man. He stopped beside her and pulled her against his chest.

Helen hadn't realized tears were slipping down her cheeks until he reached down and swiped away a tear.

"Damn! Did that skunk get you?"

"Unfortunately, yes, and the nearest doctor is twenty-two miles away."

Riley looked down at her pants leg and gulped. "You're bleeding."

She looked down then and nearly fainted for blood was seeping out slowly through her heavy pants, from her calf. The pain seemed to worsen after that.

"Let's get you back to the cabin," he said, guiding her with an arm around her waist.

After only limping a few steps, she whispered, "Wait a minute. I think I'm going to pass—"

"Out," he finished and swept her up in his arms.

That was the last thing Helen remembered until she awoke on her bed. Riley stood over her, unbuckling her belt.

She stayed utterly still when she realized he planned on removing her pants. Breathing softly, she watched him from beneath half-slit eyes. His touch was firm yet gentle and she quivered in anticipation of what he'd do; wondered how far he'd go. After all, if her simple compliments could cause him to blush, she imagined he'd be redder than an apple if he undressed her. Helen knew she should let him know she was conscious but she couldn't resist pretending. No man had ever touched her as intimately as Riley, and she craved to know what it felt like to be truly loved by a man.

No man, thus far, had ever gone this far with her for she hadn't been ready for it; hadn't been attracted enough, she supposed. But Riley attracted her plenty.

* * * *

Riley's hands paused on Helen's belt. Damn. He'd undressed a few women in his time, but those women allowed any man to undress them for a price. He'd never undressed a decent woman, but then, a decent woman wouldn't allow a man that privilege, unless the two of them were married.

But this was a medical emergency and a necessity.

He pulled the notch open then slipped his hands beneath her back, found the back of her pants and started to tug them down, lifting her a bit to free the fabric. He frowned, thinking he was imagining things; did her hips rise up because of him, or because of her? Was it possible she was playing 'possum' with him? He paused with his hands still on her waistband, pants pulled down to her thighs as he stared at her face.

No. He shook his head. She was out cold so he hurried to finish the job. Once he'd pulled her pants all the way off he grimaced at the prickly holes in her calf. Damn. The critter had done on her. Prone to faint-heartedness upon the sight of blood, Riley knew she needed him now so he managed to remain calm and conscious.

* * * *

Helen opened her eyes after she felt him move away. Her gaze followed him as he strode over to a kitchen cupboard and removed some items. He returned to her then and she decided she couldn't pretend anymore.

Riley heaved a relieved sigh. "Glad you've returned, Ma'am."

Helen choked back a laugh as his gaze swept down her body, over her white cotton underwear and bare thighs. She raised her gaze to his. "I think we've passed the ma'am stage, Riley."

There it was again; that cute blush on his face, but no reply.

She laughed. "No need to be embarrassed. There might come a time when I'll need to undress you."

"Helen, stop it," he said roughly. "You're hurt so how can you make jokes?"

Feeling chastened, Helen frowned and felt heat seep into her cheeks. She sat up on her bed and looked in dismay at her calf. "That old skunk sure as all get out stuck me, didn't he?"

"Yea, lass, he sure did. The answer to any wound is cleansing, so grit your teeth and hold still. You might want to not look so why don't you lie down again."

Helen complied and cringed, tears filling her eyes when he cleaned the wounds with soap and water he'd retrieved from the kitchen. She felt him pat it dry and started to sit up when he pressed on her shoulder with one hand.

"I'm not done yet. So, this next step will burn like hell, but it's necessary."

He held up a bottle of some brown liquid—antiseptic—he found in the cupboard.

Before Helen could even think to pull away or tell him no, he splashed the brownish liquid onto her leg. She shrieked and grabbed his wrist, preventing him from pouring it again. "Are you crazy? Why didn't you give me a chance to prepare!" she wailed.

"If I gave you a chance to think about it, you wouldn't have allowed me to do it. Now hold still, clutch the bedding, or something," he murmured as he went about dabbing at the wounds with a clean cloth, sopping up the dripping antiseptic.

Tears filled Helen's eyes at the sting but she remained rigid, knowing the ordeal would soon be over. Once he'd bandaged her leg up she felt a bit better, even though her wounds felt as if they'd been scrubbed with a brush.

"I want you to stay in bed."

"You know I can't," she protested as she squirmed to sit up. "I've got those fishermen coming in tomorrow."

"I'll change the beds and clean up the place. You stay put."

"Oh, Riley, she groaned. "That's not why I hired you."

"Sure it is. I'll do anything that needs doing around here. Now stay in bed. I'll be back to make us something to eat in a bit."

She felt her lower lip tremble and her voice as well. "You're so good to me. Thank you."

He smiled. "You're welcome. No thanks necessary, though. I know you'd do the same for me."

She went on to explain to him exactly what needed to be done with the other cabins.

* * * *

Riley locked the cabin door and left, garden rake and rifle in hand, glad he knew how to use the weapon.

He'd grown up in the big city of Dublin in Ireland, and crime was rampant. Wherever there was poverty, it seemed that way. Therefore, from a young age, his father had taught him how to load, aim and shoot a gun. His aim had always been good. Luckily he'd only had to use a gun a few times before he left Ireland, seeking work opportunities in America. Sure, he could have taken over his father's grocery store business, but he'd hated being stuck inside all day. He wanted to feel the sun on his body, warm summer breezes, even the snow in winter, and Minnesota provided him all of those things.

He cleaned up the Owl's Nest, then moved onto the other three cabins. After removing bedding, cleaning out cupboards and readying them for winter, the job took up most of his day. Only Home Sweet Home would be winter hardy. From what Helen had told him, they'd be spending the winter chopping wood, winterizing the cabin, and making repairs, including building on two more bedrooms.

After she'd explained her ambitious plans, he was embarrassed to tell her that he didn't know much about building, but could repair things that were already made. She said she had another couple men coming in to build the addition onto the cabin and he could be of the most use to them in cutting down the trees necessary for the project. He'd been happy to hear that and confident that he could do the job since cutting was his line of work.

When he returned to the cabin, he found Helen asleep on her bed and closed the door softly.

He started in on insulating the cabin and when it grew too dark to work, day turning into evening, he stopped. He peeked into Helen's room and found her asleep still and he wondered if maybe he shouldn't wake her. Deciding against it, he went outside to fetch some of the firewood he'd chopped that morning.

The cabin had two fireplaces, and he shivered when he thought how those were the only source of heat for a long winter. The insulation he'd installed would help, but next time they went to town, he'd talk with the few shopkeepers to see how they kept their homes warm. Maybe he could install some sort of heating system, other than depending on firewood.

Once he loaded up the woodbin, he turned to the kitchen. His stomach had been rumbling for the past hour. Jamming his hands on his hips he sighed. He was awful in a kitchen, having never had to cook for himself. His mum had in Ireland, his sisters too, and at his lumber job the company provided all meals.

Helen was in no condition to cook so he peered inside her small ice chest, found ground meat of some kind and pulled it out. It had been wrapped in white butcher paper and now, as he stared at the hunk of meat, wondering how to prepare it, he wished he'd thought of pulling it out earlier.

"Hi."

He whirled around and found Helen standing in the kitchen entrance. She smiled at him and she looked sleepy though more alert than she had earlier that day. She'd dressed in her tan trousers and shirt, and wore slippers on her feet.

"Why aren't you in bed?"

His scowl nearly made her laugh aloud. "Cause I'm feeling better and my stomach's growling, feed me, feed me."

"Mine too. I just found this meat in the ice chest and was trying to figure out what to do with it. Uh, any idea what kind of meat it is?"

"Moose."

"You're joking."

Now she laughed. "Nope, I'm not. One of the neighbors on the lake gave it to me. Just haven't had a chance to cook it yet. With just me here all winter last year, I kept things quick and simple.

"Why don't you take a chair and I'll cook this up in a pan?"

"I don't feel like moose meat, but bacon and eggs I could handle. You sit down. I know you've worked all day and I'm feeling better."

He protested, mildly, but gave in and sank down into a chair at the table.

He watched Helen pull thick-cut bacon and eggs from the ice box, admiring how sweet she looked as she efficiently and quickly prepared them food. She toasted some thick slices of bread in a cast iron skillet. Then she cooked half of the bacon and fried up six eggs. She set the coffee pot to percolating on the stove, then pulled a jar of orange marmalade jam out of a cupboard and set it on the table, along with dishes and silverware.

They ate, speaking little. Riley was so hungry he cleaned up his plate in record time.

Without a word, he watched Helen rise from her chair, fry up two more eggs and brown more toast for him. He gave her a grateful look when she slid the eggs and toast onto his plate. While he ate, she drank her coffee and watched him eat. Somehow, the feeling of her eyes on him made him feel wanted, needed, and he liked that—a lot.

He sank back in his chair, his hunger satisfied, then felt self-conscious. He felt her eyes on him still, and suddenly he felt embarrassed by his worn, brown flannel shirt, dungarees with suspenders. He raised his eyes, half-slit now as a lethargy stole over him. He took in his fill of her, devoured her. He smiled slightly when he saw her skin pinken and she bit her lower lip.

"It's going to be a long winter," he murmured and he sank against the back of his chair.

"They're all long, I'm afraid."

He heard the tremble in her voice and saw her clasp her hands tightly in her lap. He frowned, wondering at her skittishness. Then he thought about the long winter ahead, sharing a cabin with her.

"I'm talking real long, unless…"

"Unless?" she whispered.

Riley's gaze traveled over her hair, her lips, down her throat and over her chest. He knew she understood him and he saw the look in her eyes that told him she wanted him every bit as much as he wanted her. If they were meant to be for just this one year… Still, he hesitated.

"Unless?" she asked again as she slowly rose from the table and came around it. He didn't reply but heat tore through him as he looked up at her standing beside him now. She reached down and fingered a lock of his hair, twirling it around her finger.

He took her hand in his. "Do you understand what I'm saying?"

* * * *

Helen started to nod saw a look in his eyes that frightened yet thrilled her at the same time. "I...I think so."

He stood up and shook his head. "No, you don't, or you wouldn't have stumbled over your words. You're an innocent young woman and I'm beginning to think, unless you're positively certain you want to be my woman, I'll need to bunk down in one of the other cabins."

"Oh! You can't. Not a one is winter ready."

"Then before winter settles in I'd better make sure one of them is, hadn't I?"

She didn't reply but nodded as she tried to disguise what she knew was a forlorn expression on her face.

"It's late," he said abruptly. "I'm turning in."

"But..."

"Yes?" he inquired.

Helen had enjoyed the company of men in the past, but this feeling inside her was new and frightening and heavenly—all at the same time—yet she knew he was right; she wasn't ready for this kind of...passion.

When she didn't reply, he said, "Like I said, I'm turning in."

He started heading for the front door, ready to leave the cabin.

"Where are you going?"

"To the cabin next door. I'll be fine there during the next month or so."

Tears filled her eyes yet she nodded. "All right, but tonight you can still sleep in the extra bedroom."

"Thank you, ma'am. I appreciate it."

She sighed as she watched him stride out of the kitchen to the small bedroom down the short hallway. So he'd returned to the formalities again, she mused. But what could she do? She couldn't blame him for wanting to sleep in a separate cabin, knowing the nature of man in general. It wouldn't be fair to put temptation so close. After the fishermen left in a week, she'd help him make one of the other cabins winter ready for him so he wouldn't freeze to death.

It had been one very long day—for both of them.

* * * *

Helen woke up the next morning before dawn. As she stumbled out of her tiny bedroom, fully dressed and ready to make breakfast for her and Riley, she moved quietly into the kitchen area. The sun was just starting to rise, the narrow stream of rays illuminating the kitchen area of the cabin. She moved as quietly as she could. Then she heard footsteps on the stairs outside and breathed a relieved sigh when Riley opened the door and strode inside, his arms filled with firewood.

"Mornin'", he said with a nod and headed for the hearth. He dumped the wood into the bin and slapped his hands together. "You feeling better?"

"Yes, much. Thanks for all of your help yesterday. I shudder to think what I would have done if I'd been by myself."

He shrugged. "You were here last year all by yourself. You probably would have managed fine."

To her mind, she hadn't managed well, which was why she'd come looking for a handyman. She'd been miserable and cold, barely able to sleep at night, even with a fire going. With Riley here, this winter would be much better. It couldn't get any worse, she mused dryly.

Helen made breakfast for the two of them. They had just finished eating when she heard the sound of tires on the dirt road.

"Guess that means the fishermen have arrived," Riley said as he rose from his chair. "I'll go out and direct them to the Owl's Nest."

"I'll come with you. This is the same group I had last year. If I don't come out, they'll come in here looking to talk to me. Besides, I'll likely be feeding them breakfast, too."

Outside, three men disembarked from a vehicle that had lost its wax shine miles ago. One of the men, old enough to be Helen's father, grinned and stepped over to her, swiping his hat from his head.

"Why, Miss Helen, you are a sight for these sore old eyes! How ya been?"

Helen grinned, reached out and took his extended hand. "Just fine, thank you, Mr. Simmons."

With a sly glance at Riley, the old man said, "See ya got yerself hitched over the past year." Heat suffused Helen's cheeks and she opened her mouth to reply when Riley stopped her.

"She sure did," Riley said smoothly, taking her hand and pulling her against his side. "Took me right into the family business and put me to work too," he said with a boisterous laugh.

Which set all three of the men laughing.

Helen was stunned by Riley's words. What game was he playing?

"Come on," Riley invited. "Follow me up to your cabin while Helen makes you some breakfast."

"Magical words you've said, boy. We love Helen's cooking."

Helen set to work cooking eggs, hash, bacon and cornbread. Within moments, the men returned; two sat down at the table and the third sat on the divan. Soon the food was ready and Helen filled their plates. Helen dished up a plate for Riley and for her, too, and handed him his plate. Riley and Helen took up position against the cupboard and ate.

Soon, only the sound of chewing and scraping of forks against plates could be heard.

Helen smiled as she watched the men finish their food, then Mr. Simmons rose. "Thank you, Miz Helen. Let's go hit the lake, boys." He grinned at Helen. "Maybe we'll be lucky to catch some supper for all of us. How's that sound?"

"Sounds wonderful," Helen said, "As long as you all clean those fish before I cook them up."

Riley ambled over to the door and opened it, standing aside to let the men pass by.

"Sure thing, ma'am," said the one man Helen didn't know as he stood beside the table.

He'd hardly spoken a word but he didn't need to speak; the dark sneer on his face made her uncomfortable. She didn't trust him. She turned to Riley and caught him studying the man, his body seemingly relaxed where he leaned against the door jamb. Yet she had a feeling, from the hard look in his eyes and the set of his jaw he was far from relaxed.

Mr. Simmons and the other man named Steve Jackson had already left.

A loud bang drew Helen's attention. Riley had apparently slammed the door shut but now opened it. "Better leave, or you'll miss the boat."

The man gave a lethargic shrug. "I'm not much for fishing. I'd much rather stay right here. Maybe Miz Helen here needs help with kitchen clean-up."

"Oh, why…" Helen started, but stopped when Riley strode toward the man.

Stopping directly in front of him, he met the man's eyes with a glare. "Misses Flaherty has her husband to help her clean-up. Now get going."

The man smirked and jerked his head at Helen. "Don't see no ring on her finger." Then the man's eyes settled on Helen. "What? The husband can't even buy his wife a wedding ring?"

Riley's anger got the best of him. He grabbed the man by the back of the shirt and scuttled him across the floor and out the open door.

A shout of pain filled the morning air and Helen gasped, "Riley! Why, you can't treat the paying guests that way!" She raced around Riley and came to a skidding halt when she saw the fisherman picking himself up out of the dirt, grumbling. The man stared daggers at Riley before stalking down to the lake.

Helen whirled around and snapped, "Whatever were you thinking? You stay out of my business. I could lose business because of what you did!"

Riley leaned down, nearly nose to nose with her. "You're angry with me because I protected you?"

"I don't need protection. I lived up here by myself all last winter and did fine, thank you very much," she sniffed.

"Uh-huh. I see how you did. This place is in a shambled condition. This house isn't fit to live in for the winter months. And you've got a hell of a lot of work, lady, in order to make it habitable. Now, then, you either want me to stay and help you or you don't. You wanted a handyman, you said," he reminded her.

"I did—do. But you're behaving like you're my own personal bodyguard. I don't need one, never have."

"The man doesn't respect you. He could have harmed you, maybe tried to…have his way with you, for Christ's sake. You think I could stand by and let that happen?"

She felt heat seep into her cheeks. He had a point. Yet, somehow, she hadn't felt threatened by the fisherman. But then, was it because Riley was with her? She chewed on her lower lip even as tears filled her cycs. "You're right," she said softly. "I didn't feel threatened cause you were here. If I'd been by myself, I guess I would have felt differently."

159

She nodded. "Thank you, Riley."

"You're welcome," he said grouchily. He strode inside the cabin and picked up a bucket by its handle.

Helen saw screwdrivers, hammers and the like in the bucket and asked, "Where are you going?"

"To finish up things at one of the cabins. I'll be back in a couple hours."

Helen watched him leave and when he disappeared down the road she heaved a sigh. He'd made his point, and while she hadn't liked his high-handed attitude, she had appreciated his being here.

She made moose hash for that evening's supper, cooking the ground up moose meat in a fry pan with onions, garlic, herbs and added diced potatoes and carrots. She covered the kettle with a tight cover on one of the wooden stove's burners, and went to made the beds. Then she washed the dishes from breakfast. She continued where Riley left off; cutting strips of woolen blanket and shoving them in between the logs. Soon the moose hash was done and she took it off the burner and left it, ready for supper.

Helen left the cabin, then walked up the road to the Owl's Nest to see if she'd forgotten anything for the fishermen. She arrived at the cabin and saw that everything was in its place, wooden floors were clean, beds were made and the cabin ready for her guests. She saw their luggage had been tossed on the floor in the corner of the two bedrooms and she smiled. Fishing was a priority to these men, not unpacking.

She left the cabin, blankets in hand and headed for the cabin next door where she heard Riley at work, pounding away at something. Lover's Lane cabin was tiny, meant for two—a very cozy honeymoon couple cabin. Stepping across the lawn she reached the steps and found Riley just inside the front door, pounding a nail into a piece of wood trim.

"What are you fixing?" she asked.

"Ow! Damn."

Helen gasped when the hammer clattered to the floor. He'd hit a finger.

He didn't look at her but rubbed and squeezed the injured appendage.

"Let me look at it."

"No," he said, not looking at her. "It's fine." Now he did lift his eyes to hers. "Don't sneak up on me like that and I won't hurt myself."

Helen felt heat seep into her cheeks and she murmured, "Sorry, I didn't even think…what are you fixing?"

He took up the hammer again. "The molding around the door frame was loose so I just tightened it up some."

Helen nodded. "Thank you. I noticed that earlier and had placed it on my mental list to fix." Tilting her head to one side, she added, "I don't know if anyone else would have been so observant, though. I brought more blankets to cut up into strips. Maybe I'll start working on this cabin, filling in those holes while you finish your work. Is that okay?" she asked, hesitating when she saw the intense stare he gave her.

She was relieved when a slow grin spread across his lips. "I'd appreciate the company."

With a laugh, Helen said, "You'll get used to the quiet soon enough. Then it'll be an adjustment for you when you return to the city. You'll see."

They worked companionably together for several hours, until little daylight remained. As they walked back to their cabin, they saw a fire had been set in one of the pits by the water's edge. The fishermen had returned and as Helen and Riley drew up alongside them, she caught the odor of cooking fish.

"That smells heavenly," Helen said as she paused beside the fire.

The fishermen were seated on tree stumps they'd rolled down to the pit and with metal plates and forks in hand were digging into crisp fried fish.

"Best walleye fishing ever, Miz Helen," Mr. Simmons said. "You're welcome to join us," he added. "We've got plenty."

"Oh, why, thank you, but we'll pass. I've supper ready in the house. Good luck in the morning!" she said as she turned and made her way up the embankment to the cabin, Riley following her.

Inside, she served up cornbread and the moose hash. She laughed aloud when she saw the hesitancy in Riley as he frowned down at a spoonful of hash.

"I guarantee you'll be surprised at the first bite," she announced.

He raised his eyebrows. "As in surprised good or surprised bad?"

"Try it and see."

"Ladies first."

"Oh, my, you really don't trust my cooking do you?"

"Not true. Your eggs and bacon were great. But, well, eating an innocent wild animal like moose is another story."

"Alright, watch this…" She dug into the hash with her fork and slid it inside her mouth, murmuring delightful sounds and closing her eyes in ecstasy. Then she opened her eyes to see him looking at her suspiciously. She laughed again and took another bite.

She heard him sigh as she savored the hash, then watched him as he tentatively slid a bit off his fork into his mouth. His eyes widened and he said, "Darn, if that isn't the best thing I've ever tasted! Geez, I think I could get used to this—every day."

Helen sat back and took delight in watching him clean his plate then ask her for seconds. After supper, Riley insisted on helping her clean up.

They laughed and talked and laughed more and learned about each other.

When they finished, Helen dried her hands on a dishcloth, strolled over to the window at the front of the cabin and gasped at the sight before her eyes. "Come here, Riley. Look!"

He joined her. "Jeepers, what is that?"

"Aurora Borealis."

"Thought you could only see them in Alaska," he replied.

"We're far enough to the north that at certain times of the year, fall, in particular, we can see them, too."

They stared out the window in reverent silence for a long while, watching the roiling of the northern lights paint the sky. Helen felt him so near, his broad shoulder at her back, brushing against it. She closed her eyes and sniffed his scent—a combination of northern woods, leather and tobacco, though she hadn't seen him smoking. She sniffed again and decided he didn't smoke cigarettes but likely tobacco in a pipe. Helen raised her eyes higher and met his intent gaze. Heat suffused her cheeks again when she realized she'd been watching him.

"Helen—"

"Riley," she said at the same time.

He took her in his arms and dipped his head, his gaze on her lips. Helen slowly lifted her arms up and around his waist, then higher, delighting in the muscles in his back. Lord, but it felt wonderful to feel him against her and she tipped her head back, allowing his lips to settle on hers.

His kiss was gentle, tentative, a peck really, but enough that it ignited a flame in Helen she'd never experienced before. She tightened her arm around him and he deepened the kiss. After too short a time he released her and took a step back. She didn't like the fact he was frowning at the floor.

"Helen?" he said then, meeting her gaze. "I'm not sure this arrangement is going to work out between us."

She gasped, "Why not?"

"Because I want you—the way a man wants a woman—which is not the way a man should feel about his employer."

She bit her lip and crossed her arms across her breasts, unsure how to reply. Her heart beat rapidly in her chest. He liked her—apparently he more than liked her! The feeling was mutual. But then sadness filled her; she had a feeling he wouldn't be able to stay and work for her if he had strong feelings for her in a romantic way, and she couldn't leave this place, not even for him. Still, she needed him to stay. If he didn't, she wasn't certain she could spend another lonely winter on her own, no matter how much she loved her home.

"Well, then, if you feel you must leave then there's not much I can do, is there?" she said, disappointment settling in.

"Who said anything about leaving?"

"Why, you said you don't feel about me as an employee should feel about his employer, didn't you?"

"Sure, I did, but I've a way to solve the problem."

Helen saw his lips form into a deep grin and she felt herself responding. "And what would that be?"

He took her into his arms again. "Seems the only thing I can do is marry you."

She laughed. "The only thing?"

"For now. Don't you agree?"

Helen nodded eagerly and laughed when he swept her up into his arms and twirled around in a circle. When he stopped he kissed her again and lowered her to the floor. He pulled her against him and held her for a long while.

Finally, he moved back, took her hand and pulled her to the window again.

"Would you just look at that," he whispered.

"I am," Helen replied, her eyes focused only on him.

She would be safe, warm and loved this winter. What more could she want? At this moment all of the sights in the northern sky weren't important to her—just Riley.

"It's something else, isn't it?" he asked.

"It most surely is," she replied, still looking at him, this man she would marry.

"Hey," he said, meeting her eyes. "You're not looking at the northern lights."

"No. I'm looking at something much, much better, husband to be."

"Ah, you're sure then."

"Yes, but are you?"

"From the minute I picked you up off the pavement I knew you were the lass for me."

Her eyes widened. "Truly?"

He nodded.

"When would you like to get married?"

"The sooner the better, don't you think?"

"Yes, absolutely, positively." She frowned then. "But are you certain you'll be able to live all year up here, being away from city life?"

He gathered her close, kissed her again and murmured against her lips. "With you in my arms every night, yes. Where's the nearest preacher?"

"Down the road in Orting. Tomorrow soon enough for you?" she asked, pulling back from him to look into his eyes.

"Now. It has to be now."

"We won't find a preacher to marry us this time of night!"

She saw the sensual, glittery look in his eyes when he said, "You doubt my ability of persuasion?"

Shivers traveled up her spine as she looked at the set of his jaw, the dark, intent look of desire in his eyes. "No."

"Good." He stepped back from her, turned and pushed her toward her bedroom door, aiming a playful slap to her bottom. "Then go put on your prettiest dress!"

* * * *

They arrived in Orting at midnight. Riley nearly broke down the preacher's door until the man answered. He took one look at Riley and promptly married them in his parlor, not in the church located next door to his modest house. The poor preacher had to rouse his tired wife from bed, but from the resigned look on her face, it likely wasn't the first time a couple wanted to get hitched in the middle of the night.

Helen made a beautiful bride, dressed in a sunny yellow day dress and a small straw hat perched on her head. The best clothing Riley had was an old woolen rumpled suit jacket that had belonged to his father—dated—old—but perfect in Helen's eyes. He looked wonderful.

After the ceremony, they immediately drove home. When Riley opened the passenger door to let Helen out, he couldn't stop looking at her. He closed the door, picked her up in his arms and she laughed as he carried her over the threshold.

Memories were made that night. But the memory that would remain foremost in Helen's mind, for all the days of her life, was the two of them, gazing up at the night sky in autumn as the myriad of lights from the aurora borealis entertained them, binding them together—forever.

The End

About the Author

Nancy Schumacher writes romance as Nancy Pirri, and erotica as Natasha Perry. Nancy has been a member of Romance Writers of America and her local chapter, Midwest Fiction Writers for several years. She is also one of the founders of the local Minnesota RWA chapter, Northern Lights Writers (NLW).

Nancy is also known as 'Dame Sapphire' and is a member of the author promo organization Jewels of the Quill, www.jewelsofthequill.com. Her stories with the Jewels have won EPPIE (EPIC-Electronically Published Internet Coalition) awards in 2008 and in 2010.

On January 1, 2011, Nancy opened her new digital and print on demand publishing house, **Melange Books, LLC,** www.melange-books.com.

Breath of God
by Lori Ness

Betsey knew, without opening her eyes, she'd overslept. The sleepy twitter of birds in the trees outside her window had given way to energetic debate, indicating that they were well along with the business of their day.

She sat up. Sunbeams spilling across the hand braided rug confirmed her fear. She was late! She hadn't made breakfast; she had to get Erik up and both of them ready for school—

"Betsy!" Karl Swenson's shout silenced the birds and jolted his daughter out of bed.

Tangling her foot in the quilt, Betsy crashed to the floor. Wincing, she scrambled up and grabbed her dressing gown before rushing down the stairs.

Her father stood in front of the stove, glaring into the interior where a fire should be burning. The familiar fragrances of fresh milk and corn wafting from his clothing in place of the scent of coffee only served as an accusation to her dereliction of duty.

Betsy rubbed the sore knee resulting from her fall and hung her head.

"The stove is cold." Karl's thick accent emphasized his disgust.

"I overslept, Papa. I'm sorry."

"The chickens were making such a noise I checked and found out they hadn't been fed or the eggs collected." He pointed to a pail near the door, with brown eggs piled inside.

Betsy gulped and looked down at the floor.

"Are you sickening for something?" The dairy farmer took a step closer and peered at his daughter; the bushy, sandy brows which reminded Betsy of sheaves of wheat drew together in a frown. "Your eyes are as red as Mrs. Jeppson's Sunday hat."

"I had homework." Betsy blushed because she hadn't been doing schoolwork; she'd burned the kerosene lamp by her bed into the early morning hours and wept over the last chapters of Ivanhoe. The love story, so beautiful, had her tears watering the pages like spring showers.

"I have fed and milked the cows. I have a field of corn that needs to be picked. Is a man expecting too much to want food on the table when he comes in for his breakfast?"

Six year old Erik, blonde and stocky like his papa, appeared in the doorway with his suspenders trailing to the floor and one shoe on. "Time for breakfast?"

Karl Swenson ignored the hopeful question from his only son. "School foolishness again keeps you from chores. Clothes need washing and the bread box is empty. Apples rotting on the ground in the orchard. You stay up late and ruin your eyesight on books." His voice rose with each sentence.

Betsy bit her lip and kneaded a fold of her nightgown. Not just books—she'd discovered magazines and several were even now hidden under her bed. Her teacher had encouraged her to borrow them, declaring they would open her eyes to the wide vistas beyond a Minnesota dairy farm. A fascinated Betsy had spent hours studying pictures of faraway places.

"I'm sorry, Papa," she apologized again, scurrying to the stove. "I can scramble eggs now for your breakfast and I'll do the baking as soon as I get home from school."

Karl slammed his hand down on the oak harvester table. "You have no time for school. Many things must be done around here, today."

Betsy almost dropped the iron skillet. "No school?? But, Papa, I have three more years until graduation—"

Her father's cheeks looked as ruddy as Mrs. Jeppson's Sunday hat. "No school!" He spat the words in her direction and stomped out of the house.

Her head pounding, Betsy ordered Erik upstairs to finish getting dressed and followed him up to get herself ready for the day. Back in the kitchen, she lit the stove and toasted bread. After they'd eaten a sketchy breakfast, she set him to work sweeping the hearth and polishing the fireplace andirons with a soft rag torn from an old sheet.

As she cleaned the kitchen, Betsy wondered why she'd been so foolish. This wasn't the first time she'd neglected her chores, but she'd never imagined seeing Papa so angry. Her stomach ached at the memory of his declaration regarding school. Why had she stayed up so late last night?

As she got out the washtubs and lye soap, Betsy blinked back tears, her eyes burning from the strain of hours of reading by the kerosene lamp. Papa had a right to be so angry. A man needed a full belly to strip corn from the stalks by hand under the hot September sun.

Filling the tubs meant many trips to the pump in the yard. Anyone who did the laundry developed strong arms doing the washing and hauling water. With each pail she heated on the stove and poured into the tubs, Betsy felt as if she were drowning her dream of becoming a teacher.

With her mother gone, Betsy lost all support for higher education or even finishing high school. Papa had been indentured as a farm hand at the age of eleven when he arrived in America from Norway and had difficulty reading a newspaper in English. He didn't understand his daughter's passion for knowledge.

Betsy put the sleeve of another work shirt into the wringer and turned the crank. If only she hadn't neglected her household duties in favor of the glorious escape of reading. Now Papa would ban her Saturday afternoon visits to the library in town and she would never get to finish the serial in her favorite magazine. A tear splashed into the rinse water as Betsy squeezed out one of Erik's shirts, remembering just in time that the buttons would never survive a trip through the wringer.

The clothes line stretched like a tightrope between an elm and a maple tree in the back yard. Papa and Mama had taken her to the circus once when it came to town. She'd never forgotten the winking sparkles on the performers' costumes and the scent of roasted peanuts. Her favorite memory, however, was hearing Mama's giggles and Papa's deep belly laugh at the clowns and their silly tricks.

She couldn't remember hearing him laugh since Mama…Betsy sighed as she lugged the basket of damp clothing and the tin can filled with clothes pins to the end of the clothes line.

Lefse, a black barn cat named for his exploit as a kitten of sneaking into the house and devouring a half dozen of the flat pastries, wound around Betsy's legs and mewed complaints of starvation.

"You're plump as a market hog," she scolded him. "Go guard the grain and earn the milk Papa squirts into your mouth each morning at milking."

The thought of never going back to school gnawed at her like the sharp teeth of a varmint chewing through a feed sack. She stretched on her toes to hang a pair of Papa's work pants by the legs. The wind pounced and shook the pants as Lefse would shake a mouse to break its neck.

Lonesome for company, Erik wandered outside to join her. After rubbing Lefse's belly, he looked up and Betsy smiled at the black smudge on his nose. His eyes grinned up at her, blue as the autumn sky stretched over their heads.

He held up grimy hands. "My teacher would holler at me for having dirty fingernails, Betsy. It's fun being here at home. Can I play now?"

Poor Erik thought they were simply enjoying a day off. With a pang, Betsy realized that he would also suffer from a lack of schooling. If they somehow lost the farm and a farmer was only one disaster away from doing so, her brother's only choice would be to work as a laborer for someone else. The breeze ruffled his straw blond hair and Betsy noticed that a button was missing from his shirt. She'd neglected both the house and her family.

Her brother stuck out his tongue and tilted his head back.

"What are you doing, you silly boy?" Betsy picked up the last shirt and a couple of clothes pins.

"Tasting the wind."

"And what does the wind taste like?"

He gave her a mysterious smile. "Just like apples and leaves and cinnamon."

Betsy stuck out her tongue too, but couldn't taste anything. Erik had such an imagination!

"And just a little bit like maple syrup." Erik loved maple syrup as a sweetener—in cookies and on oatmeal and everywhere he could get it. They boiled their own from the trees on the back quarter of their farm.

"You'd be happy if I'd let you drink maple syrup by the gallon." Betsy grasped the handles and lifted the empty clothes basket to rest on her hip.

Erik crouched to study an ant hill, grimacing when a gust of air kicked up a puff of dirt. He grabbed a sleeve from one of the shirts snapping in the wind and used it to wipe his eyes.

"Erik! That's clean! Or it was clean." Betsy's shoulders slumped when she saw that the black smudge of soot across her brother's nose had now transferred to one of his father's work shirts.

"Sorry, Betsy!"

She took down the shirt. "I haven't emptied the tubs yet—I'll wash it again."

"It's the wind's fault—it threw the dirt in my face, Betsy."

"We can't do without the wind." She ducked under the line of flapping clothes. "Without wind, how would the windmill turn? And the clothes wouldn't get dry. Mama always said, "There's no such thing as an ill wind—"

Her brother abandoned the ants and scuffed along behind Betsy through the long grass. "What else did Mama say about the wind?"

He sounded so interested, he always was when she slipped and mentioned Mama. But she didn't want to talk about her. Instead, Betsy dangled the basket by one handle and pretended the warmth of the sun on her shoulders was the touch of loving hands. But she'd already let Erik down today by antagonizing Papa about school.

"Folks say it's an ill wind that doesn't blow good to someone."

At Erik's puzzled expression, she forced herself to share a memory, one she kept locked away like a precious gem in a jewel box. "Even if the wind might not be helping us, someone else needs the breeze. I used to be afraid when the wind would howl on stormy nights, so Mama taught me a poem to help me be brave."

"Like Hickory, Dickory Dock?" It was Erik's favorite and as a little boy, he always checked their grandfather clock in the hope of seeing a mouse swinging on the pendulum.

Betsy paused on the steps of the washhouse and chanted:

"Wind is the breath of God ruffling our hair,
Changing the weather from stormy to fair.
Bending the grass and rustling the leaves,
Shaking the apples down from the trees."

Catching her breath, she remembered the last time she and Mama had picked up windfalls. They had been in high spirits, with Mama teaching her to juggle three apples and chasing her with a tiny green worm who had poked his head out of a hole. She blinked at the memories washing over her, the sweet smell of ripe fruit crushed underneath, the sound of wind tossing the branches overhead and the plop of apples dropping to the cushioning grass. Mother and daughter dodging between the gnarled trees amid the giggles of two year old Erik as he toddled around with an apple clutched in his baby hands.

Pressing her hand against her stomach, Betsy fought to hold in the hurt. For a moment, her mother had been there with them again and the realization that the happy time in the orchard had been part of their last day together brought hot tears welling up. Mama had been wrong, there were ill winds. One had blown across Betsy's life that day, one which four years later still possessed the power to dry up laughter with its scorching breath.

"Betsy?"

Erik's anxious voice made her manage a smile for his sake. "Papa missed his biscuits this morning. Help me finish the washing and then we'll take a picnic out to him in the field."

"Hurray!"

Like anything else on a farm, brisk breezes were not to be wasted. Erik helped his sister strip the beds and they carried armloads into the washhouse to soak in the washtubs.

Excited at the prospect of even a small outing, Erik worked hard, humming as he steadied the heavy flour sack so his sister could refill the canister. Betsy mixed bread dough and set it aside to rise. She sent Erik out to gather some windfalls. Along with the bread and biscuits, she'd bake a pan of apple crisp and a pie.

Mixing biscuit dough, she tried not to think about the future. Her brother arrived, panting as he hauled in the fruit. When he asked what he could do next, she asked him to get out the pie tins.

The sound of him poking around in the cupboard receded as she wondered whether she should have Erik start peeling apples. No, his skills weren't up to the task, but he could help cut out biscuits—

"Hey, Betsy! What's this silly thing?" The little boy held up a metal colander with a wooden pestle rolling inside.

She gasped and dropped her spoon into the floury mixture in front of her. Drawing a deep breath, she ordered, "Put that back, Erik!"

"Can I take the silver cone down to the pond and strain for frogs?"

"No!" Betsy jerked the colander out of his hands and whirled to replace it in the cupboard. Kneeling, she gazed blindly at rows of dusty, capped Mason jars that lined the long unopened storage area.

Sitting back on her heels, she gazed at the colander. Someone had cleaned away the applesauce. Closing her eyes, she remembered…

* * * *

Kitchen windows steamed from the fog of boiling water. Sara Swensen opened a window to allow the late September breeze to play peek-a-boo in her handmade organdy curtains.

Betsy stood on tiptoe to peer into the depths of a pot bubbling on the stove. "The apples must be mushy enough by now, Mama!"

"I'm raising such an impatient dumpling, Betsy. Apples have to be very soft before they can be made into applesauce."

"Can I measure out the sugar?"

Erik, his blue romper-covered bottom planted on the floor, clapped plump hands together to call attention to his successful stacking of two wooden blocks on top of each other.

Bending to hug her son, Sara praised, "Such a clever little man!"

Excited by the attention, Erik knocked over the tower with his elbow and burst into a wail of dismay.

His mother planted a kiss on top of his head. "Don't cry, my little potato cake. Build me a barn for Papa's cows."

As the baby chuckled over his handiwork, Sara poured softened apples into the colander. When it was nearly full, she inserted the pestle and began to roll the heavy wooden implement, crushing the plump fruit. Betsy stuck her finger into the sauce oozing through the holes and transferred the warm, tart mixture to her tongue, groaning in pleasure.

"Let me take a turn and smush the apples, Mama."

"Betsy, keep up the wheedling and you'll grow up to be a fine cook or a rich beggar."

Pushing a chair over to the table, Betsy stood as tall as possible as her mother triple-tied an apron around her waist. "Your mama's going to start fattening you up like a hog bound for market. You're as thin as a baby willow tree."

A leaf, red and gold like the windfalls in the pails, blew in the open window, skidding across the oil cloth before drifting to the floor. Erik jumped up to chase it with the eagerness of a kitten in pursuit of a bug, pouncing when the leaf came to rest against the dry sink.

Betsy brushed the hair out of her eyes with the back of her hand, crooning as the pestle rolled in her fingers. "Smush, mush, hush. Smush, mush, hush."

A bead of sweat rolled down, tickled the corner of her eye. The pots boiling on the stove made the kitchen seem as humid as mid-August. Betsy loved the hours spent learning how to bake, sew and clean, watching her mama scour the tiles so clean that they could eat off the floor if they had a mind to do something so foolish.

Mama made every moment a game, teaching Betsy to square dance using the mop and broom for partners or making up silly rhymes about why a pig's tail was curly or how daisies knew when it was time to poke their white bonnets up through the spring grass. And then there were those hours spent sitting in Betsy's room and making plans for her future. Serious talks about becoming a teacher, the secrets to making a husband happy and the joy of raising children.

While Betsy pressed the pestle against the metal sides of the colander, her mother used the tongs to place empty jars into a pot of boiling water.

"Always boil the jars, Betsy. They must be clean or you can make your family sick."

Every word her mama said during these magical times seemed to be written down in her mind in the beautiful colors of the Northern Lights, never to be forgotten.

Turning, Betsy saw her mother come in with her arms full of wood to replenish the supply for the stove.

As she brushed dirt from her calico apron, she smiled at her daughter. "Your papa has promised we'll have electricity one of these years and we'll also get a telephone. We'll get a radio, so on winter nights we can hear music from faraway places."

Her mother had come from a wealthy family in Minneapolis, enjoying the pleasures of gas lighting and graduating from a woman's teaching college. Instead of educating a group of children, however, her dreams had shrunk to teaching one daughter about the joys of knowledge and the household arts. But she never had expressed regret.

"Music from faraway places?" Betsy loved to dance around when her mother played the pump organ in the parlor. "Like St. Paul?"

Betsy's best friend, Libby Hanson, had moved to St. Paul to live with her grandparents when her father had been killed in an accident. The girls exchanged letters and while Betsy could only describe farm life, Libby wrote about cable cars and picture shows. St. Paul sounded like an exotic country to Betsy.

"Music that your father and I can dance to." Sara swayed to an inaudible tune. "If we lived in the city, we'd have electricity, a telephone and a fancy bathroom."

Frowning, Betsy ignored the reference of to her parents dancing. "But we couldn't keep cats and cows if we lived in the city. And how could we make apple sauce without apple trees?"

A kiss pressed on the top of her head made her shiver with happiness. "Don't fret, my Betsy. We won't be moving to the city. Your papa loves this farm and I love your papa. We're very happy here. God even paints the sky for us with green and pink lights. We don't need a radio to have fun—"

Her mother's hug suddenly became a heavy weight on Betsy's shoulders and she winced away from the oppressive contact. Sara Swenson staggered away and leaned against the table.

"Mama!" Betsy started to climb down from the chair. "Your face is as red as Mrs.Jeppson's Sunday hat!"

That Sunday hat was a family joke. The widow had worn the hat to church as far back as Betsy could remember, a scarlet confection crowned with matching plumes that became more and more shopworn with each passing year.

Whenever Papa saw a cardinal, he'd say, "There's the bird who donated some of his feathers for Mrs. Jeppson's Sunday hat."

But Mama didn't laugh and it made Betsy's tummy feel funny. The flush coating Mama's cheeks gradually faded, leaving her face bleached as white as Betsy's petticoat.

With unsteady hands, Sara Swensen used the tongs to remove the jars from the boiling water and set them in a row on the towel spread across one end of the table.

Papa had once told Betsy, "When your Mama's happy, even her voice smiles."

Betsy didn't hear any smiles when Mama said, "My head aches, Betsy, so I'm going to lie down for a minute. Add sugar to the applesauce and fill the jars. Please be careful not to burn yourself. I'll help you clean up the mess when I come downstairs. Please take care of Erik for me."

Mama rested her hand on the doorpost as she left the room and

Betsy glanced at the windows to reassure herself that the sun hadn't disappeared behind a cloud. But it wasn't gloomy out there, just inside her heart. She felt queer, as if something fluttered in her tummy. Poor Mama. She'd been having these headaches more and more, spoiling their fun together.

But pride at having been given the responsibility to finish the final batch of applesauce took over as Betsy added sugar, measuring twice to make sure, and ladled the warm sweet mixture into the waiting jars. Erik had curled up on the floor and gone to sleep, one of the blocks that Papa carved still clutched in his fist.

Betsy wiped up the applesauce on the oil cloth covering the table and added the peelings and cores to the bucket of apple chunks destined to be fed to the pigs and the chickens. She decided to leave the colander, sticky and awkward, for when Mama came back to help her heat water to wash the supper dishes.

She punched down the bread dough that had puffed up so high in the heat from the applesauce making for the final time and covered the pans with a dish towel. When the fire died down a little more, she could pop the bread inside and Mama would wake up to the delicious smell of baking bread.

Betsy swept the kitchen and wiped off the dust on the window sill that had blown in along with the leaf. The kitchen had cooled down a little, so she went and got a small quilt to cover up Erik who was snorting like a baby piglet in his sleep.

Glancing at the clock, Betsy realized it was almost time to start supper. Why wasn't Mama up yet? She climbed the stairs and peeked in. The window was opened; Sara Swensen loved fresh air, breezes blew through every room of the house until autumn's chill took over. Betsy's mother curled up on the wedding ring quilt covering the bed, one hand tucked under her cheek. The other hand lay palm up beside her.

Betsy took the limp hand in hers. It felt cool and slack to the touch. At least Mama wasn't running a fever. Unfolding the wagon wheel patterned quilt at the foot of the bed, Betsy draped the comforting material over her mother and closed the window before tiptoeing back downstairs...

"Betsy!" Erik tugged her back into the present by yanking on her apron strings. "Why are you staring in the cupboard? Did you see a mouse?"

She placed the colander back inside and closed the door on the jars in their orderly rows and the memories. Knees aching from kneeling on the tiled floor, Betsy remembered her father's words from this morning, "Apples are rotting on the ground in the orchard." A ten year could be forgiven for mistaking death for sleep, but Betsy still shuddered from the thought how she had failed her beloved mama when she needed her most. If only she'd gone upstairs earlier, perhaps she could have saved her.

Realizing Erik was gazing at her with a puckered expression around his mouth, as if deciding whether to cry, Betsy clapped her hands together. "Guess what! I've got a penny in my pocketbook for you to pay my big helper."

Her brother was quite willing to be distracted from the cupboard's contents and ran upstairs to get his bank. Betsy checked the oven before cutting out biscuits and arranging them on the baking sheet. Erik arrived, puffing, clutching his bank, which was made of iron and very heavy.

He watched her until she wiped her hands on her apron and fetched the penny. Grinning with excitement, he placed the penny into the dog's mouth. With a whir, the iron canine jumped through the hoop held by a man in a bright red jacket and deposited the coin into the barrel on the opposite side of the bank.

Laughing in delight, Erik hopped up and down and Betsy found herself smiling, yet envying his joy. If only finding happiness could be as easy as putting a penny in a bank, but a hundred dogs jumping through a hundred hoops couldn't bring back her mother.

When the biscuits were done, Betsy wrapped them in a napkin along with cold tongue and a chunk of homemade cheese. She accompanied Erik down into the root cellar and let him fish out juicy pickles from the brine in the pickle barrel. A couple of apples and a jug of buttermilk completed the picnic lunch.

On the walk to the field, Erik skipped ahead, darting to chase after a brown rabbit and flapping his arms to imitate birds in flight. They found Papa giving the mare a drink from the bucket he carried on the back of the wagon. Grundel, the black and white dog who always followed him around the farmstead, lay panting in the shade of a huge hickory at the end of the field, a tree whose roots always reminded Betsy of enormous bent fingers clawing into the earth.

Karl Swensen straightened while Erik raced forward and wrapped his arms around his father's knee, which was as high as he could reach. "I want to play in the corn, Papa!"

After being lifted into the wagon, Erik picked up two ears of corn and tried to juggle.

Betsy cleared her throat. "We brought your lunch."

Her father turned towards her and she saw the weariness carved in the lines of his broad face. "It's a good time to take a break."

Neither of them spoke while they ate, Karl nodding at Erik's chatter and only smiling when his small son offered to turn a somersault.

When they finished, he plucked his red bandana from the pocket of his dusty overalls and wiped his mustache. "Good biscuits, Betsy."

"Please take care of Erik for me." Her mother's last words echoed inside Betsy's head, drowning out the chirp of the birds in the hickory tree and the rustle of the corn leaves. She clenched her fists and said, "Papa?"

He turned from soaking his bandana in the water bucket to look at her, his eyes the same clear blue as Erik's, the blue of the sky.

"Please, Papa, don't blame school, it's my fault. I stayed up late reading, not doing school work. I promise to take care of the house and I understand if you won't let me go back to school, but you have to let Erik go. He must have the chance to learn." Betsy set her teeth into her lower lip and pinched a fold of her calico skirt.

Karl mopped his brow. "With your hair pinned back, you look like your mama, Betsy." Typing the damp cloth around his sun-tanned throat, he sighed. "Sara wanted you and Erik to get an education—book learning was very important to your mama."

"I miss her very much." The words squeezed out of Betsy's throat.

Her father closed his eyes. When he spoke, his voice sounded gruff with emotion. "I'm sorry. I shouldn't have bellowed like a bull this morning—you've done a woman's work for the past four years and you've done a good job raising Erik."

Words of praise. Betsy couldn't imagine any of her friends' fathers apologizing to their children and her voice sounded husky in her ears, "Thank you, Papa."

His hand, thickened and scarred by years of toil, squeezed her shoulder with gentle pressure. "A man must acknowledge his faults, Betsy. Your mama would take a broom and shoo me back from the heaven's gates if I told her I took you out of school." He nodded. "You and Erik have fun this afternoon because tomorrow you're going back to school."

Betsy rubbed Belle's rough mane and the mare blew through her nostrils. "Maybe we should get Belle a straw hat on our next trip to town, Erik. A red hat, as fine as Mrs. Jeppson's Sunday best."

Erik, convulsed with giggles at the thought of the horse wearing a hat with feathers, had to be told twice that it was time to go back to the house.

As they walked away to the jingle of Belle's harness, the wind made waves in the long silky grass which bowed around their feet and the relentless motion, combined with relief that Papa hadn't banned school, made Betsy dizzy. Erik tried to sing the song she'd sung to him earlier, but he could only remember the line about the wind shaking the apples down from the trees.

"I like to eat the apples God shakes down from the trees, but I'd rather throw them. Will you play under the trees with me, Betsy? I promise not to throw at you as hard as I can." He flexed his arm to show his muscles and then looked disappointed that his shirt sleeve didn't bulge like Papa's did.

Betsy hadn't set foot in the orchard since Mama died. But the trees held a great attraction for Erik, who loved to stalk the cats with pocketfuls of little green apples for ammunition.

Memory suddenly slanted white hot light into a chink in the darkness of the cupboard with the colander and the dusty jars. Mrs. Nelson, the neighbor lady who stayed with them while Papa fetched the doctor, must have washed it.

Betsy didn't remember much about that day after Papa had run down the stairs to tell her that Mama was dead. Forgotten until now was what she'd overheard Mrs. Nelson telling a group of ladies at the funeral. But now those words jumped into Betsy's head, along images of black armbands and the sounds of sobbing.

"The poor young woman had put up over a dozen quarts of applesauce before she took sick. The children were outside when I got there, the babe chewing on a twig and watching his sister hurl jar after jar against the house. Broken glass everywhere and fresh made applesauce dripping down the boards. Child didn't even seem to realize what she was doing…"

Betsy stopped to gaze at their house. For a moment, she could almost see the white paint marred with brown streaks.

As if it were happening all over again, the pain crushed her chest, tears blurred the grass as she carried out shining brown jars, the sound of breaking glass delighting Erik into laughter. Clanging pot lids together his new favorite game, he loved loud noises.

"I broke them because I thought making the applesauce killed Mama," Betsy whispered.

She blinked and the memory of the brownish streaks vanished. Dropping the hamper, she ran forward and pressed her nose against the sun warmed boards. She sniffed. Not a hint of apples. Papa had repainted the house and never mentioned the incident. Never asked her to make applesauce, one of his favorites.

Only then she realized the colander had been sitting in the cupboard for four years, ready for use. The pain eased as Betsy remembered the rolling motion of the pestle in her hands, the pride of wearing a woman's apron, even if it had to be triple wrapped around her waist, and the leaf dancing across the yellow oil cloth, blown by the breath of God.

Erik collapsed, stuffing the last biscuit into his mouth while a blue jay hopped closer, hoping for crumbs. When her brother beamed at her, Betsy felt a rush of love, as warm and rich as new made applesauce. She stooped to kiss the top of his tousled head.

When Erik tossed the rest of the biscuit, the bird snatched up its prize and sprang into the air. Together, they watched the blue jay land on a tree branch.

The breeze hurried the clouds along overhead and blew against Betsy's forehead in a gentle benediction. "The breath of God ruffling our hair," she murmured.

"Let's go pick up the rest of the windfalls, Erik, and you can help me make applesauce this afternoon. We can have a fight but you must promise not to throw as hard as you can."

He jumped up and turned a somersault, sprawling on his back and giggling. Betsy laughed, too, as overhead the blue jay fanned out his wings and launched itself into the waiting arms of the wind.

The End

Note from the Publisher

The Northern Lights Writers of Minnesota, Chapter #199 of Romance Writers of America, was founded eight years ago, to assist authors along the road to publication. Some of the members have accomplished their dreams of publication, some have not. This book, Romance and Mystery Under the Northern Lights, is a compilation of stories written by several of the Northern Lights members—a dream fulfilled.